FIRST TIME WE LAUGHED

Timing is Everything Series, Book 2

CHRISTINE MILES

For Denver.
I will miss you.

Books by Christine Miles

ADULT CONTEMPORARY ROMANCE

Timing is Everything Series

Last Time We Loved (Book One)

First Time We Laughed (Book Two)

The Time We Met (Book Three)

This Time It's Forever (Book Four)

YOUNG ADULT

Pacifica Academy Drama Series

Me, Shakespeare and the Anti-Love Club (Book One)

The '68 Camaro Between Kenickie and Me (Book Two)

Teddy Brewster's Hold On Me (Book Three)

Silver Bells for Me and (Saint) Nicolas (Book Four)

You and Me Dancing to Gershwin (Book Five)

Summer in Winter Wonderland (A Cozy Mystery)

Prologue

"THAT'S QUITE A SMILE," Jackson commented. "What are you thinking about?"

Jillian sipped her wine while admiring the floor-to-ceiling windows lining the living room. In daylight, the uninhibited view of Lake Estes in Estes Park, Colorado, was stunning.

She swiveled right to find Jackson watching her, wearing his own *quite a smile* as he lounged in the barstool beside hers.

Mierda. He was a beautiful man. The word beautiful didn't even do him justice since he looked like he belonged in a magazine modeling boxer briefs, or in this case basketball shorts.

She sipped more wine. "I was just wondering how many women you've brought to this amazing house you call a *cabin.*" Not a complete lie after she'd walked into his family's second home with him a few hours earlier. However, the wonder had lasted maybe five minutes.

Then she'd become focused on other things.

The corner of Jackson's delectable mouth inched upward. "Are you sure you really want to know the answer to that question?"

Her memory went to the master bedroom where they'd been

wrapped around each other until a different kind of hunger had brought them downstairs. Between their unhurried, libidinous time together and Jackson sitting near her while resembling a god, every part of her tingled. "Because I now know you're not only good at kissing"—she smiled—"I'm certain I can handle the number."

Jackson leaned forward and motioned for her to do the same.

When their heads were side-by-side, he quietly answered, "I've brought a total of one other woman here for a party we held a few years ago after starting the firm."

Jackson Lovett was either a damn good liar or being completely sincere. Considering what Jillian knew of him one month into their exclusivity, she sensed it was the latter and knew why. "That's because when you're *not* at work, you're at home."

He shot her his mind-melting grin. "Or with you."

She straightened and arched her right eyebrow. "That's only been the last few weeks." She paused, then asked, "Did you love her?"

"No." He shook his head. "It was nothing like that."

She placed her wine glass on the kitchen's island counter and slowly turned it left. "Can I ask you another personal question?" What Jillian wanted to ask probably wasn't the *smartest* thing to do, but she was curious and Jackson seemed perfectly comfortable with sharing.

"Go for it."

"Do you believe in love? The kind that ends with 'And they lived *happily* ever after'?"

His grin slipped. "That's how fairy tales end and love isn't that simple."

She couldn't argue with him and said, "Then how about this question."

He raised his eyebrows.

"Do you believe in soul mates?"

"Yes." He picked up his wine glass, drank, and set it beside hers.

"Because of Alyson and David? And your brother and sister-in-law?"

"Yeah, but also my parents. They're celebrating their thirty-ninth wedding anniversary this June and have always been in sync. A team. Even through rough spells. But," he added, "I think all of them are lucky and the exception. That kind of love is rare."

She nodded. "My older sister found it, but our parents *weren't* lucky." She stared at the counter. "They've been divorced for over a decade after years of a mostly loveless marriage." It had been incredibly awful to watch, too. Why the hell was she even thinking about any of that?

"So it sounds like you've never been in love, either."

"No." She glanced up to find him watching her. "But I agree with everything you said."

Jackson eased off of his barstool and nestled himself between her bare legs. "I think we should move this outside to the deck."

Jillian gaped at him. "It can't be more than twenty-five degrees outside."

He pressed his mouth to hers. Within seconds their kiss became hot and voracious.

Jackson slid his fingers up and down her thighs as they leisurely broke apart.

Santo cielo. He was the reason she'd asked about love and soul mates, and why she'd briefly pictured her parents' marriage. But she and Jackson had only been dating a month.

"There's a propane fire pit out there and a hot tub." His grin became naughty. "And me. I don't think you'll freeze, Miss Castillo." He squeezed her thighs. "It'll be so quiet out there."

She also never thought she'd be a "lucky one."

Jillian took a shaky breath. "I'm still going to need more than this T-shirt, Mr. Lovett."

A short while later, he sat in an outdoor chaise on the deck and guided her onto his lap.

She wiggled her body into Jackson's warm arms, the nearby propane fire pit giving off a generous amount of heat. She then buried her face into his neck that smelled of his cologne and her perfume. *Them.* She breathed him and the incredible silence deep inside of her. But as she slowly released the air, two tiny words and a realization drifted through her misty mind.

Oh, no. She was in *big* trouble.

Chapter One

ROWDY CRIES of success and moans of failure exploded from the living room.

Jillian blinked several times, then reached for the frozen margarita on the table. She brought the cold glass to her dry lips. The chill, salt, and tequila slid down her throat, easing the heat that had enveloped her at the memory of her first time here. The Lovetts' *cabin*.

She eyed Jackson, sitting on the edge of the sectional couch in the living room. His ten-year-old nephew, Brendan, sat beside him, followed by Jackson's brother, Will, followed by David, Jackson's best friend since childhood. The four were focused on the massive T.V.

Alyson Douglas dropped to the empty seat beside Jillian at the dining room table and pulled her long, auburn hair into a messy knot on her head. "Can one of you please explain what it is about video games that turn smart, successful men into middle school boys?"

Another explosion of rowdiness reached where they sat. Brendan even sprang from the couch and exchanged an enthusiastic high-five with his Uncle Jackson.

Jillian dragged her gaze from them to take another, longer sip of her margarita.

"It's *Call of Duty*," Jillian's younger sister, Claudia, offered. "It's pretty badass."

"But we prefer GTA," Claudia's girlfriend, Afton Diaz, added. "It's way more thrilling."

"But just as violent," Jillian mumbled under her breath.

Alyson tilted her head right. "GTA?"

"*Grand Theft Auto*." Claudia grinned at Afton. "Her innocence is so sweet, right?"

Afton giggled. "Yep. I get why you *used* to have a crush on her."

Alyson's face became the color of a ripe cherry which made Claudia and Afton quietly laugh while snuggling each other's sides.

"*Detener*!" Jillian set her glass down. "Would you two leave her alone?" She then mouthed "Sorry" to her best friend.

Alyson nodded and leaned forward. "Are you doing okay?" she softly asked. "You've been really quiet all day."

Jillian managed a warm smile. "I'm fine. I knew this would be a little awkward." She once again glanced at Jackson, concentrating on the video game.

Still, it hadn't been quite as awkward as Jillian had initially feared. Jackson had been either outside on the deck with everyone else at this Labor Day weekend barbecue or playing *Call of Duty*, ultimately giving her the same distance she was giving him.

Alyson clasped Jillian's left hand and squeezed. "You didn't have to come today."

"Of course I did. You and David deserve to be celebrated." Her best friend's recent engagement to David Preston was another reason the Lovetts had decided to throw a barbecue. "I'm also the maid-of-honor, a role I take *very* seriously."

"But Jackson's the best man."

Jillian sighed. "Al, I promise everything will be fine. Perfect even." *And it would be.* "I can't wait to help you start planning."

Her friend laughed. "I think I'm still processing that I'm marrying David."

Also known as the love of Alyson's life who she'd met over twelve years ago in college.

"Can you believe it?" Her best friend's gaze drifted to her fiancé, also absorbed in *Call of Duty*. "Because I can't believe it." She held out her left hand and stared at her ring, a square, shimmering diamond set in a simple, yet elegant platinum setting. "Jilly, what if right now is a dream?"

Desiring a man she couldn't have, sitting a room away *right now*, was not Jillian's idea of a dream and she said, "This is all very real. But if you still need convincing, Claudia, Afton, and I could overpower you, then carry you down to the lake and throw you in."

At that moment, the video game paused, and the guys stood and stretched.

Jackson's lean, absolutely perfect upper body became almost outlined in his snug T-shirt.

Why in the hell did Jackson Lovett have to look like he did? And be smart and successful and funny and an incredible—his Colorado sky-blue eyes caught Jillian's.

She looked at Alyson. But...*dammit.* No more spying on him from this moment forward.

David turned and walked their way. When he stopped at the table, he lowered his head, and he and Alyson shared a long kiss.

Yearning mingled with sadness spiraled through Jillian, even though she was the reason she was alone and had been for months.

"How's the game going?" Alyson asked David, interrupting Jillian's solemn thoughts.

He straightened. "Jackson's right about Brendan. That kid's unbeatable."

"David," Claudia stated. "There's something Afton and I have been meaning to tell you."

His gaze swung from Alyson, who shrugged, to Jillian, then to Claudia and Afton.

"Alyson gave us the shortened version of your history months ago," she continued, "and if you hurt our girl again, we'll take you somewhere you'll never be found *and* make you suffer."

Afton placed her chin on Claudia's shoulder and nodded.

His face flushed as he said, "Understood."

Gracie, Jackson's six-year-old niece, suddenly rounded the corner, clip-clopping in pink dress-up shoes and wearing a sparkly pink dress. A tiara completed her princess ensemble.

She stopped at David's left side. "Hi, Uncle David."

He cautiously eyed Claudia and Afton for another second before smiling at Gracie. "Hi, beautiful." He lowered himself to her height. "Where are you going all dressed up?"

She fixed her tiara, currently slipping off of her adorable blonde head. "I'm getting married, too."

He playfully crossed his arms. "Really? Who are you marrying?"

"You!" Gracie grabbed his arms. "So come on. Let's go." She tugged him forward.

He stood and grinned at Alyson. "Guess I have a wedding to get to."

Gracie led him into the living room.

Alyson giggled as Jillian's phone burst into the rippling ring tone.

"It's Campbell or Hayley." Alyson winced. "I've been half expecting one of them to call us today since the MacGregor wedding is the biggest one we've ever put them in charge of."

Jillian shook her head. "It's not them, and they're fine, Al. They have Felicity's team helping them." She picked up her phone and answered. "Hey, how are you feeling?"

"Awful," her older sister, Brynn, declared. "I know you and Claude are in Estes Park today for the barbecue, but I really need to talk to you."

That didn't sound good.

"Let me go somewhere quiet." Concern and confusion swirled through Jillian while she scooted from her chair. To Alyson, Claudia, and Afton, she said, "I'll be right back."

Claudia straightened. "Is it the babies?"

"I don't know." Though it had to be Brynn's pregnancy. Still, if something terrible had happened, Jillian had no doubt their older sister would be hysterical at this moment.

Jillian darted for the staircase, up the steps, and went right. She walked swiftly into the master bedroom and out onto the balcony that hung above the main deck. When she reached the railing, she said, "Okay. What's going on?"

"I'm on mandatory bed rest for the remaining weeks of my pregnancy." Brynn moaned. "That's nearly two months. Jilly, what the hell am I going to do in bed for two months?"

Jillian gripped her phone. "Are the babies okay?"

"They're fine," Brynn assured. "I've been experiencing mild contractions and my blood pressure has been high. Too high, according to my doc." She sighed. "I love these boys with everything I have, but…I hope you never get pregnant with twins."

Jillian relaxed her grip on her phone and stared at Lake Estes, shimmering under the Colorado sunshine. "But everyone's okay?"

"Not even close since my doctor's edict has put us in a position where we'll need help around here, especially with Sebastian. Marcos has a big case right now and his parents are still working. You know Dad's too far away, and I hate the idea of having a stranger helping around here for two months." Brynn paused for a breath, then said, "Mom's determined to fly out here and help us until I give birth."

Mierda. Jillian swallowed her own moan.

"I think she was already online looking for flights before we got off the phone," her sister continued. "I can't have Mom here for two months, bossing us around like she does. If my doctor is worried about my blood pressure now—and Marcos? When I told him, he went for a bike ride. I haven't seen him since, though he did call to check on me. And thank God his parents took Sebastian with them to Breckenridge for the long weekend—"

"Brynn, you need to breathe." *They both did.* "Your blood pressure has probably skyrocketed in the minute we've been on the phone." Jillian's probably had, too, at the thought of their mother dropping her life on the Big Island of Hawaii to come here for two months.

"Jilly, you know if I tell her 'thanks but no thanks' she'll never let it go. She'll be on her death bed, still chastising me for refusing her help when I was pregnant with her grandsons."

She stayed silent at her sister stating nothing but the truth.

"Then I had a thought," Brynn tentatively added.

Jillian watched a fishing boat drifting across the lake while listening to her idea.

Daisy's Bouquets, the flower shop she co-owned with Alyson, was doing better than ever. They had weddings every weekend, sometimes two. They were doing double the business from this time last year. She was also now Alyson's maid-of-honor. Jillian's life had become the definition of swamped. But how could she say no to her older sister's plea? Brynn never asked for help. Claudia wasn't an option due to her schedule as an ER nurse at a hospital in the south Denver metro area. And Jillian didn't want their mother here anymore than Brynn, more so even.

That thought left her with no other choice.

"*Sí.* Call Mom and tell her." Jillian would somehow make all of this work.

How much sleep did she really need?

JACKSON'S GAZE wandered to the staircase for the third time.

Jillian had been up there for a while. Based on the way she'd raced up the steps, something big must have happened.

He glanced at Alyson, still at the table and talking with Jillian's sister and girlfriend. They, too, kept eyeing the staircase, so whatever happened probably wasn't work-related since Alyson would have gone up there with her.

And, *shit*, why did he even care?

"I now pronounce us married."

Jackson turned at David's vow.

His good buddy knelt in front of Gracie giving him her little girl smile that had a way of melting and breaking hearts at the same time.

David kissed her hand. She threw her arms around him. They hugged, then he tickled her which caused shrill laughter to explode from her tiny body. She wiggled away from him and ran onto the deck to where her mom, Jackson's sister-in-law Savannah, sat talking with other guests.

His friend stood and mumbled, "Jillian's still not seeing anyone, so stop being a chickenshit and go up there."

Jackson frowned. "She's on the phone. And what the hell would I say to her?" Being cut off at the knees by a woman while standing in the cold, Colorado spring rain had a way of making a guy unwilling to approach her, single or not.

"Just off the top of my head," David replied, "you could start with *Hi, Jillian.*"

Jackson ran a hand through his hair. "She hates me." Though

he had caught Jillian watching him. But only because he'd snuck another peek at *her* for the millionth time that day.

He'd known she would be here and had spent the week preparing himself for this day. When she'd walked into the house with Claudia and Afton, however, Jackson's memory had gone right to the weekend he'd brought Jillian here in March. The heated, unforgettable memories had been hanging around him all damn day, too. Though playing *Call of Duty* had given him something else to focus on for a while. Or more like a *short* while.

"Jackson," David began, "she was pissed, it was months ago, and you two are going to have to figure it out. Being the best man and maid-of-honor?"

Right. But that did remind Jackson he had something pretty big in store for David and Alyson. It was an idea he'd been rolling around since they became engaged a week ago. He'd need help planning everything, and Jillian had been the first person to cross his mind as the maid-of-honor and Alyson's best friend. Jackson legitimately needed to talk to Jillian, but the fact they'd exchanged no more than one half-assed smile all day had given him zero confidence to approach her. Plus, she'd been sticking close to Claudia and Afton. Until this very moment.

"Take a chance. She might surprise you." David stepped back. "Hey, I've been meaning to ask you if your mom's feeling alright?"

Jackson glanced at his mom, shaking with laughter as she sat between his dad and David's Aunt Eileen. Interesting that David had also noticed her fatigued, pale appearance from earlier in the day, but Jackson answered with honesty, "Will and I talked to her. She said she was fighting off a cold." Based on her continued laughter, she appeared to be winning the fight.

David nodded, then headed for Alyson, still at the table.

Her eyes and face lit up. No doubt David was looking at her

the same way. They were soul mates who'd found each other at the University of Colorado Boulder, then lost each other due to tragedy, and reconnected ten years later.

Soul mates like his parents, and Will and Savannah who'd also met in college.

David called reconnecting with Alyson after so long fate.

Jackson called it luck. No one deserved it more, though, than his best friend.

Take a chance. She might surprise you.

Or Jillian might tell him to take a flying leap into Lake Estes. Recalling the disappointment and irritation on her face before she'd left him *that night*, Jackson would probably be taking his life into his hands by going up there. But he had this idea and couldn't shake the feeling Jillian would want to help him. On that thought, he headed for the staircase. It's not like he had anything to lose at this point. Except, possibly, his life.

His steps turned wobbly as he veered right, having a strong idea where she would have gone to have a private conversation that hopefully had ended by now.

When he reached the master bedroom doorway, he poked his head around the corner while keeping his eyes off of the bed. A spot where they'd discovered even *more* compatibility.

His shoulders fell, however, at the sight of Jillian on the deck and still on the phone.

She paced left to right and pushed a lock of shoulder-length, almost black hair behind her ear as she spoke quietly into the phone.

Jackson couldn't help but stare at her profile…sensuous curves…toned legs.

When they'd met at Becca Preston's—now Ridley—birthday party in February, he'd been drawn to Jillian for many reasons. Watching her, he was reminded of reason number one, followed by the vivid memory of sliding his fingers down her soft legs in that bed—

"See anything you like, Mr. Lovett?"

He blinked her into focus.

She arched her right eyebrow as she slid her phone into the pocket of her shorts.

That eyebrow thing she did, along with her smart mouth and throaty voice, were just more reasons Jackson had been hooked by Jillian Castillo.

"Hi, Jillian." Heat absorbed Jackson's face at being caught ogling her from the doorway of a bedroom like some creeper in a true crime documentary. He forced himself to step forward. "Everything okay? You've been up here a while." *Shit.* Now he really sounded like a stalker.

She narrowed her sultry, dark eyes. "That's a pretty friendly, personal question and observation, considering we haven't seen or spoken to each other since April."

So much for "she might surprise you."

He ambled toward her. "If memory serves, that wasn't my choice." Or being left in the pouring rain with nothing more than an umbrella, ignored apologies, and frustration. "Jillian, having a client who's an asshole doesn't make me one."

She smirked. "The jury's still out on that."

His jaw tightened. "Really? You're still that pissed? And after everything—"

"Jackson, there is no 'everything'. We were *together* for just over a month." She lifted her shoulders. "That's called a speed bump in time."

Her words sliced through him, but he managed to simply hold her stare.

A thick, tense silence rippled between them.

What the hell had he been thinking, coming up here? That was the last time he would take advice from his long-time friend who was seeing the world through a happy-in-love lens.

Jackson also smirked. "You're right. We had fun. That was that." He leaned against the doorframe which led to the deck. "It was bound to end." Though it hadn't felt like that at the time, it probably would have burned out. And he knew this from past, first-hand experience.

She stepped by him and into the room. "Something's come up. I have to grab Claudia and Afton so we can leave."

Which meant something big had happened in her world.

He sighed. "Jillian, I didn't come up here to swap insults or rehash what happened."

She stopped and faced him.

"We're adults, it's over, and we need to move on. Especially for David and Alyson."

She remained silent but gave him a curt nod.

"I have an idea on something to do for them and I'd really like to talk to you—the maid-of-honor—about it." He paused before adding, "I was hoping you could help me with it, too."

After several seconds, she replied, "I'm listening."

"You said you need to leave, and I need longer than a minute." He straightened. "Can we meet up for coffee next week at that joint in the Highlands?"

She released a quick breath. "Okay. Day and time?"

"I'll text you on Tuesday and we'll figure it out then."

She frowned. "You still have my number?"

Jackson swallowed a frustrated sigh. "Yeah. But obviously you need my number again." Wow, did he feel like a complete jackass—

"No, I don't. Talk to you next week." She practically sprinted away from him.

He still couldn't stop himself from asking again, "Is everything okay?"

"It's fine," she threw over her shoulder before disappearing from view.

He turned to stare at the lake, wondering for the umpteenth time what the hell had *really* happened with her—them—in April. Outside of him ending up in business with the devil.

Chapter Two

JILLIAN LET herself into Daisy's Bouquets. As the bells over the door tinkled, she flipped the sign from "Night-Blooming Jasmine" to "Morning Glory." Once inside, she paused to admire their space in the Sloan's Lake neighborhood where they had moved at the beginning of June.

They'd recently changed the window display and interior decorations to reflect the fast-approaching fall season. Bouquets featuring flowers with warm colors, such as sunflowers, orange and deep red roses, burgundy calla lilies and red dahlias, complemented the harvest inspired decorations. They'd also, in the front right corner, recently created a wedding consult spot. Examples of artificial wedding bouquets and table arrangements representing each season sat on built-in shelving. A bistro table with three matching padded chairs completed the corner.

Jillian smiled at the warmth, the intoxicating fragrance many of the flowers radiated, and the overall coziness. Yes, this space was quite smaller than their former spot in the Highlands, but it would be theirs for as long as they wanted. Their landlords—David's Aunt Eileen and Uncle Hugh—had made that clear when she and Alyson had signed the lease.

When it came to Daisy's Bouquets, the struggles were behind them.

Her smile dipped, though, at the thought of being away so much for the next two months. But then she reminded herself for the millionth time it was temporary. When Brynn had the babies, Jillian would return to working right here where she belonged.

She walked behind the counter and stored her purse.

As much as she would miss being in the shop on a daily basis, spending more time with her five-year-old nephew, Sebastian, would be a fun change. Spending more time with her older sister, however—Jillian shook her head.

Brynn was the one who was *most* like their mother, but she needed help, and the only alternative was Eva Castillo coming out here.

Jillian and Brynn would be just fine.

She opened a file folder labeled "Daily Orders" they kept on the counter next to the register. Campbell Grey, their other full-time employee, had drawn the longest stick for working the four-hour, Labor Day shift. Apparently, a few orders for today had come in yesterday; two birthday bouquets and one get-well-soon.

She turned to head toward the backroom when the bells over the shop door jingled.

Thatcher, Alyson's husky, trotted inside, followed by his human.

Jillian arched her right eyebrow. "You realize he's here more than Hayley." Their only other employee who worked part time because she was a college student.

Alyson laughed. "I know, but now we're in a dog-friendly space."

Thatcher stopped in front of Jillian, his mouth hanging open in a pant while his fuzzy tail flapped back-and-forth.

She bent down to rub his face while Alyson joined her behind the counter.

"Okay," her friend said, laying down a sheet of paper, "I think I have a doable schedule for while you're gone."

Jillian straightened, and their eyes caught.

"But are you really going to be fine with working up in Boulder during the week and being on Saturday wedding duty?" Alyson frowned. "That leaves you with one day off."

Ideal? *Hell no*. Still, Jillian really didn't have a choice.

"Al, I can't expect you and Campbell and Hayley to cover for me during the week and *also* do the weddings." She leaned against the counter. "Especially Felicity Mayhew weddings."

In March, Daisy's Bouquets had hit the big time by partnering with Felicity Mayhew, also known as the most sought after wedding coordinator in the metro area. Although she'd aligned herself with another locally-owned flower shop at around the same time, Felicity always reached out to Daisy's Bouquets first.

Alyson gave Jillian a soft grin. "I just don't want to see you wear yourself out. Because you now have another pretty important job."

She returned Alyson's grin. "I promise I'll be fine." It's not as if she had anything better to do than work and be her best friend's maid-of-honor. After the potent time with Jackson and splitting from him, Jillian had decided an indefinite break from men was what she needed most.

Thinking of Jackson reminded her of his mysterious plan for Alyson and David, and him requesting Jillian's help. He had yet to text her about meeting up some time this week. He'd definitely caught her off guard, too. In more ways than one. Between that, Brynn's rough pregnancy, and her sister needing help, Jillian had been a tad bitchy to Jackson on Saturday.

"So I have some wedding news." Alyson laughed.

No matter the tension with him, Jillian had to put her best friend and David first until the wedding day. She had no choice. It was also the right thing to do. Then she and Jackson Lovett would once again go their separate ways.

"We set a date!" Alyson threw her arms around Jillian. "*This* New Year's Eve."

Jillian froze for a few seconds before releasing her friend and leaning back. "Are you being serious? Because that's only—"

"A few months," Alyson interjected. "I know. But we want to start our life on the first day of the new year. We also don't want to wait any longer than we have to," she quietly added.

Jillian understood their haste. But New Year's Eve? *Santo cielo.* Was that even possible?

"We don't want anything fancy. Just us, with our family and closest friends."

She nodded. "That sounds perfect for you two, but you'll still need a place to get married and hold a reception." There was also no chance in hell any spot in the Denver metro area nice enough for a formal wedding *and* reception would still be available this close to New Year's Eve. The bride and groom—especially the bride—had to know that. "Where are you two thinking?"

Alyson smiled. "My parents' house in Evergreen. Or Hugh and Eileen's house in Denver. Or *possibly* the Lovetts' cabin." She lifted her shoulders. "I'm leaning more toward Evergreen or Estes Park because it'll be winter. Better chance of snowy landscapes."

And David, Jillian strongly suspected, probably didn't care where the wedding happened as long as it happened. Alyson was, after all, the love of his life and vice versa.

Jillian straightened and grinned. "I think those are fantastic options." *Intimate. Snowy. Romantic.* What she thought of as the perfect wedding, too. But she shoved the thought aside and asked, "Have you talked to your parents about this? Or Hugh and Eileen? Or the Lovetts?"

Alyson shook her head. "Not yet. We just decided all of it last night."

The shop phone started to ring.

As her friend scooped up the receiver, Jillian picked up the "Daily Orders" folder and walked to the backroom.

With the work table filling the center, and the utility sink and shelving lining the back wall, their shared work desk barely fit in the front, right corner. A tight space for sure, but as much as they'd loved their former spot anything was better than being associated with that rotten-to-the-core Marsden Enterprises.

She set the folder on the table while recalling Jackson's statement from Saturday.

Having a client who's an asshole doesn't make me one.

Maybe not. But considering Marsden Enterprises had kicked them—Daisy's Bouquets—out of their space in the Highlands right after buying the building in late February, Jillian still couldn't believe Jackson's choices in April; the other reason she'd ended things with him.

As far as he knew, it was the *only* reason.

Jillian sat at the table and stared at the first flower order until the words swirled together.

Now she was the maid-of-honor to his best man, on top of possibly helping him with something related to their friends' wedding happening on New Year's Eve. She also had to somehow juggle helping out her older sister in Boulder while being a florist and co-owner of a small business in Denver.

She took a steady, deep breath, exhaled, then lifted her chin.

No matter the craziness she'd have to endure the next couple of months, she'd without a doubt take it over having her mother in the state of Colorado.

JACKSON LEANED back in his chair and glanced at the time on his office phone. Just after ten. Jillian also had to be well into her workday by now.

He picked up his cell, but when he went into text messaging he paused to stare at the screen, specifically her name in black, bold print. He then re-read the last text she'd sent him thirty minutes or so before they'd met up for dinner. What had been their final date.

You're losing points, Mr. Lovett. Her response to his, *I'm running late. I'll be there soon.*

The reason Jackson had been running late was because he'd found out his architecture firm had won a notable project—a high-end shopping mall for locally-owned businesses.

Unfortunately, it was being spearheaded by Downey Development. Or more accurately Keith *Dickhead* Marsden, the company's "silent partner."

Jackson had spent over an hour closed up in his office, talking over *the win* with Zach, his business partner, and David, their former partner who'd left architecture in July for his music. They'd discussed the pros and cons of going into business with Nelson Downey, the company's CEO, with the guy probably being Marsden's mouthpiece more often than not. But the pros had far outweighed the cons. So Jackson had foolishly hoped explaining all of that to Jillian would help her understand, from one small-business owner to another. He'd spent their entire dinner trying to find the right opening and words to tell her about the huge, important project that would have his firm ultimately aligned with Marsden for months.

He continued to stare at her message in their thread he'd been unable to delete.

You're losing points, Mr. Lovett.

Shit. That had turned out to be a massive understatement.

Strong-willed, sassy Jillian Castillo had *not* supported his—

their—decision to move forward, bringing their "speed bump of time together" to an abrupt end. Though he'd half feared that reaction, he still couldn't shake the feeling something else had been going on since she'd been acting a little…off…for about a week. He'd probably never know for sure. The best he could do between now and Alyson and David's wedding was to put his frustration aside and reach out to Jillian, strictly as maid-of-honor, and hope they could work together on his plan.

Jackson straightened and was about to text her when his office phone's intercom beeped, followed by "Nelson Downey is on the line. Can I transfer him?"

He swallowed a sigh before answering, "Yeah, Marjorie. Put him through."

As the phone rang, Jackson set his cell down, took a deep breath, and picked up the receiver. "Good morning, Nelson. What can I do for you?"

"I need a meeting as soon as possible with you, Ember, and that Diane what's-her-name."

Jackson narrowed his eyes. "Her name's Diana Shepherd. She owns Life Force. That successful chain of new age stores?" Something he knew nothing about, but it didn't change the fact the older woman had built an impressive local empire.

Diana deserved as much respect as the so-called great Ember Leventhal who was fast becoming pain-in-the-ass number two when it came to this project.

"Right, right," Nelson muttered. "When can you get all of us into your office?"

Jackson sat back. "Can you tell me what this is about?"

"Ember's rethinking the spot she initially chose for her store."

Of course.

"Okay. But what does that have to do with Diana?"

There was a pause on Nelson's end before, "After a closer

look at the plans, Ember has discovered Diane has a better location. We need to work this out before Ember backs out."

Because Downey Development needed the so-called great Ember Leventhal's name attached to this high-end shopping mall going up on the edge of Cherry Hills Village and Greenwood Village, the Denver area's most affluent suburbs.

"And we—*I*—need you at the meeting," Nelson continued, "in case there has to be a discussion on design changes to accommodate whatever Ember wants. Make it happen by Friday, Lovett." The line went dead.

Jackson slammed down the receiver.

We. He knew damn well who Nelson had really meant with that two-letter word.

He gritted his teeth for several seconds, then again picked up the receiver.

"Marjorie, I need you to call Diana Shepherd's office immediately to schedule a meeting for this week in our office."

"Specific date and time?"

"Just make it ASAP. Let me know as soon as it's on my calendar, then call Nelson Downey's office and give his assistant the info."

"Okay." She hung up.

Since this week was already heading in the direction of shit, he needed to text Jillian about meeting up for coffee to discuss and, hopefully, start planning what he had in mind for their best friends.

Jackson picked up his cell but paused when he saw he'd missed a call from his mom who'd also left a voicemail. He'd listen in a minute. He then chose Jillian's name and paused to think about what to type.

He finally settled on, *Hey. It's Jackson. What day and time would work best for you to meet up this week?*

Yeah, she'd told him she'd kept his number, too, but there was no way for him to know if that had been the truth or said out of guilt because he had kept hers.

Jackson next listened to his mom's message. She rarely called him during the workday, so he couldn't help but wonder if something was going on, especially since he'd just seen her over the long, holiday weekend.

"Hi, Sweetheart. Dad and I need you to come up to Longmont for a family dinner. We're hoping Friday evening would work? Call me back when you can. Love you."

Family dinner was typically on Sundays.

Okay, since starting the firm a few years earlier he hadn't been the best son when it came to going up to Longmont on a regular basis. But why would his parents push dinner up to Friday? It sounded like he was expected to be there, unlike on Sundays. Which wasn't a problem now that he had no life outside of this office. He also hadn't been interested in dating since Jillian and he'd been drowning in work. Regardless, his parents' request seemed strange.

Jackson chose his brother's name and texted, *Hey, did you get a call from Mom about a family dinner this Friday night?*

Will, Savannah, and the kids almost never missed Sunday dinner. Will had to have gotten a call from their mom, as well, but Jackson wanted to know for sure.

He stared at his message to Will, read that it had been "delivered," and closed out of text messaging. No matter his confusion, he had to get back to work. So he again set down his cell, refocused on the designs for the shopping mall filling his oversized computer monitor, and did what he did best. He shut out the world and became Jackson Lovett, co-owner, managing partner, and lead architect of now LW Architecture + Interiors.

Chapter Three

JILLIAN SIPPED her red wine while watching some thriller on Netflix that really hadn't captured her attention. Though she had the apartment she shared with Claudia to herself, which was always nice, her busy brain couldn't focus on anything but two things at this moment.

Her phone, beside her on the couch, chirped with another text from Brynn.

You can get here any time you want in the mornings. Marcos will get Sebastian to school.

Helping out her sister and family was the number one thing on her mind and would begin tomorrow morning after the number two thing on her mind.

She texted, *Okay. I should be at your house by ten.*

Jillian couldn't imagine her morning coffee meeting with Jackson—number two thing on her mind—lasting longer than thirty minutes. Maybe forty-five? She had no idea what he was planning for their best friends, but she didn't want the meeting to go any longer than it needed to.

She'd placed him into the category of favorite mistake in April and that's where he'd stay.

I'll have a list of things for you to do when you get here. See you tomorrow! Brynn had followed up her statement with the red heart emoji.

Jillian released a heavy sigh before setting her phone aside.

List of things for her to do? *That didn't sound good at all.* But Brynn and her family needed help, so Jillian would have to suck up whatever her older sister threw at her…with a pleasant, sisterly smile on her face.

She sipped more wine and nestled herself deeper into the couch cushions.

Thank God Claudia had a late shift at the hospital and would then be going to Afton's afterward. Jillian wasn't in the mood for her sister's current obsession with *Grand Theft Auto.*

Their second floor apartment in the city's Washington Park—Wash Park—neighborhood was modest and the appliances needed updating. But she and Claudia had done their best to add life to the space when they'd moved in together over three years before out of financial necessity.

As of late, Claudia's work schedule and relationship with Afton had kept her sister rarely at home. It certainly felt as if Jillian lived alone. Now she'd be the one who was rarely home, but not for very intriguing reasons. A handful of months ago, though, that hadn't been the case.

Jackson's striking, grinning face drifted through her mind.

She'd been in big trouble the second they'd introduced themselves at David's sister's party back in February. Then they'd had an amazing first date, followed by a second, and third and before she'd realized it, she'd been way in over her head when it came to Jackson Lovett.

Something she'd *never* experienced or expected.

After watching her parents slog through a miserable marriage…which had included infidelity on both sides…keeping her heart and soul to herself had been Jillian's priority throughout her dating life. Yes, Brynn had found love and happiness with Marcos. Claudia, on the other hand, would most likely never settle down with one woman since she enjoyed serial monogamy. Jillian had been like Claudia, too, until meeting a smart, successful, sexy architect.

She sighed and tried to concentrate on the movie that made no—

Her phone burst into song.

When she glanced at the screen, the tension in her neck and shoulders magnified. She stared at the caller's familiar face filling the screen for several seconds until she answered, "Hi, Mom." She followed that up with a large sip of wine.

"I just got off the phone with Brynn," Eva Castillo answered. "Your sister has assured me that she'll let me know if all of you *do* need my help. Or if something happens with her and the babies, *God forbid*. But you are to call me immediately if anything else happens."

Jillian kept a second sigh in check at her mother's dramatics over Brynn's situation. That, from what she understood, wasn't highly unusual when a woman was pregnant with twins.

"I still don't understand," Eva continued, "where your decision came from. I was more than ready and willing to help your sister and Marcos with everything they would need."

Jillian frowned at the judgment oozing from her overbearing mother's voice

"What I've been hearing from your sisters since I never hear from *you*, is that the business is doing better than ever. Why would you choose now to step back in order to help Brynn when I have a much more flexible schedule and could help for a couple of months? This choice of yours doesn't make sense, and I don't agree with it."

Por supuesto. Because Eva Castillo was never wrong.

Jillian managed to politely say, "We all agreed it would be

much easier for everyone, including you, for me to help them out since I *live* here." Not a total lie, either.

"I assured your sister I had no problem coming to Colorado to help. With your father now living on that *farm* in Argentina, one of us needs to be present for you girls and I live significantly closer to Colorado than he does."

Mierda. Just what Jillian and her sisters didn't need. And farm? Their dad had moved to the Mendoza region of Argentina last year to help run his cousin's *vineyard* and winery.

"I made that clear to Brynn, too, so what aren't you two telling me?"

Jillian finished her wine and set the glass down on the coffee table. "Mom, everything will be fine." But what she really meant was that they'd be fine without *her*. "I have to go."

"Jillian, *háblame.* Why am I always your enemy?"

She was in absolutely no mood for this and said, "Someone's downstairs. We'll talk in a few days." *Or not.* She hung up and tossed her phone onto the coffee table.

No matter what Eva Castillo said, she was more interested in doing the talking than listening. Something Jillian had witnessed and experienced time and again for years. It had really become noticeable while watching her parents' marriage disintegrate into mutual hate.

Brynn, older by four years, always insisted their parents had loved each other and could remember those days, though vaguely. Being older also meant she hadn't been around to watch the final years of their parents' tumultuous marriage.

Jillian narrowed her eyes.

Their childhood home in Lakewood had turned into World War III. Lines had been drawn with no zones of neutrality in the house outside of bedrooms. Their dad had moved into Brynn's old room during the final, painful stretch. When their parents had actually been at home, their weapons had been raised voices and angry words, especially from their dad who had a temper. It had been a rotten situation. She and Claudia had rarely invited their friends over as teenagers, also known as the worst, darkest time for all of them living in that damn house.

Jillian sat back and stared blankly at the T.V.

Brynn had been lucky, in more ways than one. Maybe if Jillian had been the oldest—if her parents had ended up like Jackson's and Alyson's—she would have approached her dating life differently. But she'd kept her heart and soul to herself, only to be caught completely off guard when she'd met *him*. She'd never truly thought she'd make a real connection with a man.

Jackson's and Alyson's parents were still happy, in love, and meant to be together.

Soul mates.

Her memory drifted to that first night with Jackson at his family's cabin.

She'd asked, *"Do you believe in soul mates?"* Even Jackson, raised by parents who felt that way about each other, had admitted "that type of love is rare." She'd agreed with him, too.

Where did that leave a skeptical woman and man with other things going against them?

All alone is where it had left *her*. Though Jillian knew via Alyson and David that Jackson had also been single since April, it wouldn't last forever. He was, after all, *Jackson*.

Pangs of envy and loneliness and sadness spiraled through her insides at the thought. Emotions she had no right feeling since Jackson was right—she'd initiated their split. But for more reasons than *that project*. Still, she'd meet up with him in the morning and listen to what he had in mind for Alyson and David who deserved a maid-of-honor and best man carrying no drama. That thought would get her through their best friends' wedding, too.

———

I'M HERE. *Got us a table by the window.*

Jackson hit send, then settled back into the chair. His right hand trembled a bit as he brought his coffee cup to his mouth.

Why was he so damn nervous? Yeah, he was not one of Jillian's favorite people, but it's not like she despised him. Or did she?

He frowned.

His firm had indirectly ended up in business with the company behind her flower shop losing its space crawling distance from this coffee joint. Jillian and Alyson had loved their spot here in the Highlands, too. Being given thirty days to get out right after Marsden Enterprises bought their former building had been a huge shock. Then they'd run into a few problems while searching for a new space in March. Everything had worked out, but it hadn't been easy.

Jackson sighed before taking a quick drink.

After going through what they had until moving into their current space, could he blame Jillian for despising him? At the same time, taking the shopping mall project had been the best *business* decision for his firm. Nothing personal about it. But that brought him to the now, trembling at the thought of seeing Jillian who must have only agreed to meet him for David and Alyson's sake since she'd made her feelings clear *that night.*

The memory, even this many months later, caused him to wince.

He focused on the coffee shop's door. Seconds later, Jillian stepped inside.

She went straight for the counter that had slowed in busyness since he'd arrived.

As hard as Jackson tried *not* to check her out, his gaze started at her hair pulled up into a tight ponytail, slid over her tight, black

T-shirt and equally tight jeans, and stopped at her black-and-white checkered Vans. The shoes looked even more worn out since he last saw them.

The first time he'd noticed the Vans he'd teased her that maybe it was time for a new pair, to which she'd sassily replied, *"Comfy shoes are like a good man, Mr. Lovett. Hard to find."*

She suddenly turned from the counter, and their eyes locked.

Jackson tried on a friendly smile while ignoring the buzzing in his head that her sultry dark eyes had caused from the moment they'd met.

She responded by sipping her coffee before heading his way.

He straightened as she sat in the chair across from him. Silence, outside of an employee at the espresso machine heating milk and various conversations, settled between them.

"Good morning," he finally said, then tried not to cringe.

During the handful of weeks they'd been together, everything had been effortless, including talking. And the laughter. There'd been so much talking and laughter.

"Hi," she murmured.

Now it felt as if they were more strangers at this moment than the day they'd met.

How could that happen between a man and woman with off-the-charts chemistry? Something he hadn't experienced since Brooke Marshall in high school. Did that even count?

"So I have to be up in Boulder by ten," Jillian stated. "What's on your mind?"

Her comment made him pause, then he couldn't stop himself from asking, "Boulder? Do you have a delivery that far away?"

She sipped her coffee and replied, "Do you remember me telling you that my older sister, Brynn, is pregnant with twins?"

He nodded. "Yeah. Of course I do."

"Well, she's in the last couple months and it's become a little…difficult."

He raised his eyebrows. "That doesn't sound good. Are she and the babies okay?" Could that also have been what caused her to leave so suddenly on Saturday?

"Yes, but Brynn's on bed rest. She and Marcos will need help around the house and with Sebastian." She hesitated before adding, "And it was either me helping them or our *mother*."

Right. Her mom—Eva?—who lived on the Big Island of Hawaii. To the massive relief of Jillian and her sisters. He and Jillian hadn't been together long enough for him to hear the story of what sounded like an extremely strained relationship. He had, however, picked up enough here and there to understand she would step up to avoid being in the same place as her mom.

"What about the shop?" he asked. "David told me you guys have gotten to the point where you're turning wedding and event business away." News Jackson had liked hearing since he had genuinely been interested in Jillian *and* her shop.

She gave him a small smile. "Yes. It's fantastic, too. I'll miss being there during the week, but Alyson worked out a temporary schedule with Campbell and Hayley filling in for me as much as possible." Her smile slipped. "But I'll be working all Saturday weddings."

He absently drank his coffee. "It sounds like you're going to be pretty busy the next couple months." He needed help with his idea—her help would be ideal, too—but would she even have the time? "I don't want to add to your already full schedule. Maybe I should—"

"Jackson, I'm here, you have my attention, and it's Alyson and David. *Dígame*," she added. "I have to get up to Boulder."

"I want to throw David and Alyson a combined bachelor and bachelorette party."

She arched her right eyebrow. "Okay. I'm listening."

He released a quick sigh at that eyebrow thing she did which had knocked him sideways from day one. "You know David doesn't drink, so taking him out for a guys-only night won't work." Jackson needed to stay focused no matter how damn good Jillian looked right now.

"I know. And Alyson isn't one for a *real* girls-only night."

"That's what I figured," he continued. "I also can't help but think David and Alyson would rather be together than have separate bachelor and bachelorette parties."

She laughed.

Jackson let the throaty sound fill his head. Which then buzzed.

"*Absolutamente.*" She leaned back. "They're wanting such a small wedding, too, this might be a good way for everyone in their lives to celebrate them."

He shot her a quick grin. "Exactly." This was officially going better than he expected, but he still had to ask, "Do you think you'll have time to help me pull a pretty big party together?"

Jillian lowered her gaze to the table.

"I think it should be us—the maid-of-honor and best man— that make it happen."

She pursed her lips.

"But I'll understand if the timing isn't right." If Jillian did say no to helping him, Jackson could always enlist Becca, David's sister, who was a newlywed herself.

Jillian stayed silent for several more seconds, then straightened. "No. I'm in. They absolutely deserve something big like this."

He slowly expelled the air that had become lodged in his chest.

She leaned forward. "We'll make this happen no matter what. Agreed?"

Knowing exactly what she really meant, he nodded once. "Done." A hundred-pound weight came off of his shoulders at Jillian's willingness to put aside her dissatisfaction with him.

He'd certainly hoped she would agree to help him for their

best friends, but nothing was official until it was official. He also fought the strong urge to have them shake on their deal.

"Where and when are you thinking about having this bash?" she asked. "Alyson told me yesterday they chose New Year's Eve as the wedding date but weren't certain on the where yet."

He finished his coffee. "Yeah. David caught me up last night. So I was thinking the Saturday after Christmas?"

She cracked a smile. "Makes sense. The where might be a bit more difficult. They're considering a few different places to have the wedding and reception that would also be great party places." She paused, then said, "Your family's *cabin* is one of them."

Jillian broke their eye contact as his mind again went to their perfect getaway that weekend in March. Which seemed to appear at the worst moments. Like right now as he sat less than a foot away from her, looking comfortable but so damn good at the same time.

He cleared his throat. "David told me all of that, too." He'd also given Jackson the job of bringing up the possibility with his family when he saw them Friday night for the impromptu dinner. "I was thinking my house might work for the party. What do you think?" Jillian had spent quite a bit of time there before their abrupt end.

She lifted her shoulders. "Maybe. But before you sacrifice your house for a bachelor-bachelorette bash, let me do some research on alternative options."

He smiled softly. "I can do that."

The coffee shop sounds surrounding them faded into silence as they stared at one another.

Why the hell had she *really* ended things with them? Had she been looking for a reason before *that night*? But why? If that had been the case, he'd undoubtedly given her one.

Jillian pushed back her chair and stood. "I have to go. I'll be in touch when I get some info on possible places to throw the party."

Jackson opened his mouth to respond, but she turned and nearly fled the coffee shop.

Shit. Maybe this wouldn't be the best thing to do after all. For either of them.

Once outside, he paused to inhale the warm, late summer morning air deep into his lungs. Then his phone inside his suit pocket started to vibrate and ring.

"Hey," he answered.

"Everyone's set for the meeting tomorrow morning at nine *sharp*," Marjorie stated. "It's also on your calendar. I blocked off a couple of hours."

Holy shit. He hoped it wouldn't last that long. But he said, "Thanks. I'll be in shortly."

Jackson walked in the direction of where he'd parked his SUV.

Okay. He could and would plan the party with Jillian. It *was* his idea.

Though the situation wasn't ideal, Jackson couldn't help but think planning the party with her help might be a damn good distraction from other areas of his life, namely work.

Chapter Four

THE DOOR OPENED and Marcos smiled.

Jillian returned his grin that really didn't reach his weary brown eyes. "You look tired."

He stepped aside to let her into the house.

She removed her sunglasses. "You've lost some weight since I last saw you, too." Her smiled faded at the fact it had only been about a month ago when she'd been here for Sebastian's big fifth birthday party. "This pregnancy is taking its toll on you both."

Her brother-in-law ran a hand through his thick, black hair streaked with gray, then sighed. "We were warned at the beginning it might be a high-risk pregnancy because of Brynn's age and being so petite." He brought back his smile surrounded by the beginnings of a salt-and-pepper beard which he always grew for the fall and winter months. "We're okay, though."

Jillian followed him deeper into the house.

"Thank you for coming to our rescue," he said over his shoulder. "I love your mother—"

"*Mentiroso.*"

Marcos chuckled as he reached the kitchen table. "Okay, *love* may be a strong word." He picked up his laptop bag and faced her. "Regardless, she probably would've caused unnecessary problems. And Sebastian will definitely have more fun having his Aunt Jilly's attention."

She joined him at the kitchen table. "How is my sister?" she quietly asked. "Really."

He sat on the table's edge. "She loves being at her job and now has to work from home. She's also not used to sitting for longer than the average-length movie. And now she's stuck in bed—for the most part—carrying two boys, who according to her seem to love kicking each other and her in the process."

Jillian flinched. "That bad." At least she now knew what she was up against since she'd be interacting with Brynn the most until she gave birth.

She'd have to tread extremely carefully for both their sakes.

"Go up and see Brynn." Marcos straightened. "I need to get to work. Brynn put a list together for you and wrote out Sebastian's schedule for the rest of the week."

Jillian arched her right eyebrow. "He's five and has a schedule?" *Increíble*. And that to-do list was starting to sound a tad on the ominous side.

He fought a smile. "He's in a youth soccer club and has many friends who have birthday parties. In fact, there's one this weekend. I know you won't be taking him to the party, but I'm sure Brynn will have you take him shopping to pick out the gift. You'll be fine, Aunt Jilly."

As Marcos went right, in the direction of the garage, she frowned.

How was it her five-year-old nephew had more of a social life than she did?

She shook the irony aside, eyed the staircase, then took a deep breath before jogging up the steps. Once she reached the landing, her shoes sunk into the plush, taupe carpeting. She passed Sebastian's superhero-themed bedroom and bathroom, what would be the twins' room once they were born, and the lone guest room and guest bath.

Jillian could just hear Brynn and Marcos's bedroom television. She paused in the doorway of the master suite that filled the upper west corner of the house and grinned softly at the sight of her older sister sleeping. She was propped up against the headboard with pillows.

Brynn wore a yellow sundress and had her long, nearly black hair pulled up into a knot. Her sister's laptop sat nearby on a lap desk. Some papers were scattered around the bed, as well.

Jillian walked toward the bed where she eased onto the edge.

Brynn's eyelids fluttered open. "Hi," she murmured. "How was the traffic?"

"Not too bad." She rested her hand on Brynn's tummy. "How are the boys?"

Her sister shifted into a more upright position. "Quiet…for now." Brynn flashed Jillian a sappy smile. "Marcos has been amazing since I was put on bed rest." She placed her hand over Jillian's still resting on Brynn's stomach. "I know your life has officially become crazy busy."

Jillian's mouth became a hard line since she strongly suspected what was coming next.

"But it can't *only* be about work, family, and friends, so I had a thought last night that I talked over with Marcos. You need to have some fun. Put yourself back out there?"

Brynn just couldn't help herself when it came to the topic of Jillian's personal life.

"To find your own Marcos? And David?" Her sister squeezed her hand. "Claude and I still think it's strange you haven't dated *anyone* since that last guy. Jackson? But Claude did tell me she thought you really liked him."

Fabulosa. Now her *sisters* were talking about her personal life behind her back.

"Jackson and I weren't meant to be, and dare I ask where you're going with this?"

There was no reason to tell her nosy sisters about helping Jackson plan the big party for Alyson and David until absolutely necessary. Perhaps she'd even wait until the invites went out.

"Marcos works with a couple of attorneys we think you might like."

She withdrew her hand from underneath Brynn's. Though they meant well, Jillian had no interest in dating a lawyer for many reasons that included she wasn't like Brynn who had chosen an attorney. "Where's that to-do list? Marcos also mentioned a schedule for Sebastian?"

"Jilly, please think about letting us set you up?"

"*Detener!*" Jillian stood. "You're making me *loca*." She held out her hand. "The list?"

Her sister released a huge sigh, rustled through the papers on the bed, then produced a piece of white paper with a typed list and what looked like a printed calendar. "Here are both. Sebastian has soccer practice after school, but you'll have enough time to bring him home for a snack and to let him change his clothes. School lets out at three-fifteen, but I suggest getting there *at least* ten minutes early to get ahead of the car line chaos."

Jillian arched her right eyebrow. "What the hell is a car line?"

Brynn winced. "You'll find out soon enough. Oh, you'll probably want to take the Suburban since it has Sebastian's booster seat which is required for his age and size."

Car line? Booster seat? Driving that bright-white boat called a Suburban?

Jillian scanned the to-do list...with *ten things* needing to be done? Including a trip to the grocery store that had a lengthy list of its own.

She closed her eyes.

Santo cielo. Between this reality, her obligations at the shop and as maid-of-honor, and now helping Jackson plan a bachelor-bachelorette bash, what the hell had she gotten herself into?

━━

JACKSON EYED DIANA SHEPHERD who looked like a small, frizzy gray rabbit about to be devoured by wolves named Nelson Downey and Ember Leventhal.

Downey leaned back in the conference room chair, examining Diana. He placed his folded hands on his round gut that stuck straight out and over his suit pants; the buttons of his white dress shirt being pushed to their limit due to his massive stomach.

Jackson's client loved five things—blondes, golf, five-star dining, money, and himself. But not in that order. Looking at Downey, the five-star eating had clearly caught up with him. The guy wasn't tall, either, which contributed to his squat shape.

Downey gave Diana a condescending smile that accentuated his double chin.

It was the same damn smile Jackson was beginning to loathe and dread.

Diana's thin, folded hands resting on the conference table, tightened.

Based on Downey's looks and unbearable character, the attractive blondes he consistently displayed in public had to be absurdly well-paid escorts. Or hoping to be Mrs. Nelson Downey some day since he was one of Denver's wealthiest businessmen.

"Mrs. Shepherd—"

"It's *Ms.* Shepherd." Diana's pale-blue eyes, behind thick, round glasses, sharpened to a point. "I've been divorced from my third husband for two weeks and earned that title. What you two are doing to me isn't fair. Life Force is just as successful as Miss Leventhal's clothing line."

And score one for the lady dressed all in gray. Jackson had also noticed she bore a strong resemblance to a teacher in a *Harry Potter* flick he'd once watched with Brendan and Gracie.

Somehow smothering a grin, Jackson glanced at Downey and his partner in this crime, the so-called great Ember Leventhal.

The clothing designer, a local celebrity of sorts, yanked her gaze from her phone.

"*Ms.* Shepherd," Ember began, "I need the bigger space more than you do. And my stores draw more customers in one week than any high-end box store in the city of Denver."

Ember Leventhal's black eyes would match the color of her soul if she had one.

She smirked at Diana. "I appreciate the fact you're also a successful business owner, but this new shopping center is the big time." She went back to her phone.

Jackson swallowed a sigh.

And score one for the lady in the tight, bright-red suit. Because she was right.

"Moving me to that northwest space"—Diana gestured toward the plans on the conference room table—"between the specialty ice cream shop and store for pets won't help *my* financial bottom line. I need to be next to the independent bookstore with the coffee and wine bar because of the clientele they'll attract." She sniffed. "I'm also very allergic to cats and dogs."

Downey raised his thick shoulders. "If you can match what Miss Leventhal is willing to pay in rent for that space—"

"Which is *not* the original amount, Mr. Downey." She raised her chin. "You and Miss Leventhal worked out that new fee as a way to get *me* out of that spot."

They'd probably had help from Keith Marsden, too. But still. Diana Shepherd definitely had fangs and claws. At the same time, she'd lost and knew it.

"Now I'll have to add this meeting's turn of events to my list of things I'm discussing with my spiritual advisor later today."

Diana stood. "If you'll excuse me, the destructive energy in this room is suffocating my chi."

Downey straightened. "I'm afraid we'll need an answer before you leave."

She glared at him. "You'll get my answer when I'm ready to give it."

Downey and Ember shared a wide-eyed stare before irritation settled into Downey's face.

Fighting another smile, Jackson stood and followed the petite woman to the door.

Although he understood Diana's unhappiness with being "moved" to a less-desirable spot, he had to grudgingly concede the space Ember was bulldozing her way into was highly valuable and, in reality, too big for the new age store.

Diana halted, settling her defeated eyes on him. "You seem like a reasonable, courteous young man," she murmured. "But your aura is awfully dark for someone your age."

Jackson stayed silent because he had no idea what she was saying.

"I don't suppose there's anything you can do to stop them?" she softly asked.

He frowned since this was the aspect of his work he despised. At the end of the day it was, for the most part, about people making money. "I'm only the hired help. I'm really sorry."

She nodded and gave him a tentative smile. "Come visit us at my flagship store in Larimer Square. After two hours with me, your aura will be glowing."

Jackson watched her head for the stairs.

Had the eccentric businesswoman just propositioned him?

He shook his head, shut the door, and faced Satan's associates giving him twisted smiles.

"Ember has a couple requests she'd like to discuss now that we're alone," Downey stated.

Jackson approached the table as dread crept through him.

"My store in Cherry Creek North has two stories and I want a second story at *this* location," she declared, her soulless eyes never leaving Jackson's face. "I also want my store to face *west*. Sunset light is flattering, and women buy more when they look ageless in the store."

He stared at the designer while wanting to laugh and tell her where she could shove her damn shopping theory.

"We can certainly accommodate those simple requests. Right, Lovett?" Downey asked.

Jackson quietly inhaled, then said, "All of the stores are one story. Having one, two-story building doesn't make sense from a design standpoint." He flipped through the plans until he found the section that faced *west*. He angled the sheet toward Downey and Ember and pointed at the area. "If you want a west facing store, I recommend you choose one of these spaces."

She put her phone down for the first time since entering the building. After giving the plans a cursory glance, she wrinkled her nose. "They're too small. If you can make them bigger, we'll talk. And there must be something you can do to make the mall look *pretty* with my two stories." She grabbed her phone and purse. "I have another meeting." She and Downey stood at the same time. "Thank you for everything, Nelson. You'll keep me posted on this?"

His client nodded, though his eyes were locked on Jackson.

Ember flounced past Jackson without a second look or word.

Scorn had settled into Downey's plump face. "Lovett, what the hell are you doing? You know we—I—need the Ember Leventhal store because of the area. Her store will draw every rich soccer mom living in Cherry Hills Village, Greenwood Village, and beyond." Downey pointed at the conference room door. "Diane what's-her-name should consider her store lucky to be in the same place as Ember's."

He gritted his teeth at Downey's continued disrespect toward Diana and his determination to give the so-called great Ember Leventhal everything she wanted. But Jackson knew trying to accommodate her illogical demands would be nothing more than a huge waste of his time. He managed to calmly say, "There's no valid reason she needs two stories or a west facing store."

Downey shuffled forward and peered up at him. "If I were you, I'd consider the challenge she's presented as a way for you to stay the architect on this project or I could give it to another firm before I walk out of this building."

Jackson's jaw turned to steel while he met his client's cold, hard stare.

"I'll check in early next week and expect you to have a design for Ember to look at." Downey strolled out of the conference room.

Jackson breathed deeply through his nose while counting backward from ten.

Once his blood no longer felt at boiling point and he knew Downey had to be out of the building, he grabbed the plans and rolled them up…while fighting the compulsion to tear the sheets apart. He then marched from the conference room into his office and shut the door behind him. A little on the hard side, too. When he was behind his desk, he tossed the plans next to his computer with enough force the paper landed against his pen holder, causing it to topple.

He sat in his chair and stared at the plans. "*Shit.*"

Bidding on the project back in early March had seemed like an advantageous decision for the firm that had been *his* idea he'd taken to David and Zach over three years ago. Because of that, the firm's success had been his number one priority from day one. Yeah, his relationships with family and friends, and his personal life, had taken a hard hit. But the firm wasn't just his livelihood— he had a staff of six, plus Zach. Almost everyone in this building also had families of their own. As such, Jackson had considered *everyone's* best interests when he'd chosen to go after this high-end shopping mall project featuring locally-owned businesses.

Great concept. Great location. Great project. Hugely profitable.

How could he *not* have gone for it?

Jackson rubbed his eyes and sighed.

Not too long after he'd submitted their bid, he'd found out that Keith Marsden had his greedy, dickhead paws buried deep into Downey Development and Nelson Downey. Who was turning out to be as big a greedy dickhead as Marsden. Then in a *holy shit* twist they'd won the job, and Jackson's professional and personal life hadn't been the same since.

He recalled the shock, disappointment, and irritation on Jillian's face when he'd finally told her about the project. Then she'd dumped him, gotten into her car, and drove away. Now, months later, he really had no personal life and Nelson Downey had him by the balls when it came to the *entire* project.

The overall profits and recognition would be incredible and make LW Architecture + Interiors a go-to firm for high-end commercial projects throughout the metro area. Another reason he'd gone after and taken the project. But getting into business-bed with Downey/Marsden was turning into a soul-sucking experience.

Maybe that's what Diana had meant by his aura being dark?

His phone, sitting on his desk, buzzed with a text.

Jackson straightened, willing it to be—

His shoulders slumped at his brother's name.

Don't forget to drag yourself from work tomorrow night and be at the house on time.

Right. Family dinner in Longmont that was always on Sundays. Until this week.

Btw, Mom told us to get a sitter for the kids. Weird, right?

Jackson stared at Will's newest message.

Weird? More like unheard of since their parents loved everything about being grandparents. They were even Will and Savannah's babysitters. So, yeah, their mom's request wasn't remotely close to normal.

He texted his brother, *Big time. What do you think is going on?*

Jackson sat back, now staring at his phone.

Family dinner moved to this Friday *and* without the kids? For some reason, their mom wanted only him, Will, Savannah, and their dad at this particular family dinner.

No idea. But S and I are trying to stay positive.

That's all Jackson could do, too. But as he moved aside the plans he'd tossed onto his desk, another round of dread crept through him.

Chapter Five

JILLIAN CAREFULLY MANEUVERED her sister's bright-white boat posing as a SUV into the elementary school's car line; this chaos reminding her of leaving a concert or sporting event. The main difference being the cars in this line, driven mostly by moms yakking away on their phones or texting, featured insignias belonging to BMW, Cadillac, Land Rover, and Mercedes.

She gripped the steering wheel.

Today was only day two of her nanny-maid-servant responsibilities and she already detested *this* job. During her first car line just yesterday, she'd been honked at for waiting too long to make a left-hand turn into the parking lot because of her inexperience driving an automobile double her car's size. She'd also been honked at for merging into the actual line too late, then yelled at by an older woman—maybe a teacher?—for not pulling forward to pick up Sebastian. Leaving the parking lot she had, once again, been honked at for waiting too long to make a right-hand turn, afraid she'd cut off an approaching driver.

Jillian inched forward as a BMW SUV merged in front of her.

After privately bitching about it to Brynn—who thought the story was *hilarious*—her sister had suggested Jillian walk to the school since it only took twenty or so minutes. But Jillian had figured she really needed the practice, with the weather still being nice, driving her sister's boat through car line.

She glanced in the rearview mirror.

The mom in the fancy SUV behind her had one eye on the chaos and the other on the phone she held in her hand.

Tomorrow's weather would be similar to today's, seasonably sunny and warm. Perfect for a mid-afternoon walk. It would probably be a nice change for Sebastian, too.

His alphabetical group fell into sight, and she straightened.

Her nephew looked adorable in his khaki shorts, blue polo shirt, and new sneakers. Jillian couldn't help but smile and give him an enthusiastic wave…that he barely returned.

She stopped the boat in the correct location and smiled at the surly woman from yesterday. She, however, ignored Jillian while signaling Sebastian to head to the passenger side.

As soon as he'd buckled his tiny body into his booster seat located in the back and behind the passenger seat, he looked at her and asked, "Is it Friday yet?"

It was only his fourth week as a full-day kindergarten student. Based on his enthusiastic chattering this time yesterday about school, she'd been under the impression he loved his class. So at this moment, his big, dark eyes looked too crestfallen for a five-year-old.

Jillian shot him a sympathetic smile. "Sorry, kiddo. You've got one more day." She followed the same BMW around the playground. "Tough day at school?"

"I'll say," he grumbled. "My friend Adam pushed Carly off a swing at recess, then ran away. The teacher thought I did it 'cos I was helping her and she was crying."

Jillian glanced at her nephew. "Didn't Carly tell the teacher who really pushed her?"

Sebastian looked at her with wide eyes. "She was bawling pretty bad."

Jillian giggled.

Talking to and spending time with her precocious nephew would definitely get her through the next couple months and had already turned into a daily bright spot.

"You're doing better today," he added. "No one's honking at us."

"Thank you, Sebastian," she murmured.

Within ten minutes they were approaching the house. A dusty, full-sized pickup truck with a trailer holding an assortment of landscaping equipment blocked the driveway. Jillian was forced to stop alongside her Subaru parked on the street.

"What's this all about?" she asked more to herself than Sebastian.

He poked his dark head out the passenger window. "It's yard day. Niall's here!"

Her sister and brother-in-law paid people to take of their yard? *Increíble*. But it's not like Brynn or Marcos had the time, especially now. Her sister had never been into yard work anyway.

"Sit tight." Jillian spotted a somewhat scrawny guy dressed in a landscaping uniform leaning against the trailer while chugging a bottle of water. "Excuse me?" She headed toward him. "Could you please—?"

The guy burst into Spanish, threw his hands up, and speed-walked for the open garage.

"*Solo quiero que muevas tu camioneta*!" she replied, but he kept walking. "Great." She headed in the same direction to find this Niall.

She was halfway up the driveway, giving Sebastian a quick check, when she heard, "Oh, shit! Sorry."

Jillian turned to find a tall, toned guy wearing a baseball hat, a black T-shirt with a pair of worn jeans, and black boots jogging toward her. She came to a gradual stop, meeting him in the middle of the driveway.

He removed his aviator sunglasses, revealing striking hazel eyes. Based on his youthful, exuberant face and impressive physique, Jillian placed the guy somewhere near his mid-twenties.

"I lost track of time." He then called over his shoulder, "Carlos!"

The "guilty" employee walked into the garage.

"*Necesito que muevas el camión fuera del camino,*" the young guy said to Carlos.

Jillian arched her right eyebrow at his perfect Spanish.

He faced her and shot her a crooked smile.

"Thank you. I told him the same thing, but I guess he didn't hear me."

"No worries." The guy pulled off a work glove. "I'm Niall Donnelly."

She grasped his hand. "Wow. The only thing missing from your intro is the Irish accent."

He laughed. "I could introduce myself with one if you want." He released her hand. "But I have to warn you, my Irish accent falls right around embarrassingly terrible."

She returned his grin.

"So, you must be the aunt helping out for the next several weeks?"

She peered at him. "Yes, but how did you know that?" And why would he know that?

The pickup truck gurgled to life, and Carlos slowly moved the load forward, unblocking the driveway in a matter of seconds.

"Hi, Niall!" Sebastian ran toward them, stopping at Jillian's right side.

The two did a quick fist bump.

"Actually," Niall said, now blocking Sebastian's playful

punches, "it was this guy who told me that his crazy aunt would be helping out around here."

Jillian looked at Sebastian. "I thought Aunt Claudia was the crazy one."

Sebastian lost his balance while swinging at Niall who caught him before he fell to the ground. "Mom says," he said on a deep breath, "you're both crazy."

Por supuesto. And clearly Niall was a family friend and their weekly landscaper.

"Sebastian, does your crazy aunt have a name?"

"Jilly."

"Jillian," she clarified.

Carlos scurried by them and in the direction of the backyard.

"Jillian," Niall began, his mouth curving into a smile, "how's your sister feeling?"

"She's good." Jillian stepped backward. "Too good. I think she's going to enjoy having me as her servant." *Probably more than enjoy*. "I need to get that thing parked and unloaded."

She tried *not* to make herself look foolish backing the boat into the driveway. After almost grazing a tree on her second try, Niall guided her in using forward and stop gestures.

"I'm not used to driving something so big." For some reason, she felt compelled to explain herself to this eye-catching young guy now helping her unload the back filled with numerous baby items she'd purchased on sale from Target…because there wasn't enough baby stuff crammed into the twins' room. "That older, blue Subaru over there is mine."

"A practical, fuel-efficient choice." Niall grabbed the two boxes of diapers and followed her into the house. "I drive an older Jeep Wrangler. Loads of fun, but not fuel-efficient."

Jillian halted at Brynn in the kitchen, making a cup of tea. This was the first time she'd seen her sister out of bed since becoming their nanny-maid-personal servant.

Brynn's dark eyes brightened when they spotted Niall. "Hey there." She waddled forward to ruffle Sebastian's hair. "Did you introduce him to your aunt?"

"Nah. He did it." Sebastian climbed onto one of the two bar stools situated at the island counter. "I'm hungry. That lunch Dad made me didn't cut it."

Jillian shared a quick laugh with Niall as he set the diapers on the table.

"I'll grab the rest," he said.

Before she could express her thanks, he was gone. She then faced her sister whose head was tilted slightly right, eyes locked on the direction Niall went.

Jillian set her bags on the nearest countertop and arched her right eyebrow. "Seriously, Brynn. Are you kidding me?"

"Oh, come on, Jilly." She giggled. "I'm pregnant with twins, bigger than a blue whale, and bedridden. Not dead. And before that Jackson guy, you would've beaten me to it."

Without a doubt.

Jillian turned and started to unpack one of the reusable bags.

"What're you guys talking about?" Sebastian asked.

Outside of putting a call into a person who would be able to find a place for Alyson and David's bachelor-bachelorette party, Jillian had managed to keep Jackson far from her mind. Until now. Still, she had no intention of contacting him until she had a reason. Their unexpected reunion was temporary and about business.

But, *dammit*, he'd looked so incredibly edible yesterday in his dark gray business suit.

She frowned as she finished unpacking the bag.

Jackson Lovett would look edible in a potato sack. If only she could hate him for it, too.

Niall staggered back into the kitchen, loaded with reusable bags crammed with various household and baby items. He tried to set them carefully on the kitchen table, but each bag landed with a thud, followed by papers plummeting to the kitchen floor.

"I got it." She stepped forward and dropped to her knees. Niall joined her, their eyes connecting over the scattered newspapers. "You didn't need to carry the bags in all at once."

He nodded and said, "You have really pretty eyes."

Jillian froze for several seconds as her cheeks became hot. "They're just brown."

"Deep brown." He stared at her. "They're expressive, too. You're sad about something."

She jumped to her feet and placed the newspapers on the table.

Where the hell had that come from? This kid had only known her for maybe ten minutes.

As Niall rose, she turned and marched back to the counter.

Brynn pierced her with a wide, questioning stare.

Fabulosa. Of course her sister had caught Niall's out-of-the blue flirtatiousness.

"Is Marcos ready for Sunday?" Niall asked.

"Absolutely," Brynn answered. "He hasn't been to a Broncos game in a couple years. He's also happy you offered to do the driving."

Marcos had playfully taunted Jillian last night before she left about how he'd be going to the Sunday afternoon football game. The fact he was going with the much younger Niall Donnelly caused her to pause while unpacking another bag. She'd assumed he was attending the game with a colleague. Apparently, Niall had become *really* good friends with the Ortegas.

"Niall, will you take me to a game?" Sebastian asked. "It would be so super cool."

"Someday. When you're a little older. Brynn, we're almost done for the day. Jillian?"

She forced her mouth into a smile and glanced Niall's way.

"It was very nice meeting you." He shot her a sly grin before heading for the door. "I'll see you guys Sunday."

The second he left, Brynn asked, "What was that?"

"What was what?" Sebastian asked.

Jillian held on to an exasperated sigh. "I have no idea what you're talking about."

"You know exactly what I'm talking about."

"Mommy, I don't know what you're talking about."

Jillian whirled from the counter with an armful of onesies. "Brynn, you're hormonal. I'm going to put these in the boys' room."

Brynn narrowed her eyes. "You two totally had a moment."

"Who had a moment?" Sebastian whined.

Jillian left the kitchen and jogged up the stairs.

Niall's perceptive comment filled her head; his words bothering her way more than his compliment about her eyes and her sister's borderline snarky statements.

How was it that a guy she'd known for a handful of minutes had noticed her emotional state? She'd assumed she'd been hiding her feelings pretty well, too, since no one in her immediate circle, outside of Alyson, had sensed anything was wrong. Claudia had been the only one to meet Jackson, so he was nothing more than a name to her other family members. Hadn't really been more than that to Claudia, either.

Jillian walked into the twins' room and went to the dresser where she paused.

Unfortunately, Jackson had ended up being someone significant to Jillian that she *never* expected and was something he'd in no way been ready to hear.

Chapter Six

YOU'LL TALK *to your parents about Al and I possibly getting married at the cabin?*

Jackson pulled into his parents' driveway and parked beside Will and Savannah's SUV.

He eyed his childhood home as the dread he'd been battling returned. Something wasn't right. He had a feeling, despite "staying positive," his brother and Savannah felt the same way.

He re-read David's text, then responded the only way he could.

Yeah. But I wouldn't worry about their answer. Have a good show tonight.

Jackson suddenly wished he was at home, getting ready to go watch David and his jazz band play at their usual place. He also couldn't help but wish in that scenario a certain woman would be going with him. There was a good chance she was going, too, but as Alyson's date.

Thanks! Tell everyone I said hi.

As a way to ignore the dread that had worsened as tonight approached, he'd lost himself in the Downey Project. He'd worked until the second he had to leave the office to be here on time. Longmont wasn't a quick jaunt from lower downtown Denver, especially on a Friday night.

He released a deep sigh and hauled himself from his SUV.

Once inside, he spotted his family members sitting at the dining room table. His mom and dad sat next to each other at one end while Will and Savannah occupied the table's right side. The four were chatting, but Jackson's dread tripled in strength as his instincts picked up the sober mood. Not a typical occurrence in his boyhood home. This house had almost always been light-hearted, even when he and Will had gone through their teenage, brotherly torture phase.

"Hi, Sweetheart," his mom murmured when he arrived at the table.

Jackson's pulse gained momentum at her frail appearance, blood-shot eyes, and drained expression. The fact his dad appeared no better made him glance at his brother and Savannah, their eyes round with anxiety and concern.

He slowly pulled out the closest dining room chair and sat. "Hey." He tried on a smile. "So this is supposed to be a family dinner, but I don't smell anything cooking." Also not a good sign because on true family dinner nights this house smelled like a five-star restaurant.

His mom grinned. "Dad's in charge tonight and is grilling fish."

Okay. That certainly wasn't unusual. Jackson still couldn't stop himself from glancing again at his brother who barely lifted his shoulders.

"You look tired," his mom softly continued. "You're working too hard again."

Total understatement. But *shit*. He was in no mood for a conversation that had been a popular topic in this house since he started the firm.

"You do look like crap," Savannah offered. "Are you living at the firm now?"

His sister-in-law, who he'd known since he was seventeen, meant it as a joke, but Jackson wasn't about to laugh. "Work's kicking my ass a bit right now, but no. I really don't want to talk about work, either." It also wasn't the reason they were together like this on a Friday night. "Mom, what's going on?"

His parents exchanged a somber yet determined look. Which meant his instincts had been right. Something was wrong. Big time.

"I went to see my doctor a couple weeks ago," his mom began, "because I haven't been feeling quite right for a while." She gripped his dad's hand.

Jackson exchanged a swift look with his brother and Savannah. He couldn't help but wonder, based on their wide eyes, if they were also remembering how pale and exhausted she'd been the first part of Labor Day weekend.

His dad pulled her closer to his side as she looked at Savannah, Will, then him.

But she'd explained all of it away as fighting off a cold.

"The doctor ran some tests," she continued, "and discovered advanced cancer that started in my ovaries."

Silence descended.

The seconds ticked by as his mom's admission settled itself around and between them.

Jackson frowned and leaned forward. *No.* He had not heard her correctly.

"She instantly referred me to an oncologist who confirmed the diagnosis on Tuesday."

He froze while processing the words "advanced," "ovarian," and "cancer."

"Mom, what are you saying?" Will asked.

She sighed. "It was caught too late, Sweetheart. The cancer

has spread." She and his dad shared a quick, defeated look. "The oncologist said surgery would be invasive at this point."

No. This couldn't be happening to their mom. She'd just turned sixty in June. She'd only been retired from her almost forty-year career in education for one year. Their parents had also celebrated their thirty-ninth wedding anniversary in June.

"But what about other treatments? Like chemo?" Will asked.

She hesitated, glanced at his dad who slowly nodded, and again concentrated on them. "I decided not to undergo treatment. It took meeting with two more oncologists before I found one—a woman—who understood that I..." Her voice wavered and she quietly inhaled. "I can't spend my final months feeling sicker than I already am only to prolong the inevitable."

Jackson eyed Will, staring out the dining room window, then Savannah, staring at the table, then his dad, who kissed his mom's forehead. But the longer he sat there, trying to process his mom's unexpected reality, his confusion and shock made him ask, "Why did you keep something like this from us? We also knew something was wrong last weekend, but you—"

"We were waiting for the official diagnosis from the oncologist that didn't come until Tuesday." She squeezed his dad's hand. "We also needed time to think and...discuss the treatment options *my* doctor thought would be viable."

"Which you've already rejected," he persisted. "Mom, that doesn't make any sense."

"Jackson, it wasn't your decision to make," Savannah argued.

His sister-in-law was right. But it didn't stop him from saying to his mom, "It doesn't change the fact that it sounds like you've decided to lie around and wait for death."

Her eyes became round before hurt flashed through them.

He looked away. Had he just said something that rotten to his mom? *Who was dying.* Which made him the biggest dick on the planet right now. But still, why wasn't she fighting?

"Jackson, outside." His dad stood. "Now." He walked to the sliding-glass door and shoved it and the screen open.

After a deep breath, Jackson also stood, walked past his dad, and well into the backyard. As soon as his dad shut the doors, he said, "Mom doesn't give up which means she's not thinking clearly. You can't really be supporting this."

His dad stopped in front of him. "And you need to watch your mouth. Having a tough time at work is no excuse for what you just said."

"Dad, this has nothing to do with work." Jackson pointed at the dining room windows. "You're letting Mom give up. How can you do that?"

As his dad's face transitioned into the ferocious mask Jackson hadn't seen since high school, he knew he'd officially gone too far.

He shoved his hands into his pants pockets.

"I'm going to let those comments slide," his dad quietly said, "and only because it's clear to all of us you're having a piece-of-shit workweek. But you'd better not say anything like that to me again. Do you understand me?"

Jackson nodded while a strained silence fell between them. But after several seconds, more honesty spilled out of him. "I'm sorry. But it feels like you and Mom gave up." He made eye contact with his dad. "Why *can't* she be one of the lucky ones?"

He knew he sounded like a naïve kid rather than a rational adult. Yet, imagining his mom gradually succumbing to a vicious cancer poisoning her body was too much to comprehend.

"It was caught too late," his dad replied. "Way too late. I've been with your mom for every doctor's visit. And her decision to forego treatment was difficult for me, too." His dad's eyes became shiny. "But she has my full support and needs the same thing from you, Will, and the rest of the family. She's going to need all of us as much as possible," he firmly added.

Jackson stared blankly into space.

"This isn't much consolation, but we can give the three of you some stuff to read. To help you better understand what we'll be facing in the upcoming months."

Jackson shook his head, turned, and walked toward the backyard's fence gate. "I can't do this. I have to go. I'll…stop by tomorrow. Tell Mom I'm sorry." He headed for his SUV, recalling the last time he'd experienced this level of shock and helplessness.

He'd been nine years old and riding his bike, trying to keep up with his brother who had just turned twelve. Will had received his first skateboard. He'd been an obnoxious older brother when they'd been kids. That day Will had been acting invincible, too, not wearing a helmet and tearing down their neighborhood sidewalks as if he were Tony Hawk. The car filled with oblivious teenagers backing down the driveway hadn't seen him coming.

As if in slow motion, Will had flown sideways at least ten feet. All these years later, Jackson could still hear his brother slamming into the concrete. Where he'd laid as if he were dead. He'd stared at his older brother—crumpled on the street as the teenagers in the car rushed to help him—before adrenaline had hit. Jackson riding his bike back home to tell their parents what had happened remained a massive blur to this day.

He climbed into his SUV and slammed the door shut.

His mom was dying. And there was nothing he could do but stand by his family and watch. Helpless. How would his *dad* be able to watch the woman he loved and had been with for over forty years become even more sick and eventually—

Jackson eyed his phone he'd left in the center console.

David had asked him to talk to his parents about the cabin being a possible location for the wedding that was only a few months away.

He frowned.

Shit. Would his mom…be here in late December? To watch her "third son" marry *his* soul mate? And how the hell was he going to tell David, who'd lost his parents over ten years ago in a horrific car accident, that his "second mom" was *dying*?

It was in that moment Jackson realized he didn't want to be alone. Not tonight. *Her* face then drifted through his dazed mind.

Appropriate? Not even close for reasons that included Jillian's current feelings for him. The chances of her being available on short notice were also slim. But he had nothing to lose.

He grabbed his phone and texted, *Hi. Are you busy tonight?* He then started the engine.

Will and David were the ones he went to during absolute shit moments in life. And Zach, another close friend, but he was married with a baby girl.

If Jillian said no or was busy, he'd plant himself at a bar near his house.

Jackson was at a light, about to get on I-25, when her response came through.

No. But I don't have any news yet on a space for the party.

He hesitated, then typed, *This isn't about the party. Can we talk in person?* He paused before adding, *Please?* Seconds later he merged onto I-25 and hit the gas pedal.

He rolled down every window in his vehicle. Other drivers were moving at the same rapid rate now that it was pushing eight o'clock.

Jackson focused on the road and the wind, loud and whirling around him. He almost didn't hear his phone ringing in the passenger seat.

He grabbed it, sighed at the caller's name, and answered, "I know it's a lot to ask."

"Jackson, what's going on?" Jillian asked with a hint of exasperation. "We're not friends and never have been."

That was a statement he couldn't get on board with since,

from their beginning, they'd talked and laughed together as if old friends. Everything with them had been effortless. But he shoved those thoughts aside. "I'm asking you to make an exception this one time."

His mom was dying.

Silence fell on her end until, "Okay. I'm at home."

He released a quick breath. "Is Claudia there?"

"No. When she's not at work, she's with Afton at her place."

He changed lanes to pass a slow driver. "Thanks, Jillian. I'll be there soon." He dropped his phone in the passenger seat and placed his head against the headrest.

The noisy wind continued to swirl around him while he sped toward Denver. Farther away from Longmont and his family struggling with a new reality and multiple unknowns. Except one. Leaving like he had probably made him the worst son on the planet, especially after what he'd said to his mom.

His dying mom.

He loosened his tie even more, tugged it over his head, and dropped it next to his phone.

Tomorrow he'd make up for being a bad son. But now all he wanted, at this moment, was to forget.

Chapter Seven

"JILLY, you haven't been to a show in a month," Alyson stated. "Please come tonight?"

Jillian stared out her living room window, watching for *him*.

"I know for a fact," her best friend continued, "that Jackson won't be there. He's up in Longmont having dinner with his family."

She frowned.

He was supposed to be in Longmont with his family? So why on earth had he texted her about needing to talk? She'd also heard the slight edge in his voice during their brief conversation. The main reason she'd said yes to his odd request.

"Becca and Matt will be there," Alyson added.

What the hell had happened with his family that would cause him to text her that he needed to talk? She knew they were hard on him when it came to his work. He'd told her that during one of their many getting-to-know-you chats. While he'd disclosed that fact, the implication he didn't always appreciate their concern for the work hours he kept had been heavy.

"*Jilly?*"

She blinked a few times. "Al, I'm just not feeling up to it

tonight." She kept her eyes trained on the sidewalk. "Three days as my sister's servant felt like three weeks." *And it was only the beginning.* "The wedding tomorrow is so damn big I need to get some sleep. I promise I'll try to make it to next week's show."

Alyson sighed. "Okay." She released a quick laugh. "The backroom at the shop does look and smell like a sea of orange and red roses. It's pretty incredible."

"Have fun tonight and I'll see you in the morning." She picked up her wine glass and sipped while continuing to stare out the window.

She couldn't believe a conversation with his family about his long work hours would cause him to text that he needed to talk. Frustration, definitely. But he'd sounded so *serious*. Not at all like the man she'd grown pretty close to in such a short span of time.

Easygoing. Funny. Loyal. Confident. There'd been none of that in his voice earlier.

Something extremely big with his family had rattled him.

Her phone began to vibrate and ring. When she glanced at the screen, a tiny moan escaped. She was also tempted not to answer, but this person would keep calling until she did.

"Hi, Mom."

"I'm calling to see how it went with you and your sister the last few days."

Jillian took a longer sip of wine. "It went fine." She paused before asking, "Why? Did Brynn say something different?" As much as she loved her older sister, Brynn had always had the habit of *embellishing* the truth to their mother.

"I haven't talked to your sister."

Yet.

"I don't like this arrangement. You two have always had a complicated relationship and the last thing she needs right now is unnecessary stress. Marcos doesn't need it, either."

Jillian pressed her lips together, then said, "I have no intention of causing Brynn or Marcos any *unnecessary stress*. And Brynn asked for my help." For the same reasons Jillian had taken on helping her sister.

"Well, I don't think she'd really thought all of that through before asking you. I just know it's not a good idea for anyone."

What the hell did her mother think was going to happen over the next two months?

No, she and Brynn hadn't always gotten along, especially as teenagers. And, yes, her older sister occasionally suffered from mine-is-better thinking which could be infuriating. It also reminded Jillian of the person on the other end of this call. But she and Brynn were now adults and had, over the years, developed respect for each other and their vastly different lives.

Jillian gripped her phone. "Mom, was there something else you needed? I have somewhere to be tonight."

"Yes. I do. I've decided to come to Colorado and help your sister. It would be best."

She closed her eyes. *Mierda*. She didn't have the time or patience to deal with this, or her mother in general. "*Suficiente*! Everything's fine and we don't need you to come out here."

The harshly spoken words had tumbled out before registering in her brain.

A long, tense silence fell between them.

Jillian finished her wine and turned from the window. No doubt her mother was waiting for an apology, but Jillian couldn't get the words out. It's not like she hadn't meant them.

"Well," her mother finally said, "Brynn and Marcos will have the final say on this."

The line went dead, and Jillian stared at her phone.

Between her mother and Brynn, she'd never hear the end of this…for the *rest* of her life.

She tossed her phone onto the dining room table and marched into the kitchen where she poured herself another glass of wine.

She never should have answered.

Her mother had always had a way of getting under her skin and scraping until Jillian was pushed into a reaction. An itch that had to be scratched. A scab that had to be picked at. That was her relationship with Eva Castillo in a nutshell.

The apartment buzzer exploded from the hallway, causing her to jump.

Jillian filled her lungs with a deep breath, then slowly exhaled. She needed to get the messy moment with her mother out of her heart, mind, and soul. For some reason, Jackson Lovett needed her and she had to do her damned best to be his *friend.*

Everything would be fine.

She headed for the box beside the front door to buzz him into the building. While waiting for him to walk up to the second floor, she gave herself a quick once-over.

Thank God she hadn't changed into her pajamas the moment she'd arrived home from her painfully long commute from Boulder. She had yanked her hair free from the tight ponytail that had started to give her a headache during the drive. Then again, she had no business caring about how she looked for him anymore. On that thought, she opened the front door.

Jackson cleared the last step, looked up, and their eyes connected.

Any remaining thoughts on how she looked or her mother or Brynn left her mind at the sight of his dim eyes, mouth set in a hard line, and sandy-blond hair more mussed than usual.

"What the hell happened to you?" The words tumbled out before registering. Again.

Jackson stopped a foot away from her and slipped his hands into his pockets. "Yeah, apparently I look like shit." He shook his head. "Just didn't have the time to make myself all *GQ* before coming over here."

She sighed. "I said it out of concern." She stepped aside. "Come in."

As she followed him toward the living room, confusion mingled with a hint of anxiousness settled itself onto her shoulders. She didn't recognize this worn out, humorless Jackson Lovett. What the hell *had* happened in Longmont? Despite his occasional irritation with his family when it came to discussing his work hours, she'd always had the impression he was extremely close to every person in his immediate family.

It was something she'd greatly admired about him and the Lovetts. Even envied a bit.

She buried that thought and asked, "Would you like some wine? It's red." Or as Jackson had called it the day they'd met, "headache in a bottle. "

He stopped at her living room window. "That'd be great. Thanks."

While pouring the wine, she eyed him, mouth still set in a hard line as he stared out the window like she'd just been doing. She then met him where he stood and handed him his glass.

He peered at her. "I thought for sure you'd go to the show with Alyson. Especially after a unique workweek?"

She managed a half grin. "Wasn't feeling it tonight." She sipped her wine, then said, "I actually haven't been to one of their shows in a while."

He leaned against the wall. "Me, either." His gaze went to the window once more. "I haven't been a very good friend lately."

"David has to understand." She lifted her shoulders. "He hasn't been out of architecture that long."

Jackson took a drink while still staring out the window.

She searched her brain for something—anything—to get him talking. It was quite clear Jackson Lovett had acquired the weight of the world since she'd last seen him on Wednesday, a mere two days ago.

"How'd it go this week?" he asked, looking at her.

She forced her mouth into a smile. "It was fine. I think it'll work out great."

A grin played with the right corner of his mouth. The same corner she'd thoroughly enjoyed kissing during their short time together.

"I think you're lying, Miss Castillo." He took another drink. "How'd it *really* go?"

She sat on the edge of the dining room table. "My sister has turned me into her servant, but it really wasn't that bad."

He nodded, still fighting a smile.

"Spending time with my nephew will definitely be the best part." She sighed. "But my *mother* is convinced she still needs to come out here and help, and I'm now dealing with that."

Darkness flashed through his eyes and settled onto his face. The change was so rapid Jillian lost her breath.

He turned, walked the few steps toward her couch, and sat.

Unable to stand his confusing behavior any longer, she straightened. "Jackson, what the hell is going on with you?" She approached the couch. "What happened in Longmont?"

His head snapped in her direction. "How'd you know I came from Longmont?"

She hesitated before answering, "Alyson told me you were there as she was trying to talk me into...going to the show tonight."

He nodded once, then muttered, "Right."

Jillian eased onto a cushion, keeping her back pressed against the couch's arm. "Tell me what happened," she quietly tried again. "That has to be why you're here."

Jackson focused on her. "It's my mom. She told us tonight she has cancer and that it's"—he cleared his throat—"terminal." He broke their gaze and finished his wine in two swallows.

Jillian stared at him as her mind went into overdrive.

Nancy had terminal cancer? But she'd just seen his mom a week ago at the cabin where she'd looked—a little on the pale side and tired. Jillian had figured she'd been getting over a cold and hadn't thought about it after that. She'd also been focused on avoiding another member of the Lovett family the entire time she'd been there. When she, Claudia, and Afton had been saying their goodbyes to everyone, she'd noticed Nancy had looked better. Still on the pale side, but more vibrant than when they'd arrived.

"Do you mind if I help myself to more of this?" He held up the empty wine glass.

She absently shook her head.

How could Nancy Lovett, a lively, selfless woman with an amazing laugh, have terminal cancer? Outside of her pale features and obvious fatigue, she'd been exactly the same.

Jackson came back with the wine bottle, set it down, and sat in the same spot.

She squinted at him. "How long has she—your parents—known?" There'd been no indication at all, from either of his parents, as to what was physically happening with Nancy.

"A couple weeks," he murmured. "But they got the official diagnosis on Tuesday. She doesn't want to undergo treatment, either." He glanced her way. "We'll have to watch her get *sicker* and not be able to do a damn thing to help."

She set her glass on the coffee table and scooted to his side.

"Jillian, what if I can't do that?"

She grasped his free hand. "You're going to have to do that. You won't be alone, Jackson." She angled her head left to catch his dazed, wide eyes and a portion of her heart split. She also curbed the strong urge to pull him into her arms by gripping his fingers. "What do you need from me?" At this moment, their history didn't matter.

"You're doing it by letting me be here and listening." He

settled back into the cushions. "I can't deal with tomorrow right now. So can we sit here like this, drink wine, and watch something on Netflix? I don't care what it is."

She managed to softly say, "*Si.* We can do that."

He squeezed her hand.

Their fingers remained tightly linked as Jillian forced herself to face forward, away from Jackson. The man she'd fallen in love with now exuding shock over what the future held.

Chapter Eight

JACKSON PULLED INTO HIS PARENTS' driveway and déjà vu surrounded him. The only differences were the garage door was open, his brother and Savannah weren't here, it was mid-morning, and he'd come straight from his house. After taking a near scalding shower to help clear the red wine headache that aspirin had officially killed during his drive up to Longmont.

He sat back and swiped his phone from the center console. His thoughts then strayed to the memory of *her*, sound asleep and curled into a tight ball in the corner of her couch at around midnight when he'd awoken. He still couldn't believe he'd possessed the strength to leave instead of stretching out beside her and accepting the consequences, good or bad. But after covering her with a blanket, he'd left quietly and swiftly, locking the door behind him.

After what Jillian had done for him, he definitely owed her a text.

Hey. I left around midnight and didn't want to wake you. Thanks for last night. Let me know when you find out about a place for the party. He then tapped send and hauled himself from his vehicle. Tomorrow had arrived and he had to face it.

He heard the edge trimmer's unmistakable buzz as he entered the open garage and followed the sounds of yard maintenance coming from the back. Normally, he'd find his parents in the yard. His mom on her knees, working on her flower beds, or vegetable and herb gardens, while his dad mowed or trimmed the bushes. Today, however, his dad was working alone, wearing shit-brown shorts, his obnoxious orange Hawaiian shirt, and equally obnoxious brown sandals with white socks.

Jackson walked toward where his dad stood, edge trimming. When his shadow darkened the area, he looked at Jackson and turned off the trimmer.

Jackson gave him a quick once-over. "Who dressed you today?"

He adjusted his sunglasses. "I'm not Calvin Klein and neither are you, smartass. Your mom's upstairs, reading. When you're done talking with her, you can help me with the swing."

He gestured toward a gargantuan box with the words "Pergola 3-Person Patio Swing" printed across the top. "Your mom wanted a swing in the yard." His dad grinned. "With the way the weather's been going the last few years, I figure she'll be able to enjoy it through October. Maybe even here and there…" His voiced trailed into silence.

Jackson nodded. "Is she in the office?"

"Yes. Lately, she's been falling asleep while reading." His dad cleared his throat. "Don't be afraid to wake her up."

Jackson faced the house and, by the time he reached the sliding-glass door, the edge trimmer revved to life. He closed the door and the silence shrouded him. He couldn't remember the last time he'd been in his childhood home on a Saturday morning.

Was it always this quiet? Or was the eerie stillness a representation of the coming months? Of what he and his family—specifically his dad—were facing?

He slowly headed for the staircase.

As he approached the living room, his gaze landed on their most recent family portrait hanging above the fireplace. Unbelievably, the picture was already almost a year old.

Jackson paused on the threshold of the living room when it hit him.

His mom's illness would most likely prevent *this* year's portrait from happening.

It was her pet project. She arranged the date, time, place, and told everyone what to wear. It typically happened around Thanksgiving, too. A tradition she'd started when he and Will were little kids. The clothing coordination hadn't started until Brendan turned a year old. Last year's clothing theme had been black and white, more formal than previous years.

In that moment, Jackson recalled the Hawaiian-themed portrait taken years earlier.

A quiet laugh escaped since that picture had been the definition of terrible. It had been so awful, he and Will, the times they'd been here for dinner that year, had taken turns removing the picture from the wall, hiding it somewhere in the house, then had betted on how long it would take their mom to notice. His grin faded, though, when he remembered sharing that story with Jillian not too long after they'd started dating. They'd been swapping funny sibling stories. Her addictive, throaty laughter had caught the attention of people near them in the restaurant.

The first time he'd made her laugh like that had been at Becca's party. He couldn't remember what he'd said, but Jillian's laughter had made his head buzz then and it still did.

Jackson turned from the picture and continued toward the staircase.

As amazing as she'd been last night, being with him without saying a word, now wasn't the time to be thinking of her.

When he cleared the last step, he headed right toward Will's old bedroom that had been transformed into their parents' office years ago.

He paused in the doorway.

His mom, wrapped in a blanket, sat in the corner of their old, brown leather loveseat.

Jackson walked into the room.

Her head popped up, then she closed her book and removed her reading glasses.

"I'll never understand why you waited to tell us what was going on." He closed the door behind him. "Didn't you think we might have something to say about all of this?"

"Of course you would have. Your dad certainly did. But that doesn't change the fact I make the final decision since the cancer is inside of *me*." She put the book aside. "And if you don't like my decisions, I'll tell you the same thing I told him. The hell with you!"

Jackson straightened at the force behind her words, suddenly feeling foolish and unreasonable. Because she was, like Savannah had been last night, absolutely right.

"I will concede," she added in a gentler tone, "not telling you, Will, and Savannah when we received the initial diagnosis may not have been fair to you. And for that I am sorry." She nestled deeper into the blanket, exhaustion settled around her bleary eyes and lined mouth.

Jackson couldn't ignore the obvious that her physical decline had barely begun.

He buried the harsh reality into the deepest place in his mind while lowering himself onto the loveseat's matching ottoman. "I didn't mean to sound like a complete ass when I walked in here." He paused before adding, "Or last night before I left."

She gave him an affectionate smile.

"I happened to look at the family picture on my way up here." He sighed, then recalled his dad's comment from last night.

"Mom, I'm really sorry for the rotten thing I said to you last night and promise I'll support the decisions you make."

Jackson's memory went to the brief exchange with Jillian about watching his mom get sicker and not being able to do a damn thing about it.

"*What if I can't do that?*"

"*You're going to have to do that.*" She'd also said he wouldn't be alone.

His mom withdrew her hand from beneath the blanket, clasped his, and squeezed.

No, he wouldn't be alone. But that reminded him of who he needed to see after leaving Longmont. David slept pretty late on Saturdays since his band played until midnight or so on Friday nights. Jackson would eventually have to shoot him a we-need-to-talk text.

His mom, still grasping his hand, scooted down until she had her head resting on a throw pillow. She gave him a sleepy smile. "It is a lovely portrait. I think it's my favorite one so far."

He fought a grin. "Not the infamous Hawaiian-themed portrait?"

Her smile dipped. "All of you are never going to let that go."

Jackson started to laugh and, within seconds, she joined him.

"Those shirts were pretty awful," she said around her laughter. "What was I thinking?"

"Dad's wearing his right now, so you have at least one fan." His smile matched hers. "The rest of us burned our shirts in the fire pit at the cabin."

"I don't want to hear any more." She shook her head. "What all of you—namely you and your brother—do up at the cabin needs to stay there."

Jackson suddenly remembered David and Alyson considering the cabin as their wedding spot. And of course that unforgettable weekend in March with Jillian.

He pushed the memory into the deepest parts of his mind, as well, and said, "I was supposed to tell you and Dad last night that David and Alyson thought the cabin might be a good place for them to get married and wanted—"

His mom gasped, followed by an enormous smile that made her look like his mom from the last thirty-two years. "You have to tell them the cabin's theirs!"

Jackson angled his head back and released a quick laugh. "I think they're considering a couple of other places, too. Like her parents' house in Evergreen."

She again squeezed his hand. "Tell them to call me. I'll talk them into choosing the cabin." Her smile slowly faded. "Have you…told David yet? Them?"

He looked away as his own grin vanished. "No. I was planning on talking to him later today. You know he's up late on Friday nights now."

"Yes. I'm so happy for him, too. I also loved seeing him and Becca glowing last weekend. Those two absolutely deserve what they have found with Alyson and Matt."

Jackson slowly nodded. At the same time, he strongly suspected where this was headed.

"And I've said for years your brother lucked out when he met Savannah." She burst into laughter which prompted Jackson to lift his head. "That weekend your brother came home from school with Savannah attached to his side, your dad and I cornered him in the kitchen." She laughed again. "We told him if he blew it with her *and* didn't start taking his classes seriously, we'd yank him from CSU and put him in some all-boys school we found in Indiana."

"And he apparently bought it."

His mom's pale cheeks became pink. "I was in the middle of preparing dinner and may have been holding a knife when we were talking to him."

He laughed until his eyes connected with hers, now serious.

"It never occurred to us we would have to have the *opposite* conversation with you."

And there it was.

Jackson stood. "I'm going to let you get some rest and go help dad."

"Sweetheart, I obviously don't know what happened between you and Jillian."

That made two of them. For the most part.

"And I also know it's none of my business, but I'm not blind."

He frowned. "What are you talking about?"

"You two weren't as sly last weekend as you thought you were." She pointed at him. "I caught you looking her way without her knowledge as much as I caught her doing the same thing to you." She leaned forward. "That said, what's the problem?"

He'd gone into business with the devil. At least, that's all he knew for certain. But he said, "Mom, it wasn't meant to be." He edged past the ottoman. "I'm also too busy for anything serious right now." Not exactly a damn lie, either, considering the Downey Project and being up to his neck in thick bullshit that would not be going away any time soon.

"Jackson Richard Lovett, you need to stop letting work interfere with having a *real* life."

He froze at his mom's razor-sharp tone and words.

She released an exasperated sigh. "You're thirty-two years old and single. You have a beautiful house you're never at because Savannah was right last night. You live at your office. You love everything about the outdoors, but rarely spend time there." Her eyes sharpened to a point. "And then there's your family who hardly sees you. All of this is because of your work."

Shit. He couldn't deal with this conversation that also felt like déjà vu. Times ten. So he turned and headed for the door. "Dad's waiting for me." He placed his hand on the knob.

"I also have a strong feeling that your work is what really happened between you and Jillian, and every woman you've dated since starting the firm."

He opened the door.

"Sweetheart, I understand how important the firm is to you and your career, but your life doesn't have to be this way."

His steps faltered at the sadness that had taken over her voice and he paused.

She made it sound so simple, but it wasn't since she and no one else in his family understood what he was currently up against. On top of being "the boss." They didn't need the additional worry, either. Especially now.

Jackson looked over his shoulder at his mom, her eyes wide with concern. "Mom, I'll be fine. I promise." He stepped into the hallway and closed the door.

The Downey Project was too damn important to the firm, everyone who worked for him, *and* his career. Which meant his life did have to be this way until his neck was free of the noose-like bullshit.

JILLIAN CAREFULLY SET the vase of bright-red and deep orange roses on the left corner of the white platform, then straightened and turned.

Today's happy couple had opted to have their ceremony in an event space that opened to the outdoors. Despite the warm weather Colorado experienced in early September, the bride and groom had chosen to remain indoors which didn't take away from the elegance.

Rows of covered chairs faced the platform where the couple would exchange their vows. At the end of each row sat three LED candles that provided as much warm glow as real candles would.

A long, white aisle runner ran from the end of the last row right up to the platform's two steps. The red and orange roses in their clear vases encompassed by green filler gave the room a splash of color against all the bright white.

Hermosa.

Still, as much as Jillian loved each perfect result no matter the location, having a wedding of such grandeur had never appealed to her, cost having nothing to do with it either.

She spun in slow motion, taking in her surroundings one more time.

Something about all of this was too elegant, too magnificent, too…*perfect.*

She closed her eyes as a much better wedding scene filled her mind.

Nearby, pounding waves instead of the traditional wedding march or some other over-used song. Barefoot on the beach. Sunset. A gentle breeze coming off of the water. Warm, soft sand between each toe and getting into the hem of a simple, yet shimmery wedding dress. And the completely *GQ* groom—she opened her eyes and shook her head.

Mierda. Jackson had been heavy on her mind today.

"Jilly?"

She spun in the direction of Alyson's voice.

Her friend held the last vase of flowers going in the room. "Where were *you* just now?"

With Jackson and his mom and the total unfairness of it all. Well, that's where her mind had been before her brief trip into Fantasyland. She couldn't say any of that, though. It wasn't her place to tell Alyson about Nancy. Because it was clear Alyson didn't know, that meant Jackson had yet to tell David and that's who she needed to hear it from.

Her friend placed the vase on the right corner of the platform.

"I was admiring another job well done," Jillian replied. *The absolute truth, too.*

Alyson turned the vase slightly left, slightly right, back a bit, then stopped and sighed.

Jillian smothered a smile at her best friend's perfectionism that *always* came out when setting up for *any* kind of event they had.

After adjusting the blooms and filler, Alyson faced Jillian and frowned. "You've been awfully quiet today." She stepped forward and grasped Jillian's hand. "What's going on?"

Jillian wanted nothing more than to tell Alyson the man she loved, who had no idea she felt that way, had been given terrible news the previous night that he was still processing. But *no one* knew of her feelings for Jackson. Still, the words were right on the edge of release.

She opened her mouth, paused, then swallowed the truth, followed by a tight smile. "It was a long week. I'm looking forward to having tomorrow to myself." Again, the absolute truth.

Alyson frowned. "Are you going to be able to handle being up in Boulder Monday through Friday, the horrible commute back home, and working *every* Saturday? Be honest, Jilly."

A humorless laugh escaped. "Well, when you say it like that…" Her voice ended in a deep sigh. "Please don't worry. I'll be okay, Al. I promise." And she would be. Hopefully.

They turned in unison and slowly headed up the aisle.

"I've decided on the colors for the wedding, Miss Maid-of-Honor."

Jillian laughed. "Fantastic! Let's hear it."

"The combination is blackberry gold."

They stopped at the end of the aisle and faced each other.

At the sight of her best friend's enormous smile and glowing face, a twinge of envy tugged at Jillian's insides. An emotion that caused irritation with herself at feeling that way toward Alyson who, like David, did *not* deserve it at all.

She squashed the feeling and returned Alyson's smile.

"The base colors would be black and gold, then we'd throw in deep purple and burgundy for pops of color. What do you think?"

Jillian leaned forward. "I *love it*." Every inch of her meant those words, too.

"There you two are!"

Felicity Mayhew's voice—with the hint of a British accent—made Jillian look left.

The woman, dressed to professional perfection in a gray power suit, walked toward them. "More accurately," she continued, focused on Jillian, "there *you* are." Their eyes caught, and Felicity's widened. "Do you have a few moments to chat?"

This had to mean Felicity had bachelor-bachelorette party venue news for her.

"Yes." Jillian glanced at Alyson, watching her and Felicity. "I'll catch up with you and Campbell in the ballroom?"

"Okay." She gave them one more long, questioning glance before leaving the room.

The moment she was gone, Felicity handed over a piece of folded paper.

"I do believe your timing for the party—the Saturday after Christmas?—is working to your advantage with holiday parties being over. My assistant made calls to several popular places in LoDo and compiled a decent list for you. You shouldn't have *any* trouble choosing a location."

As Jillian grasped the paper, excitement fluttered through her at the fact she and Jackson were doing this for their best friends. Despite the unexpected and unfair twist fate had dealt Jackson and his family, they had to keep moving forward.

Jillian straightened. "This saved me so much time. *Thank you*."

She grinned. "You can really thank me by inviting me to this revelry? Alyson will always have a special place in my heart as Holly Golightly."

Jillian pressed her lips together and nodded. "*Sí.* I know. And of course you're invited."

Felicity stepped back. "Brilliant! I will let you get back to work. I, on the other hand, have a terribly nervous bride who needs my attention."

Once alone, Jillian removed her cell from her back jeans pocket. Jackson had said in his text from this morning to let him know when she had news on places for the party.

A soft smile teased her mouth while she re-read his message. And the image of him covering her with the blanket she'd wrapped herself in at some point before waking up at almost six this morning. But a deep frown replaced the slight smile at remembering the disappointment of him not being beside her, followed by the *why* he'd ended up at her place to begin with.

With a shaky breath she texted, *Hi. Thanks for the blanket. How are you doing? I have a list of potential places.* She paused for several seconds before typing, *Maybe we should meet next week? Wednesday, same place and time?* She tapped send and closed out of messaging.

Thank God her workweek was nearly over. Then she could go home, crawl into the bathtub…and try *not* to think about the surreal turn her life had taken this week.

As she approached the ballroom to join Alyson and Campbell, her phone buzzed and chimed with a text.

She halted just outside the room.

You're welcome. I'm about to leave Longmont for LoDo to meet up with David, but I'm hanging in there. Thanks for asking. Wednesday, same place and time. I'll be there.

Jackson was on his way to talk to his best friend about his mom.

She knew, from what she'd heard from Alyson and seen first-hand, how close David and his sister, Becca, were to the Lovett family, especially Nancy.

Jillian closed out of her phone and shoved it back into her jeans pocket.

Yes, Jackson had been *very* heavy on her mind. And he definitely would be the rest of the day and night.

Chapter Nine

"HEY, TRAVIS." Jackson smirked at the guy seated on a stool outside The Blues Note's doors. He pointed at the fishing magazine. "They pay you to sit there and read that boring crap?"

Travis grinned. "Got here early, did my shit, now I'm relaxing until the doors officially open in an hour." He held up the magazine. "Fishing isn't boring if you go with the right guys, Jack. You should come up with us some time."

He'd corrected the bartender a few times that his was name was Jack*son*. Not until Travis had anyone in his life ever called him *Jack*. But he said, "When the mountains call, I prefer biking or hiking." For the life of him, he couldn't remember the last time he'd done either of those activities he thoroughly enjoyed, and his mom's strong words appeared in his mind.

You love everything about the outdoors, but rarely spend time there.

He smiled tightly. "But thanks for the invite. I'm here to see one of your bosses."

Travis went back to his magazine. "Door's open. They were rehearsing, but it sounds like they must be taking a break now."

It took Jackson's eyes several seconds to adjust to the club's darkness after being in the sunlight. It reminded him of the few times he'd been in Las Vegas, spending a long period of time inside, then walking out *into* sunlight. The simple action literally a glaring reminder it was daytime and that life was happening beyond the dim, noisy, smoky walls of the hotel-casino.

He walked deeper into the spacious club and stopped when he spotted David seated at his piano on the stage. He was talking easily with a couple of his bandmates.

Jackson couldn't imagine working all day in a dark club with almost no windows.

David and his bandmate, Randy, had bought the place over a month ago from two brothers who'd been burned out on the long hours and Denver nightlife. But this world suited David for many reasons, the most important one being the fact his buddy was, at his core, a musician. Once he'd made the decision in March to leave architecture and pursue music full time, everything had snapped into place. Though no one deserved what he now had more than his best friend, Jackson couldn't ignore the pang of longing. Like the one happening at this moment. It was as if he was missing a few big pieces of *his* complicated puzzle.

Your life doesn't have to be this way.

David stood. "Guys, I have to call it for the day. I'll see you later."

In a matter of seconds, he was heading right for Jackson. And with a bounce in his step that had become permanent since reuniting with Alyson.

"Whoa." David stopped and squinted at him. "*You* look like horseshit."

Jackson narrowed his eyes.

Yeah, he looked tired for sure. But he wasn't certain how or why that equated to "looking like shit," which was basically all he'd heard the last twenty hours or so.

David grinned. "What the hell did you do after leaving Longmont?"

Jillian seated near him on her couch, quietly drinking wine and watching the movie, re-appeared in Jackson's mind for the umpteenth time that day. She'd been everything he'd wanted and needed. She'd also been close but miles and miles away from him.

"Hey." David stared at him. "What happened last night?"

Jackson sighed. "Is there somewhere in here we can talk?" Telling David at his new place of employment had not been Jackson's first choice. But as co-owner of this club, he spent a good portion of his time here, specifically Thursdays, Fridays, and Saturdays.

David's grin transitioned into a frown. "Yeah. Randy and I have a designated booth in the back that we call the downstairs office. Nobody bothers us when we're there unless it's important." He paused, then added, "Do you want a beer?"

Something stronger would be better. Out of respect for the fact David wouldn't be able to drink while Jackson told him everything he needed to, he replied, "No, I'm good. Thanks."

As Jackson followed David, he remembered a conversation he'd had with his mom years ago, not too long after his friend had gotten out of a month-long stay in rehab. To overcome a destructive and scary relationship with alcohol after losing his parents and almost losing Becca.

David had loathed the idea of staying in his childhood home while helping his aunt and uncle get it ready to sell. He'd been determined to commute to Longmont from his aunt and uncle's house in Denver. Jackson had shared that info with his mom, who'd then called David and told him he could stay with them for as long as he needed. Not too long into David's stay with Jackson's parents, she'd started calling him her "third son."

He and David sat across from each other in one of the many

booths lining the walls of the club. The actual bar took up a good portion of the club's center.

"You're not here with good news," David stated. "So just give it to me straight."

Jackson despised everything about this situation for a shitload of obvious reasons that included the chance his mom…might not make it to David and Alyson's wedding. At least, that's how it had sounded last night.

As everything came out, slightly easier than it had with Jillian, David listened, his eyes wide with shock while his mouth inched open.

When Jackson finished, David sat back, now staring at the table.

Silence, outside of sporadic bursts of laughter coming from the stage, settled between them. And stayed there until David suddenly cleared his throat.

"She's not in any pain. Right?"

Pain? That was something—an image—that hadn't occurred to him until this moment.

Jackson's mind rewound to when he'd been with his mom this morning in the office. She'd definitely looked tired and pale, but there'd been no signs of discomfort due to pain. His dad hadn't said anything of the sort, either.

"No," he replied. "It doesn't seem so right now—" He stopped at those two extra words.

David released a long, slow breath.

"But believe it or not," Jackson added, "I do have good news."

His friend raised his eyebrows.

"Mom said you and Alyson have to get married at the cabin." Jackson tried on a smile. "She wants you to call her so she can talk you guys into it. I told her you were also thinking about Alyson's parents' house in Evergreen."

David nodded once.

Jackson sat back. "I hate that I had to come here and tell you—"

"No, you did the right thing." David shook his head. "But getting married at the cabin doesn't seem very important now, you know? Al will feel the same way when I tell her..." His voice trailed into another round of silence.

"Don't tell my mom that." Jackson gave his friend a slight grin. "She'd find a way to kick your ass if you say that in front of her."

David returned his slight grin. "She'd find a way to kick my ass if I said that to her over the phone." He expelled a quick breath and straightened. "I'll call her tomorrow. I promise." He paused before saying, "I'd call her tonight, but I need to tell Al. And Becs. And process—"

"I get it, David. Trust me," he added under his breath. In fact, Jackson was still processing a reality he'd never seen coming.

"So what *did* you do last night after leaving Longmont?"

Jackson opened his mouth, the truth right there. But "I went back to the office" came out in a rapid mess of words instead. Maybe because a huge part of him wanted to keep such a private moment in time with Jillian...private. And uncomplicated.

David stared at him. "Okay. That's fair. But what the hell are you going to do?"

He frowned. "What do you mean?"

"About work?" His friend leaned forward. "I know how much *more* you've taken on since I left, especially with Zach having a wife and baby to get home to at a reasonable hour. You were supposed to bring in another architect to replace me back in July."

"I know that," Jackson muttered. "The Downey Project has had my complete attention." And did he like it that way? Not one damn bit. But that's the way it was right now.

"Then put Zach and Cruz in charge of hiring another archi-tect," David shot back.

Jackson inhaled deeply before stating, "I'm the managing partner. It's my responsibility." He wasn't trying to sound like a control freak, but it really *was* his responsibility, being in his job description. That he'd written up when creating the firm.

David continued to stare at him as he said, "Put *me* and Zach in charge of it."

Jackson peered at him.

"Which is what you should've done before I left."

He gritted his teeth. "Thanks. But don't you have enough going on?" He gestured toward the club. "Between now co-owning and managing this place"—he lowered his hands—"the band, Alyson, planning a wedding that's happening in a few months, I'd say you're tapped."

"I'll be the judge of that."

They eyed each other as a tense silence surrounded them.

"Jackson, you can't do it all alone, and at some point you're going to have to step back."

He glanced at David, watching him through frustrated eyes. Much like his mom had been looking at him earlier before he left his parents' office to go help his dad.

Jackson understood what David was *really* saying. But he couldn't step back from work. Not now. The firm—his career—would never survive if he did.

"You have to hire another architect," David restated. "Stop being a stubborn asshole and let me help you do that."

Jackson suddenly needed fresh air, the privacy of his quiet backyard, and a stiff drink. Preferably two. So he scooted from the booth and stood. "I'll think about it, talk to Zach, and get back to you next week." He turned, but then stopped and looked over his shoulder at the only person who, outside of his family, had known him the longest. "I'm really not trying to be a dick, but *this* place is your life now. Not architecture."

"Being away from the club for a couple of days here and there won't be a big deal."

He stepped back. "Okay. Thanks for the offer to help."

"No thanks required." His friend also stood. "After everything you and your family have done for Becs *and* me—" He cleared his throat. "I'll call your mom tomorrow."

Jackson nodded, turned, and walked toward the entrance-exit.

As he drove south to his "beautiful house he was never at," he'd try his damnedest not to wish he was headed for *her* place in Wash Park. Or that she was meeting up with him at his place. Considering everything that had happened the last twenty hours or so, being alone no longer held the same appeal. Unfortunately, alone was his other current reality.

▭

JILLIAN POKED her head into Brynn and Marcos's bedroom. "Hi. Just wanted to let you know I'm here."

Brynn removed her glasses. "We need to talk."

She stared at her sister while somehow managing to hold back the long, weary sigh because she knew exactly *who* they'd be discussing.

"Mom had me on the phone for an hour Friday night." Brynn shifted against the pillows.

Jillian leaned against the doorframe. "*Por supuesto.*"

"She was really upset by what you said."

"Brynn, she wasn't listening to a damn word I was saying." Per Eva Castillo's usual when it came to her relationships with most people.

"Well, telling her we didn't need her here—"

"It slipped out." Jillian had also been expecting company and had needed to get off the phone. But she wasn't about to tell her sister that. "It's not as if what I said was a lie, right?"

Her sister sighed. "No, but you never should've said it and you hurt her feelings. *Again.*"

Jillian narrowed her eyes.

"I'm the one she runs to every time you two get into a…thing. Which is *always.*" Brynn shook her head. "I'm tired of it and it's not fair. I have enough going on right now."

Jillian straightened. "Did you happen to mention any of this to Mom while on the phone with her Friday night?"

Brynn pointed at her. "She wouldn't have called me if not for what you said."

Of course her sister hadn't said anything to their mom.

She raised her chin. "You should be having this conversation with her. What do you need done?" If she could help it, she wouldn't come back up here today unless it was necessary.

"Jilly, it's not a secret Mom's difficult. But she is who she is and it's not going to change." Brynn rested her head against the pillows. "Can you *please* figure out a way to get along with her until the babies come? I can feel my blood pressure rising just having this conversation and remembering how upset she sounded Friday night."

Maybe if their pushy mother would listen every now and then, her feelings wouldn't get hurt so damn much. But Jillian crossed her arms and said, "*Si.* Your wish is my command."

Brynn glared at her. "You don't have to be a smartass."

"What do you need done today, Brynn?" she repeated.

Her sister tilted her head left. "There's one more thing we need to talk about."

Jillian pressed her lips together while taking a deep breath.

"Marcos went to the Broncos game with Niall yesterday."

She lifted her shoulders. "Yeah."

Brynn gave her a ghost of a smile. "He asked Marcos about you."

Jillian froze.

"Marcos actually called it 'pumping him for information about you'." She smirked. "I knew I saw some kind of spark between you two on Thursday."

Oh, *hell no*. She could not deal with this, now or ever.

"But Marcos didn't give him your phone number when he asked."

Jillian squinted at her sister.

Niall had asked for her phone number, too? Yes, he'd been a tad on the flirty side, but she hadn't given him the I'm-interested vibe at all. So clearly Niall Donnelly was young *and* arrogant. Even if her heart, mind, and soul weren't tangled up in another man, she would never be interested in a guy like that, no matter how good-looking.

She forced her mouth into a bright smile. "I'll make sure and tell Marcos thank you for not giving him my number. Can I go now? Are we finished here?"

Brynn raised her eyebrows. "You're single and have been for months, but you're not interested in a guy who looks like Niall?"

She shrugged. "What can I say? I like men my own age or older, so stop playing Cupid."

"Actually," her sister slowly said, "I was going to tell you not to encourage him." Brynn patiently smiled. "Niall's young and doesn't need a woman with…baggage."

"Baggage?" Jillian gaped at her sister. "But you want to set me up with a lawyer in Marcos's office?" *Santo cielo*. What the hell was happening here?

"You just said you like men your own age or older," Brynn countered. "That's another way of saying having real experience in life *and* with relationships. Jilly, Claude and I know something big must have happened with that guy Jackson because—"

"Brynn, we're not having this conversation." *Not now or ever.*

"*Fino!*" she snapped. "The laundry needs to be done. Marcos left Sebastian's schedule for the week on the kitchen table." She slipped her glasses back on and focused on her laptop.

Jillian spun from the doorway and marched down the stairs.

Mierda. The thought of her sisters talking about her and Jackson and her "baggage" caused Jillian to tighten her hands into fists. Not everyone was meant to be with their soul mate like nearly all of the people in her circle. Or fall in and out of love like Claudia did, behavior no one in her family questioned. Just because Claudia was the baby.

She veered right, into the kitchen, and stopped at the table.

Maybe falling in love—too quickly—with a man who she'd known for a fact was nowhere near ready for that kind of commitment, then abruptly ending things with him, could be classified as "baggage." But all she'd told her sisters was it hadn't worked out with Jackson. A simple and pretty accurate explanation. Still, when had having "baggage" become toxic? That's how Brynn had made it sound. No, they didn't know the *real* reasons behind the split that had led to her indefinite break from dating—one she'd end when she was damn good and ready.

Also known as no longer loving Jackson Lovett...at some point in the faraway future.

Jillian's phone buzzed and burst to life from her back jeans pocket.

"Hi," she answered. "What's up?" Though she had a strong feeling as to why her best friend was calling.

"Have you, by chance, talked to Jackson recently?" Alyson slowly asked.

Just what she suspected.

Jillian paused to formulate her answer, not certain how much she wanted Alyson to know, namely about Jackson ending up at her place Friday night. So she simply said, "Yes."

Her friend released a deep sigh. "You know about Nancy?"

Jillian pulled out a kitchen chair and sat. "Yes."

"Did you know on Saturday?"

"Yes." Jillian winced. "But it wasn't my place to tell you."

"I know that," Alyson murmured. "When did Jackson tell you? He didn't get a chance to talk to David until Saturday evening."

She leaned back into the chair. "He needed someone to talk to and called me Friday night after he found out." *The absolute truth, too.*

"Wow. That's a little surprising. You two haven't exactly been close since April. Is there something going on with you two again?"

Outside of heart-breaking news and planning the surprise bachelor-bachelorette party? "No." Jillian stared at the kitchen floor. "How's David doing?"

Silence, followed by, "He's been pretty quiet." Alyson released a humorless laugh. "But Nancy let him have it yesterday when they were on the phone and he didn't want to talk about the wedding. And it *is* happening at the cabin at Nancy's insistence. Neither of us could say no."

Jillian grinned. "Al, it'll be absolutely magical. Winter and New Year's Eve on Lake Estes?" She would, with a lot of help, make sure their wedding was exactly that way, too.

"Yeah, but..." She sighed again. "Jilly, Nancy's diagnosis is grim. What if she—"

"Alyson, you can't go there." None of them, especially Jackson and his family, could go there. "Do you really think Nancy would let anything stop her from being at your wedding?" That statement, though, caused her to think of Jackson.

What if he, someday, chose a path that included a wife and kids?

They'd never know his mom.

The mental image caused yet another portion of Jillian's heart to splinter.

"You're right," Alyson firmly stated. "Everything will be perfect."

"*Absolutamente*." Jillian picked up Sebastian's schedule for the week. "Let's talk later, okay? It's time for me to become Brynn's servant."

She continued to stare at her nephew's schedule after they hung up.

Soccer practice. Birthday party sleepover Thursday night, since there was no school this Friday for some reason. Hadn't the kids already had a three-day weekend? Shopping for the birthday present between now and Wednesday.

She dropped the paper onto the table, stood, and went to the laundry room, located between the kitchen and garage. But when she saw the two hampers full of laundry, she released a long, tiny moan. Still, being the Ortegas' servant meant keeping her mother in Hawaii.

Completely worth it.

Chapter Ten

THERE WAS a quick knock from Jackson's office doorway, then, "Hi. Do you have a sec?"

He glanced up to find Laura, the firm's lead interior designer, standing just inside his office. She gave him a huge smile he couldn't help but return.

"Of course." He waved her forward. "Welcome back. How was your trip?"

Laura approached his desk. She wore a pair of jeans with a white T-shirt that made her look even more tan. Her weeks spent in the sun had lightened her brown hair, too.

"Spectacular. Blissful. Unforgettable." She laughed as she sat in a chair in front his desk. "There aren't enough good adjectives to describe spending two weeks in Indonesia."

He kept his smile in place. Because the thought of spending two weeks getting lost in several Indonesian islands with nothing more than a backpack full of beach clothes and sunscreen caused a different type of envy to settle around him. And it hit him.

Outside of sporadic, short weekend trips to the mountains and Estes Park, he hadn't taken a *real* vacation since before starting the firm over three years ago.

"*And*," Laura added around a quick laugh, "Josh proposed while we were gone." She continued laughing as she held up her left hand now sporting a simple, yet shiny ring.

Jackson pushed his realization aside and laughed with her. "Congrats, Laura. That's great." He'd always liked Josh, too. The couple had actually become Jackson's go-to friends during ski season since they skied as well as he did, if not better. "Have you told Marjorie? I think she's still a little upset David and Alyson got engaged after he left."

Laura's smile grew. "She does like planning parties around here. And no, not yet. I'm telling people one at a time and thought I'd start with you. Being the boss and all."

Right. The boss drowning in the job description *he'd* written. Jackson somehow managed not to frown at the irony and asked, "Do you guys have a date set?"

"No, but we are thinking about having a destination wedding."

He laughed. "Doesn't surprise me a bit." The couple averaged two big vacations a year. Traveling was in their blood and absolutely nothing stopped them from exploring the world. So of course they'd be considering a destination wedding.

"What'd I miss around here?" she asked. "And speaking of weddings, did David and Alyson pick a date and place?"

He leaned back in his chair. "New Year's Eve at my family's cabin on Lake Estes."

"Oh, that sounds so romantic," she murmured. "Perfect for them, too. Anything else?"

Jackson had yet to tell anyone in the office about his mom. Maybe because he was still trying to accept everything; the changes since Friday and the changes that were coming.

His phone's intercom beeped, followed by, "Nelson Downey's on the line *again*."

His jaw tightened. "Marjorie, tell him I'm in a meeting." He glanced at Laura, watching him closely, and shot her a half grin. It's not like he was alone.

"Jackson, he's called three times today and is getting more and more *upset*."

"If it's important, he can leave a message and I'll call him back." But he knew why Downey had called three times. "I'll buy you lunch tomorrow for dealing with him so much today, okay?"

There was a long pause on her end, then, "My favorite place?"

"Done." He released a quick breath once she disconnected.

"I heard from Cruz," Laura slowly said, "that Downey and Ember Leventhal made *quite* an impression around here last week."

Jackson stayed silent, staring at the contracts piled on his desk that needed reviewing.

Between being caught off guard Friday night, doing damage control on Saturday for being a dick to his mom, talking to David, and nursing a massive hangover yesterday from checking out Saturday night, he hadn't looked at the Downey Project designs since Friday.

"Jackson? Is everything okay with that project?"

No, not one damn bit. But he said, "Downey and Ember threw me a curve ball last week, but it'll be fine." He straightened. "When are you officially back in the office?"

She stood. "Wednesday. Josh and I are still upside down with our internal clocks. But I do have my first design meeting with Tricia and Ethan Albright that morning."

Jackson smiled. "Good. Cruz told me they've been great to work with."

"Yes." She laughed. "Such a nice change from Vivienne Dunne. Though David's connection with her definitely saved all of our sanities in the long run."

Yeah. One reason Jackson had stalled on hiring a new architect. As much as David belonged in the life he now had, he'd been a damn good architect, especially when it came to working with *crazy* difficult clients. For that reason, David would have probably been a much better architect for the Downey Project.

His best friend's offer from Saturday reappeared in his mind.

Laura stepped backward. "I'll see you Wednesday."

"Okay. Tell Josh I said congrats." Jackson's gaze again landed on the contracts, then his computer. Where the most important architectural designs of his life to date were waiting to be perfected. Time, which he had little of under normal circumstances, was also of the essence.

He glanced at his colleague. "Hey, Laura?"

She stopped inside his office doorway.

"If you and Josh do decide on a destination wedding, where would it be?"

She grinned. "Aruba is our first choice. Oh, that reminds me. When Josh and I do decide on everything, we're throwing a save-the-date party."

Aruba. An island surrounded by warm, Caribbean water with white sand and palm trees.

"Why do you ask?"

He lifted his shoulders. "Just having an anywhere-but-here moment." An exotic trip like that would be perfect with the right woman. The kind of woman who could make you forget about the real world by merely being present. "Have a good night."

You can't do it all alone.

Jackson hesitated for a few seconds, then picked up his office phone.

"I'm about to leave for the night," Marjorie answered a tad on the testy side.

He couldn't blame her, either, since she'd been the one dealing with Downey all day.

"Tomorrow can you pull out those résumés we received

before David left and call the candidates I chose as possibles? They're probably no longer looking, but it's a place to start."

"Yes. I can do that."

"If any of them are still looking, set up interviews for early next week." That would give Zach *and* David enough time to work the interviews into their vastly different schedules.

"Okay. And if none of them are still looking?"

He sat back. "Get in touch with the recruiter we used and we'll start over." Only this time around, he would add a few more things to the job description of "Senior Architect."

Jackson picked up his cell and saw that his brother had texted him.

Call me as soon as you get the chance.

Shit. That didn't sound good and the possibility of more bad news meant Will would have to wait. Jackson then went into his contacts and chose another all-too familiar name.

"Hey," David answered. "I was actually going to call you. Matt and I were talking, and we need a hard game of basketball. Can you meet us at the gym?"

Although Jackson wanted nothing more than to meet up with his buddies for a hard game of basketball, he had no choice but to say, "It's not a good night for me, but thanks."

David stayed silent.

Jackson strongly suspected what his friend was thinking at that moment and added, "Okay. You win. I'm hoping interviews for a new architect can start early next week. Will that work for you?" And, really, who better to hire his replacement?

Nothing.

"David, are you there?"

"Yeah," he answered around a quick laugh. "I'm just savoring the words '*you win*' coming from you. And I think for the first time in—"

"Will early next week work for you or not, wiseass?"

"It'll be fine."

After they hung up, Jackson put his phone aside and went back to staring at the contracts.

Hiring another architect willing to take on more than what David had shouldered would definitely help. It wouldn't, however, help him with the Downey Project.

Avoiding Nelson Downey today would bite him in the ass tomorrow. Unless, of course, he could finish the redesign for his bastard client, the mouthpiece Keith Marsden, and the so-called great Ember Leventhal.

With that thought, Jackson picked up the contracts, put them aside, and focused on his computer. It's not like he had anything better to do tonight. Or anyone waiting for him outside of this building. At least, not until his Wednesday morning meeting with Jillian. A moment he found himself looking forward to, despite the highly unexpected direction their relationship had taken.

JILLIAN'S STEPS faltered when she spotted Jackson walking from the other direction. He was on the phone, but as they met outside the coffee shop, he said, "I'll take a look when I get to the office" and hung up.

The corner of his mouth lifted in a small smile while he slid his phone into his pants pocket. "Hey." He gestured at the space between them and the shop's door. "Good timing today."

"It appears so." She took in his dark sunglasses, black polo shirt, and khaki pants that of course fit him *perfectly*. Though his eyes would be the true tell to his emotional and mental well-being, she couldn't help but say, "You look—"

"Like shit. I know." He frowned. "I haven't slept well the last couple nights."

His mumbled confession made yet another part of her heart crack.

After the next few months, would there be anything left of her heart?

"Actually," she murmured, "I was going to say you look better than you did on Friday."

He brought back his small smile. "Thanks. I'm pretty sure you're the only one who thinks that." He shook his head, then opened the door for her. "But it did earn you a coffee on me." Once they were inside, he asked, "Your usual?"

The fact he still remembered her favorite coffee drink made her softly smile while she replied, "*Si*. I'll grab us a table." Of course, they had been here several times while dating.

When she was seated at a tiny table for two along the shop's wall, she went into her purse and pulled out the list of event spaces. She then slid her gaze to Jackson now at the counter, ordering their drinks.

He'd taken his sunglasses off and hooked them on the front of his polo shirt. She remembered from their brief time together him saying when he dressed like he was today it typically meant he had a "light day," meaning no meetings with clients. Still, his tight mouth and stiff posture seemed to scream the weight of his world was consuming him.

Santo cielo. Jackson Lovett needed a break from his life. Really, life in general. That thought became amplified when he sat across from her and slid her coffee in her direction.

"I'm sorry you're not sleeping well." She'd known his eyes would tell the true story.

He took a drink and held up the cup. "It's why caffeine has become my drug of choice."

She sighed. "Jackson, it's not funny. You have so much going on—"

"I know that. And I appreciate your concern, but I swear I'll be fine." He pointed at the list. "That's the real reason we're here, so let's talk about the party."

She sat back and crossed her arms. "I think I should plan the party myself." She didn't want to do that, but *a lot* had happened in Jackson's life since they met this time last week.

His forehead formed a deep V. "No. It was my idea, I'm the best man, David's like a brother, Alyson might as well be a sister, and I'm going to do this for them."

Jillian remained silent, observing his weary, distant eyes and even tighter mouth.

He leaned forward. "Jillian, I need something good in my life right now, and planning this party with *you* is—" He stopped and took another drink of his coffee. "I need this, okay?"

How could she argue with that and his surprising honesty? And could she really fault him for needing a positive distraction?

"*Sí.* I won't mention it again." Unless he started to look worse from this day moving forward. Then she would mention it again and be unyielding. "How was your mom when you saw her on Saturday?"

"Thanks. And she was good. We…talked for a bit, then I helped my dad build a pergola swing for her." He angled his head toward the paper. "So what do you have there?"

She held back a sigh. Still, had she really expected him to go into the details of his time spent with his parents in Longmont? She slid the paper toward him. "A list of several places in LoDo that are—amazingly—available the Saturday after Christmas." She picked up her coffee and sipped. "I highlighted the ones I like best. I also included their rental fees for that day."

He focused on the list and raised his eyebrows. "Are these places always this pricey?"

She lifted her shoulders. "Around Christmas, yes. And during wedding season."

Their eyes locked over the paper.

"Jillian, I'm not trying to be a cheap bastard here, but I really don't mind throwing the party at my house." He set the paper down. "It's big enough and everyone would be comfortable. I can also buy one of those outdoor heaters for the patio."

She lifted her chin. "I had a feeling you'd say that and came prepared with arguments." She went back into her purse and withdrew a notecard.

Jackson fought a smile which she'd easily take over grimness.

"I expect your undivided attention as I go through each argument I wrote down."

He released a quick laugh. "I'm all yours, Miss Castillo."

She froze, his statement dangling between them as his face turned an incredible bright red. She knew what he'd actually meant, but his phrasing felt far too…appealing.

He pointed at the index card. "I'm listening."

Jillian straightened and focused on her arguments. The party. That's why they were here. "First, now that Alyson and David have chosen your family's cabin as the place for their wedding and reception, they will have to limit the guest list to only family and close friends."

He nodded.

"But they have so many other people in their lives," she continued, "who will want to be a part of their wedding. That's where the bachelor-bachelorette party—your idea—comes in."

"Yeah. But my house—"

"Second, this is going to be a pretty big party." She arched her right eyebrow. "A gaggle of guests, food, drinking, and everything else that goes along with hosting a party that size. *Including* the clean up."

He went back to fighting a smile.

"Third, if we have the party at a spot in LoDo, guests who've been drinking can walk or Uber to a hotel easily and safely." She paused before adding, "Or take light rail home. My first choice is a bar and restaurant near Union Station." Also known as the city's main light rail stop. "It's in a great location, spacious, has a slew of pool tables, and other bar games."

He glanced at the paper. "It has to be the spot you highlighted and circled *three* times?"

"Yes. Because, fourth and final argument, I think it's perfect."

They exchanged quick smiles.

"I think it's so perfect," she slowly said, "I reserved it by paying the deposit."

He blinked. "How much did that cost? This place isn't cheap."

No, it certainly wasn't. But Alyson and David deserved it and more.

"It's not a big deal."

"Jillian, the party was my idea."

"And stopping you from sacrificing your house as the party spot was *my* idea."

"You're right, but I should still be the one paying for this."

She narrowed her eyes. "Why? Because you're Mr. Successful Architect?" *Who drives a Range Rover and lives in a beautiful home in Denver's Hilltop neighborhood.* "Jackson, just because I share an apartment with my sister and drive a Subaru doesn't mean I'm destitute."

He rubbed his eyes. "That's not what I meant."

Silence, outside of the chatter going on around them, settled into their tight space.

"I'll pay the rest. Will that work?"

She gave him a curt nod. "We have to make a decision soon. They'll only hold it for a week. If we don't book and pay the balance by then, we lose it but they'll refund the deposit."

"Okay." He brought his cup to his mouth. "Then what's next?"

She gathered the paper and her notecard. "I haven't been to

that place in a long time, so I thought it would be a good idea to check it out first."

He swallowed some coffee. "Great. When were you thinking?"

She stared at him. "Jackson, you have a lot going on. I don't mind going alone. Or taking Claudia and Afton with me."

Frustration flashed through his cobalt eyes that had brightened a bit during their conversation. Another good sign…not including the frustration she'd ignited by her honesty.

"I told you I need this," he reiterated. "I haven't been there in a while, either, so I'll go with you." He flashed her a smile. "And if you want to bring Claudia and Afton, that's cool. The one time I was around them they didn't strike me as boring."

Jillian laughed. "True. But come to think of it, I'm not sure I could trust them—namely my *sister*—to keep a secret as big as this party."

"Then it sounds like it'll just be the two of us up to our necks in party planning since my family—namely *Savannah*—isn't always good with secrets." His smiled deepened. "I'm okay with just us. Are you?"

She returned his smile. "*Absolutamente.*" Right or wrong, every single cell inside of her meant it. As much as she wanted to revel in Jackson saying it first, though, she couldn't.

With everything going on in his life, he needed any distraction he could get, with or without her right beside him.

"How does Friday night sound?" he asked. "We can meet there at around six?"

His questions caused her thoughts to scatter and fade into the back of her mind. As if a flock of startled birds. She opened her mouth to answer, but his phone started to ring.

He withdrew it from his pocket. "I have to answer this." Into his phone he said, "Hey."

What brightness had filled his eyes in their short time together disappeared, followed by darkness that filled his face, then settled around his mouth. "Fine. Just…give me a sec." He lowered his phone and stood. "I have to take this. I'm sorry. But are we good for Friday night?"

She forced her mouth into a smile. "Sure. I'll see you then."

Jackson turned and rushed out of the coffee shop.

She had a feeling the call was work related, probably about *that project* having to do with soulless Marsden Enterprises. That project he'd chosen to take due to its importance to his firm and career. He'd made that clear in April. That project which seemed to be more of a burden than a cause for celebration. Combined with his family's unexpected reality, it was no wonder he wasn't sleeping well. But there wasn't a thing she or anyone else in his life could do to ease the weight of Jackson's world. He had to do it himself.

Jillian couldn't shake the dismal feeling he'd explode before that happened.

Chapter Eleven

ONCE JACKSON HAD WALKED several steps away from the coffee joint, he said, "Okay, Marjorie. Put him through." He then braced himself for the man's nastiness.

"Lovett? You there?"

"Nelson, what can I do for you?" he asked in the most professional voice he could muster as he approached his SUV.

"I want you to answer this question," his client calmly replied. "Are you trying to ruin your career and put your firm out of business?"

Jackson stopped at the passenger side of his SUV and gripped his phone.

"Because from where I'm sitting," Downey continued, "that's where you're headed after ignoring me the last two days."

He quietly inhaled and released the air. "You're not the firm's only client, and I had a hectic start to the week." It was mostly the truth, and all the sonofabitch needed to know.

"And I left you with a thought *and* challenge last Thursday."

A challenge presented as a way for you to stay the architect on this project or I could give it to another firm before I walk out of this building.

Jackson went to the driver's side. "I remember," he muttered. But now for the fun part. Something he'd planned on doing when he got to the office after his meeting with Jillian that hadn't lasted long enough. "Just because we haven't been able to connect on the phone the last two days doesn't mean I haven't been doing the job *you* hired me to do."

Downey fell silent.

Okay. Jackson hadn't gone back to the designs until Monday night. But still.

Nelson Downey's micromanagement made him want to punch a wall.

During his client's ongoing silence, Jackson started the engine and pulled away from the curb.

"You're saying the designs are ready for me and Ember to look at?"

Jackson couldn't stop from grinning as the fun part began. "Yes. But we have a problem." Or more accurately Downey and Ember had the problem. He was simply the hired help who couldn't make the impossible become possible due to the bullshit called "red tape."

"What exactly would that be?"

He stopped at a red light. "It'd be easier to show you two what I'm talking about." And be more fun since he'd be able to see the looks on their faces. "When can we meet?"

"Ember had to fly out of town this morning for business. She's hoping to be back some time this weekend."

Jackson followed a slow car through the intersection.

Could this really be happening? Would he actually be free of this project—them—for the rest of the week *and* weekend? Yeah, he had a lot to catch up on, but at this point anything was better than dealing with Downey, Ember, and this soul-sucking project.

"Put us on your calendar for first thing Monday morning. I

also recommend you get better at answering my calls from this point going forward. I don't care how busy you are."

The call ended, and Jackson dropped his phone in the passenger seat. When he reached another light, though, he burst into laughter. In spite of the fact he had to look and sound like a lunatic, it felt good. Maybe he'd get some sleep tonight, too, even though the project had not been the only thing keeping him awake at night.

At that thought, his mirth transformed into sobering guilt.

With the exception of meeting up with Jillian, he'd been staying closed up in his office from early in the morning until evening, sometimes later. Lunch and dinner at his desk. No meeting up with his buddies for basketball games.

Downey also wasn't the only person who Jackson had been dodging since Monday. Which made *him* a sonofabitch

He was doing a damn good job of losing himself in his work, but it was simpler right now, despite the Downey Project. Most days he loved his work, too. Reading through and writing contracts, though not exciting, required his full attention. So did being *the boss*, as did meeting with clients and designing—typically the best parts of his job. Unlike David, architecture was Jackson's calling. And getting lost in his calling was often way too easy.

His family, David, some of his colleagues, thought he was missing out on a better life for himself. Beliefs that began when he started the firm, something he'd *never* regret. And what if this life he'd worked incredibly hard to build was as good as it would get? What if he wasn't meant to have what his parents had when he'd been a kid? And Will and Savannah, and David and Alyson, and now Laura and Josh? Not everyone was meant to have it all.

Jackson pulled into his normal parking spot near his office building.

The image of Jillian arching her right eyebrow earlier at the coffee joint filled his brain.

A smile played with the corner of his mouth.

Meeting and dating Jillian Cas*tillo*—he did love the way she said her last name—had been an unexpected punch in the gut. Then he'd taken her to the cabin and, afterward, considered the idea that maybe his life could be more than architecture *and* the firm. Maybe he could have it all someday. For a brief moment in time, it seemed as if Jillian might have been in the same place. But something between them had shifted, followed by being awarded the Downey Project.

He smirked as he opened the door.

Awarded? Plagued with the Downey Project now felt like a more accurate phrase.

Remembering his last few meetings with Jillian, Jackson couldn't help but think they still had a connection. That chemistry which had been instant. He'd told her the absolute truth when he'd said he needed planning the party with *her*.

What he'd left out, however, was planning the party with her was saving *him*.

Jackson walked into his office building, and Marjorie stood.

"Good. You're here." She picked up a file folder and held it out for him to take. "Résumés from the recruiter. I've looked through them and the candidates appear quite strong. Two interviews are on Zach's calendar for Monday. Do you want me to call David?" She raised her chin. "He does still owe me a stapler."

Jackson grinned. "Have at it, Marjorie." He reached for the folder but stopped. "You can give those to Zach."

She lowered the file. "You don't even want to scan them?"

He stepped back. "I trust Zach, David, the recruiter, *and* you." And, shit, did it feel damn good to let go of even that much of his job. "Once Zach and David narrow it down to the top two or three candidates, I'll step in. Until then, I'm out of it."

Her eyes became round behind her equally round glasses before she said, "Good."

He turned to head for the stairs.

"Jackson, one more thing."

He faced her.

She gave him a hesitant smile. "Your brother is up in your office. He's been waiting for about twenty minutes."

Jackson mentally went through every swear word in his vocabulary.

"Should I hold your calls until he leaves?"

"Yeah," he mumbled, facing the stairs once more.

Will worked crawling distance from Civic Center Park, a shuttle ride down the 16th Street Mall from LoDo. When their schedules allowed it, he and his brother would meet for lunch somewhere along 16th Street. But that hadn't happened in a *long* time.

When Jackson reached his office he paused, his gaze landing on his brother, hands in the pockets of his dark suit pants while he stood at the window. "You're here because you're pissed I haven't called you back." Will being the *other* person Jackson had been dodging since Monday.

Will faced him. "I reached pissed off Monday night. Now I'm simply confused."

Jackson stepped forward and pointed at his desk. "Will, I've been swamped." *And avoiding.* Based on the fact Will was shaking his head, his brother probably didn't believe him.

"After three years, don't you think it's time for a new excuse?" Will paused, then added, "Don't you think Mom deserves a better excuse?"

Jackson's jaw tightened and he turned to shut his office door. He kept his back to his brother while taking slow, deep breaths. Once his jaw relaxed, he headed toward his desk where Will stood behind the chair. "I spent a good part of Saturday with Mom and Dad. We're fine."

"So I heard," his brother replied. "But I still felt the need to check in with my little brother because I was worried. So was Savannah."

Jackson looked at his desk as guilt made a head-spinning comeback. "I'm sorry. And I appreciate it. But I've been busy. What the hell do you want from me, Will?"

"I want you to return calls and texts." Will's eyes widened. "What would be even better is you answering your damn phone every now then. There's a thought."

A taut silence landed between them as they stared at one another.

Jackson couldn't remember the last time he and his brother had been locked in a moment like this. It had to have been years ago. Probably when they were still in college.

As kids and teenagers, they'd fought over stupid shit. Like chores. Control of the T.V. Being in each other's bedrooms without permission. The car they'd shared until Will left for college. Calling dibs on having a girl over when their parents were out for the night. Ridiculous sibling stuff that had seemed so damn important at the time. But now, for the first time in their relationship, they were locked in a moment that was beyond important.

"Look," his brother quietly began, "Mom and Dad caught us both off guard on Friday."

All Jackson could do was nod at the enormous understatement.

"Savannah and I have no idea how to tell the kids, either."

At his brother's continued honesty, the irritation and tension left Jackson as if he were a balloon releasing its air.

"Does it ever occur to you that I call and text you because I need to talk to my little brother? Especially after *we* get awful news like we did on Friday?"

Shit. He hadn't expected a confession like that to ever come from his brother.

"No." Jackson sighed and shook his head. "I'm really sorry for blowing you off the last couple days."

Will cracked a smile. "You're actually admitting that's what you did?"

"It was a dick move." Jackson also cracked a smile. "I did learn from the best."

His brother released a quick laugh. "Okay. I deserved that."

"But everything you said was right." Jackson had to snap the hell out of it for not only his sake, but also for his family. "It won't happen again." Every part of him meant those words.

"Good. I'm glad you said that." Will walked around Jackson's desk. "The other reason I've been calling and texting, *and* showed up here, was to tell you Savannah and I want to take everyone out on the boat one more time this season. The weather's looking great for Saturday."

"I'll be there," Jackson assured. "I promise."

"Another good answer." He headed for the door. "My job here as older brother is done."

"Will?"

He looked over his shoulder.

"How are you doing?"

Will's smile vanished. "About as good as you, I'm sure." He paused before adding, "But I have Savannah and the kids." He opened the door. "Saturday, ten a.m. at the cabin."

Jackson faced his catastrophe of a desk. In that moment—and for the first time in his adult life—all he wanted to do was disappear for as long as possible. He knew exactly who he wanted to take, too, and the islands of Indonesia would be perfect for a disappearing act.

———

THE ORTEGAS' servant. That's what her life had become. For the time being anyway.

Jillian sighed while continuing to casually dust the shelving that flanked the fireplace in the family room. The Disney cartoon *Lilo and Stitch,* blaring from the massive T.V., was her servant's soundtrack. At the sound of Stitch brandishing a revving chainsaw and laughing maniacally, she peeked at Sebastian and grinned.

He was still in his p.j.'s, wrapped in a blanket, and sound asleep on the couch.

Some kind of cold or flu was already making its way through his kindergarten class, so Brynn and Marcos had kept him home due to his drippy nose, sore throat, and mild fever.

She went back to casually—really more like carelessly—dusting when a set of worn photo albums on the left bottom shelf caught her attention.

When and how long ago had Brynn acquired their old family albums? Their parents had been divorced for over a decade. Maybe when their mother had moved to Hawaii five years ago?

Jillian set the dust rag on the mantle and dropped to the floor. She pulled the first album out and shifted into a cross-legged position.

She couldn't recall the last time she'd seen these albums, much less flipped through them. But of course her sister would have taken them. It had probably come down to Brynn taking them or the albums ending up in the city's landfill. During and after the divorce, their parents had lost their sentimentality toward the past.

Jillian glanced at Sebastian, his breathing slow and steady with deep sleep, then opened the album. She couldn't stop from grinning at a pic of her with her sisters as little girls wearing similar, bright-red dresses while sitting in front of the Christmas tree. They'd always had to sit or stand in order during photos, too, making Jillian literally the middle child.

It had been a ridiculous Eva Castillo quirk.

Despite the cliché, middle child label, Claude had turned into the "wild child." But then Claudia *had* been the one still living at home when their parents had finally let their marriage die.

Jillian shook her head as she continued to flip through the album.

Page after page of birthday parties. Holidays. Family gatherings. Vacations.

Her grin faded, though, while noting that with each passing year, the older she and her sisters became, the less their parents really smiled for the photos. They'd also at some point stopped standing near one another in group pics; their dad on one end, mom on the other. And barely smiling. Also at some point, there stopped being pics of just *them*.

Their infidelities must have started by then. They'd hidden all of it pretty well—outside of "sneaky," whispered phone calls—until they'd officially separated during Claude's senior year. After that, neither one of them had hidden the fact they were beyond over each other, as well as their marriage.

How did love do that? Die a slow and excruciating death between two people who had met, fallen in love, gotten married, had three daughters, and had successful careers? At one time, her family *had been* the American Dream. How could something so meaningful and important become a marriage and family statistic? These questions more reasons she'd kept her heart and soul to herself all of her dating life.

She'd had absolutely no interest in marriage for fear of ending up like her parents.

But then she'd met…Her thoughts strayed to Jackson.

He'd looked so exhausted, dazed, and *lost* yesterday morning at the coffee shop. A big part of that was due to work, but another part was due to his family—another definition of the American Dream—being dealt an unexpected and unfair card in the deck of life.

Why were a couple like Jackson's parents given the gifts of a soul mate to love and a beautiful family, only to have it all turned upside down in an instant? From what she knew, David's parents had been like Jackson's and their story had also ended tragically and unfairly.

Jillian slid her eyes from her unhappy dad to her unhappy mom in a "family" picture.

The two had been so bitter and miserable by the time they'd separated, in the last decade their dating lives had been as casual as their infidelities. That was no way to live, either.

She picked up her phone she'd set on the coffee table while dusting.

Within a few seconds she was in her photos and tapping a pic she hadn't looked at in months. She'd almost deleted it back in April, too. She'd taken the selfie of her and Jackson after they'd walked out of an ice cream shop in downtown Estes Park *that* weekend.

A soft laugh escaped at the memory and silly photo of them in hats and heavy coats because the high that day had been around thirty degrees. Snow had also been on the ground. But the cold weather hadn't stopped them from playing tourist. Then Jackson had suggested they do something absurd and that was how she'd ended up with a selfie of them wearing goofy smiles while holding up their ice cream cones. The pic happened to be the only *thing* she had left from their brief time together. She also couldn't help but notice Jackson's Colorado sky-blue eyes were bright with humor and ease and happiness. It wasn't only because of their passionate moments together at the cabin. At that particular place in time, he'd been *Jackson*.

Now, six months later, the light had all but faded from his eyes, she was holding on to a picture that represented way more than a perfect day in Estes Park, and they were both alone.

None of that could be considered *living*.

Didn't she and Jackson…her parents…everyone with a heart and soul…deserve better?

Her vision blurred while she closed out of photos, then put her phone back on the table.

"What's wrong, Aunt Jilly?"

She blinked her nephew into focus and grinned at his sleepy gaze. "Just got dust in my eyes. How are you feeling?"

His little body trembled from his huge yawn. "My throat's hurting again."

"Okay. I'm on it." She put the photo album back on the shelf and stood.

That was enough family memories and how's and why's for one damn day.

The doorbell rang while she headed for the kitchen, so she veered left instead of right.

When she opened the door, she halted at the sight of Niall Donnelly, his eyes behind the aviator sunglasses. He also wore a tight white T-shirt, tight jeans, and a shy smile.

"Hi."

"Hello," she slowly answered. She glanced at the two other guys standing by the truck parked in the same spot as a week ago, then frowned. "You guys are here earlier than last week."

Niall nodded. "Yeah. Another job changed dates, so we'll be here in the mornings now."

"Alright. I'll let Brynn know." She started to close the door.

"Actually, I also knocked because I wanted to talk to *you*."

Jillian swallowed an exasperated sigh.

Mierda. She really wasn't in the mood to deal with his puppy-dog crush on her.

His face flushed. "Have you talked to Marcos since Sunday?"

She arched her right eyebrow. "Yes." The truth, though Brynn had told her everything.

He eyed her. "Based on what Marcos didn't say on Sunday and the way you're looking at me, I'm guessing I don't have a chance in hell."

Despite how adorably awkward Niall looked, she said, "No." Maybe if not for Brynn's odd protectiveness of him *and* being in love with another man, Jillian would feel differently. So she added, "I'm on a *mancation* right now." Niall didn't need to know any more than that.

He slowly nodded. "Okay. Friends it is then." He held out his hand. "We can never have too many of those, right?" He held his hand out farther. "You can shake my hand. I promise I wash them frequently."

Jillian absently gripped his hand and they shook.

What was happening here? He wanted to be friends?

"Are you doing anything this weekend?"

She squinted at him. "Excuse me?"

He grinned. "I'm taking my Jeep into the mountains to go four-wheeling, and you look like you could use a break from daily life." He pointed at her T-shirt that held a few dust bunnies.

She briskly brushed them off and said, "I thought I just made my feelings clear."

"And I heard you." Niall leaned forward and pulled down his sunglasses enough to peer over the lenses. "Friends do stuff like four-wheeling." His hazel eyes lit up with humor.

Jillian stared at him.

This kid was too damn cute for his own good. And he knew it.

"I'm not going anywhere with you, Niall."

He pushed his sunglasses back up his nose and straightened. "You can't say no to four-wheeling in the mountains this time of year. It'll be fun and you know it. What else have you got going on this weekend?"

Jillian crossed her arms. "I have to work at my *real* job on Saturday."

"You're working *two* jobs right now?" He gestured at himself. "Then you really need to get away for the day with your new friend, Niall Donnelly."

The giggle escaped before she could stop it, followed by her sister's voice in her head.

I was going to tell you not to encourage him.

"Jillian, come on. What have you got to lose? Since you're working Saturday, we'll go up Sunday. The weather's supposed to be great this weekend." He placed his right hand on his chest. "I promise you I'll be a complete gentleman...even though I do think you're *hot*."

She froze and within seconds her face felt as if she'd set it on fire.

This kid wasn't just cute. He was a tad dangerous.

"But you made yourself clear, and I respect that—"

"Hi, Niall," Sebastian said, appearing at Jillian's left side, but lacking his usual enthusiasm. "I'm sick and can't go to my friend's birthday sleepover tonight."

Niall gave him a sad smile. "Sorry to hear that, buddy. I'd give you a fist bump, but I have plans on Sunday with your Aunt Jilly." He grinned at her. "Can't risk missing that."

Her eyes widened and she leaned forward. "Niall, I never said—"

"What exactly is going on here? Why is Sebastian standing here like this?"

Jillian briefly closed her eyes at Brynn's voice dripping with irritation.

Her sister stopped behind Sebastian but was focused on her and Niall. "What are you doing here so early?"

"Schedule change. We're going to be here in the mornings now." Niall reached into his back pocket, withdrew a small, folded piece of paper, and handed it to Jillian. To Sebastian, he said, "I hope you feel better soon, little man." He turned and headed toward the work truck.

"Mommy," Sebastian whined, "my throat's hurting real bad again."

Jillian shoved the paper into her jeans pocket and closed the door.

"Honey, meet me in the kitchen," Brynn murmured to her son.

Once he'd walked out of ear shot, Jillian asked, "What are you doing out of bed?"

Brynn glared at her. "Last time I checked, this was my house. Meaning I can move about it as I please."

"You're only supposed to be up unless it's absolutely necessary," Jillian shot back. "I'll give Sebastian another dose of medicine and tuck him back into the couch."

Her sister leaned forward. "I got up to find you because you weren't answering my messages about how Sebastian was doing *and* who was at the front door." She smirked. "But now I know. I also know why it got so quiet down here. What's going on, Jillian?"

"*No es de tu incumbencia.*" Jillian headed for the kitchen. "Got back to bed, Brynn."

"It is my business*,*" she hissed. "This is my house, and Niall is *this* family's friend."

Santo cielo. Jillian didn't need this since she hadn't done a damn thing wrong. And what the hell was with her sister's crazed protectiveness when it came to Niall Donnelly? He was an adult, and Jillian was an adult. She'd made herself clear, Niall had accepted it, so no harm done by hanging out with a new friend. It's not like she had a full social calendar right now.

After giving Sebastian his medicine and getting him settled

back into the couch with another Disney movie playing, she took out the piece of paper Niall had given her...that of course was his phone number. With a big round smiley face.

Screw it. She didn't have anything to lose by four-wheeling in the mountains on Sunday.

Chapter Twelve

JACKSON'S PHONE buzzed and he withdrew it from his pocket.

Jillian had texted, *I'm almost there.*

He leaned against the building near the entrance to the popular bar and restaurant that was a quick walk to Union Station and Coors Field. He'd been to this place a few times over the years but had forgotten it's great location in LoDo. Jillian had definitely chosen a prime spot to throw a bachelor-bachelorette party for their best friends.

Thinking of her made him that much more jittery. Like he'd drunk five espresso shots before heading this way from work, a fifteen or so minute walk to this part of LoDo.

He tried to focus on all the people enjoying the unseasonably warm, mid-September night as they descended on the bar or walked in the direction of Coors Field where more bars and restaurants were located. If the Rockies had been playing that night, it would have been pandemonium in this area. And it occurred to him he couldn't remember the last time he'd been to a Rockies game which was ludicrous, considering he worked two blocks away from the field. He was a die-hard Denver sports fan, too, like everyone in his family.

It was also something else he and Jillian had connected over.

He took a deep breath in an attempt to settle his racing heart.

What the hell was wrong with him? He hadn't felt like this on their first date in February. Then again, that could have been because they'd been damn near inseparable at Becca's birthday party, then spent the week doing a combo of texting and Face-Timing before date number one. That had been, hands down, one of the best nights of his dating life so far.

Jackson sighed and shook his head.

Now they were…what exactly? Not friends, but more than acquaintances. Who had extremely intimate knowledge of every single inch—he stopped those thoughts before physical discomfort joined his adolescent nervousness. He was also in a highly public place. But when he spotted Jillian crossing 18th Street, from the direction of the ball field, his breathing slowed.

Thick hair bouncing around her shoulders. Red shirt and black pants, both hugging her enticing curves. Black, high-heeled sandals on her small feet.

Jackson focused on the pavement.

Shit. Maybe meeting up on a Friday night in LoDo to look at this place hadn't been such an awesome idea after all. It hadn't occurred to him she'd show up looking so damn inviting.

Especially since this could never be considered a date.

He raised his head and smiled as she finished her approached. He could only hope his smile reflected charm instead of the ache inside his chest. And farther down.

"Hi," she said a tad breathlessly. "Sorry I'm late. Traffic from Boulder was *awful*."

Unfortunately, her throaty, breathless voice did nothing but remind him of their first night together at the cabin. He swallowed and straightened. "No worries." His voice caught on the two words, coming out a gurgled mess. He cleared his throat. "You look fantastic." He had absolutely nothing to lose by being honest.

Honesty that earned him a blinding smile he couldn't help but return. He could also remember the last time she'd smiled at him like that.

During dinner on what would be their last date.

"Thanks. It didn't feel right to show up looking like my sister's *servant*."

Jackson shoved the memory aside and said, "So helping them is going that well, huh?"

"Brynn's transformation into the Wicked Witch of the West is now complete."

He laughed and it felt damn good, too.

She lifted her shoulders. "Other than that, it's been okay." She pointed at the entrance. "You ready to scope this place out?"

He nodded. "After you." As he followed Jillian into the joint, the tension eased off of Jackson's neck and shoulders for the first time in a week.

Yeah, she looked good enough to kiss until they couldn't think straight. And nibble here and there. But he'd take being around Jillian Castillo like this rather than glued to his desk at work, no matter the ache in his chest and farther down his body.

That only intensified while he followed her up the staircase to the joint's second floor.

The second he cleared the landing he expelled a quick breath. Then he tore his gaze off of her sauntering left toward the rows and rows of pool tables. Several were occupied with small groups of bargoers, drinking beer, talking, and laughing. Cracks of pool balls hitting each other reached where they stood.

"I forgot this place was a pool player's wet dream."

She laughed. "Nicely put. But it also has the ping-pong table." She gestured right behind them. "The two shuffleboards over there." She pointed straight ahead, and he spotted the two, long boards with no players. "It looks like the dartboards are in the back."

"Would the entire second floor be ours?" he asked, which would be more than enough space for the size of party they were planning.

"We could work it out that way."

"Good. There's definitely enough up here to keep guests entertained." He slowly slid his eyes from left to right, taking in all the pool tables and barstool seating along the brick wall. "The seating doesn't look too comfortable, though. For the...*older* guests?" And he pictured his mom and dad. But mostly his mom.

Until last Friday, he'd never thought of his mom or dad as old. They'd always been so active. They'd walked two miles every morning and night since his dad retired and sold his orthodontist practice. They'd also enjoyed neighborhood bike rides when the mood struck them and traveled for at least two weeks every summer—except this past one.

Jackson hadn't thought much about his parents forgoing their typical, big summer vacation two months ago. He'd been up to his neck in work, especially after David had left.

"You're right," Jillian replied. "I don't think they'd be comfortable on the barstools. But they could sit at the tables over there." She turned right, in the direction of the joint's upstairs bar that had several tables nearby. "I'm sure the staff would give us chairs to put near the pool tables. Don't you think?"

His parents had basically shrugged off their yearly tradition and left it at that, but he knew, without a doubt, his mom must have already been showing signs of her sickness.

He'd just been too caught up in work to notice.

Could he really beat himself up for that, though? Will and Savannah, who rarely missed the family Sunday night dinner, had never mentioned noticing a physical decline.

Jillian snapped her fingers in his face.

He blinked her into focus.

"You're thinking about your mom," she murmured.

He couldn't help but crack a grin at her perceptiveness.

She stepped toward him. "Jackson, your mom *will* be here for the party and wedding."

He nodded. "I know." But did he really believe that? "This place is perfect, so let's go for it." He needed to stay focused on the now. "What's next?"

"Confirming we do want the space for that night. I can do that tomorrow." She pursed her lips as she looked around. "I'm hoping they'll let us decorate a bit. It's pretty rustic."

"And you'll let me know when I need to pay the balance of the rental fee?"

She glanced his way. "That was our agreement."

"Okay." Because he had nothing to lose and had zero interest in going back to work or home, he said, "Then it's time for a beer. Don't you think?"

Her eyes widened at his offer, and he waited, holding his breath. Until she grinned.

"Sure."

He returned her grin and stepped backward. "The darkest beer they have?"

She stared at him. "You remember."

And a whole hell of a lot more than that. But he said, "Jillian, it wasn't that long ago." He turned and headed toward the actual bar.

A couple minutes later, Jackson handed her a glass of "the darkest beer they had" and they fell into step beside one another while strolling toward the back.

"How *is* your mom?" she quietly asked.

"She's doing okay." He took a drink of his slightly lighter beer. "I called my parents Wednesday night and talked to her for a bit." Jillian didn't need to know about Will's unexpected visit to his office that morning. Or their honest conversation. "She told me she's trying some homeopathic stuff to help with her low energy and strength."

They stopped at an empty pool table, the last one near the two dartboards.

He lowered himself to the table's edge. "Will and Savannah are taking everyone out on the pontoon tomorrow. It'll be the last boat trip for the season."

Jillian focused on her glass.

She'd seen the boat in March, all covered up at the cabin since that's where it lived and had jokingly asked if it was his. To which he'd jokingly replied that it wasn't his, but could use it and would consider taking her out on it someday if she behaved herself.

She'd arched her right eyebrow and had come back with, *"Then I guess I'll never get to go out on the boat with you, Mr. Lovett."*

"Well, that should be fun," she now said, followed by a drink of beer.

"Yeah." Yet another memory he pushed to the back of his mind. "But my mom told me she has something *big* she wants to tell everyone tomorrow." He cringed. "I'm trying not to worry." *Total understatement, too.* He wasn't certain how much more darkness he could take.

"Jackson, it could be good news," Jillian countered. "You need to try to relax."

He could think of a few *relaxing* things they could do together at her place which was way closer to LoDo than his house.

"Feel like having some fun?"

Ironically, the woman standing beside him—essentially his ex—was currently the brightest light in his life. How the hell had that happened?

"When was the last time you played?" She angled her head toward the table.

"I don't know. Years ago, probably. Why?"

Jillian arched her right eyebrow.

She really needed to stop doing that.

"It's been a while for me, too," she replied.

Jackson also clearly needed a distraction from how damn good she looked tonight. And the fact they were acting like *them* before that shitty night in April.

He said, "I was pretty good."

"Same."

He grinned. "Oh"—he pointed at himself—"so you want some of this?"

"It's on, Mr. Lovett."

Between her sassy smile, challenge, and the fact she didn't seem to be in any hurry to leave, either, he threw in, "Loser buys the next round?"

"*Sí.*" She raised her chin. "I will be pretty thirsty after I kick your ass."

Moments later, and after he finished racking the balls, he stepped to his right and flourished his left hand toward the table. "Show me what you got, Miss Castillo."

She bent forward in the typical pool player position while she held the stick like an expert. All of it being something Jackson tried *not* to admire.

Yeah, the physical pain from watching Jillian play pool would probably kill him. Yet, as the balls broke apart from her powerful shot, there was no other place on this planet he wanted to be and cleared his mind of everything but her and their game.

Chapter Thirteen

JILLIAN SANK THE EIGHT BALL, straightened, and smiled triumphantly. "Pay up, Lovett."

Jackson narrowed his eyes that were back to bright blue —*finally*—and shining with exasperation. But she'd take this Jackson over the one from Wednesday.

"So what exactly is your definition of '*a while*'," he asked as he withdrew his wallet. "Because I think I was hustled."

She laughed. "Laying money on who would get best two-out-of-three was *your* idea."

He handed over a fifty-dollar bill that she snatched from his fingers and kissed.

"And you're not a total loser," she added. "You did win the second game."

He opened his mouth but was stopped by her phone bursting to life from her back pocket.

"It's Alyson. I think I know why she's calling." She shot him a quick smile, then answered, "Hi."

"I'm at the club," her friend stated, "and you better be on your way."

Jillian's eyes connected with Jackson's.

Santo cielo. There was no way out of this conversation without some white lying.

"Al, I can't make it tonight. I'm sorry."

Jackson frowned, and she mouthed, "*Blues Note*."

He nodded at the same time Alyson moaned.

"Jilly, you promised."

"Actually, I promised I would *try* to make it to the show tonight." A promise she'd intended to keep…until Jackson had suggested having a beer, followed by how obviously he'd needed a night off from everything in his life.

Witnessing the weight of his world lifting with each smile, laugh, smartass comment, and the light returning to his perfect eyes, Jillian knew she'd made the right choice by suggesting they play pool. Even now he watched her, eyes bright with mischief— they were together tonight because of Alyson and David's secret party—as the corner of his mouth tilted up in his mind-melting grin. A grin she hadn't seen since they were together. As hard as it was not to walk up to him and kiss that yummy corner, it was another sign she'd done the right thing.

"This is probably going to sound ridiculous, but I miss you," Alyson said. "I was hoping we could really talk about the wedding now that we have a place and I've chosen the colors."

Mierda. With the exception of helping Jackson plan the surprise bachelor-bachelorette party, Jillian was failing at being her best friend's maid-of-honor. So she said, "I know you're off tomorrow. I *promise* I'll call you when we're finished."

"Alright," Alyson mumbled. "But why can't you make it here tonight?"

Jillian racked her brain for an excuse that didn't involve being at a bar with Jackson and said, "Claude and Afton want to hang out at the apartment. Drink wine, eat pizza, and play *Grand Theft Auto*." She caught Jackson quietly laughing. "After the week I had with my *other* sister, I couldn't say no. But I swear I'll call you tomorrow."

Silence fell on Alyson's end before, "Fine. Tell them I said hi." She hung up.

Jillian stared at her phone. "*Voy a terminar en el infierno.*"

Jackson placed his pool stick on the table and closed the small gap between them. "Jillian, you're not going to end up in hell for lying to Alyson about all of this."

She placed her pool stick beside his. "My best friend just hung up on me because I'm being a terrible friend and maid-of-honor."

He angled his head left to catch her eyes. "You also have *a lot* going on right now and Alyson knows that." He paused, then slowly added, "We could go to The Blues Note. You know it's only a few blocks from here."

She stared at him and that yummy spot on his irresistible mouth.

Oh, yes. They could. But that wouldn't be the smartest choice for many reasons. The fact Jackson now seemed to be in such a relaxed place meant it was time to bring this evening to an end. She'd done her job as…what? She had no idea what they'd become since partnering up to plan and execute the party for their best friends. Since getting the news about his mom, they'd actually become more than party-planning partners.

He snapped his fingers in her face.

She blinked twice.

"That suggestion wasn't supposed to be a brain teaser," he murmured.

"And how exactly would we explain showing up together?" She could clearly envision Alyson and David's wide eyes, followed by a barrage of questions.

"Lie." He grinned. "You're pretty good at lying on the fly, Miss Castillo."

She shook her head. "Thanks, but I think I've had my fill of lying for one night." She returned his grin. "It was a pretty good lie, wasn't it?"

He laughed and nodded.

Once they were outside, they veered left toward 18th Street.

"Where'd you park?" Jackson asked.

"At twentieth and Market."

"Walk you to your car? I'm going that way since I walked here from work."

She flashed him a smile. "Sure."

They lapsed into silence as they crossed 18th and headed toward Coors Field.

The area was still brimming with people enjoying the warm Friday night. It was such a nice night people were able to sit outside at their bar of choice with patio seating. McGregor Square, right across from the field, was particularly busy. As they cut through the square, her gaze swept over the tables that were occupied with people talking or watching the enormous screen displaying a baseball game, though the Rockies weren't playing.

Remembering the fact Jackson loved the Denver teams as much as she did, she asked, "Did you get to a Rockies game this summer?"

He slid his hands into his pockets. "No. Did you?"

She peeked at him. "I did. My dad flew in last month and was here for over four weeks, spending time with all of us." She smiled softly. "He took Claudia, Afton, and me to an afternoon game." She laughed. "Claude and Afton tried to get him drunk on margs at The Rio before the game, but when they weren't looking he poured some of his into *their* glasses."

Jackson laughed with her, then said, "God, I can't remember the last time I went to The Rio for margaritas." His smile faded. "That phrase seems to be my life's current motto." He shook his head. "I can't remember the last time I—*fill in the blank*."

Though Jillian hated seeing his handsome face stuck once

again in a deep frown, Jackson obviously needed someone to listen.

"You said earlier that you're going to hell for being a bad friend and maid-of-honor." He glanced at Jillian. "I'm going to end up there for being a bad son, brother, and uncle the last few years." He sighed. "I don't regret starting the firm with David and Zach, but it took over more of my life than I expected. I never meant for that to happen," he quietly added. "I've missed numerous family Sunday dinners. Time with everyone up at the cabin. Many of Brendan's baseball games." He released a quick laugh. "The kid's well on his way to being a professional gamer *and* baseball player, he's that good."

When they reached Blake Street, she stopped them and faced him.

"It sounds like you miss your family."

He nodded. "Yeah. And David. You're not the only one who's feeling like a terrible friend right now." He cracked a smile. "But if you tell the bastard any of this, I'll deny it."

She leaned forward. "Your secret is safe with me."

His eyes went to her mouth and back up; the action so fast Jillian wasn't certain she'd seen it correctly. Still, her heartbeat amplified while they continued to stare at each other.

"I'm going to hold you to that."

She dragged her gaze from his, and they crossed Blake.

"So what are you going to do about it?" she asked, the words coming out a tad bitchier than she'd intended.

Spending all of this unexpected time with him tonight had definitely rattled her core. However, she'd couldn't deny the fact she'd liked distracting him from the weight of his world and being his soundboard.

"What do you mean?"

She whipped her head in his direction. "You just said you're missing your family and best friend. What are you going to do about it?"

His steps slowed to a stop and he peered at her.

"It doesn't have to be that way," she continued. "It *shouldn't* be that way, especially now. And I hope you'll give your family your undivided attention tomorrow when you're with them." She hesitated before adding, "Just like you were with me tonight."

He remained silent, still peering at her.

"As far as David goes…" Her voice trailed off. Then the obvious hit. "Start going to the band's shows." It was something she also needed to do. "You work within walking distance of the club. And if we happen to see each other, it won't be a big deal." *Not anymore.* In fact, it would be more than okay, but Jillian couldn't say that. Still, she softly grinned. "Am I right?"

He returned her grin. "Yeah. Definitely."

She stepped toward him. "Jackson, our businesses and careers are vastly different, but I still know what it's like to co-own a business *and* be the boss."

His grin slipped.

"I understand the pressure of keeping a business going. And making sure it's successful and stays that way for yourself and everyone who works for you." She lifted her shoulders. "But it's okay to take a break and let go."

He opened his mouth, but she held up her hand.

"I know. *That project* is important to you and the firm. Everyone can see what all the pressure is doing to you, though." She lowered her hand. "Maybe if you start to let go of other parts of your job, you'll have the time you need to make your way back to your family?"

Jackson slowly nodded. "Believe it or not, I'm working on it."

"Good." She smiled. "You probably need to have fun more often, too."

He brought back his grin. "Like I am right now?"

She arched her right eyebrow. "You can do way better than listening to my thoughts and advice while standing on a busy street in LoDo."

Jillian had seen his fun, relaxed side, especially during their weekend together in March. He was awfully good at it, too. He just had to let go of being Jackson Lovett—architect, business owner, and boss—every now then, which was what he'd done that weekend.

She could only hope he'd continue to "work on it" and take her other advice seriously.

"What do you think should be next on our party to-do list?" he asked when they reached her car. "We have the place and games that will be provided at the place."

She leaned against her car. "I'm thinking the guest list should be what we tackle next." She frowned. "We may even want to do a save-the-date. Because of the time of year?"

"Makes sense. But compiling a guest list is going to take longer than either of us can spare on a Wednesday morning."

"Agreed." She eyed him, eyeing her. "Thoughts, Mr. Lovett?"

The corner of his mouth eased upward. "Are you…busy tomorrow night?"

She froze.

"We could meet up somewhere quieter than LoDo or the Highlands." He leaned forward. "You bring your cell, I'll bring mine, and we'll put a list together?"

She gaped at him, her answer on the verge of release. But was it the right answer? The *smartest* answer? Nothing he'd said or suggested was wrong and unreasonable. It actually made sense to put together the guest list when they didn't have to worry about being anywhere else.

"Jillian, that wasn't supposed to be a brain teaser, either." Jackson straightened. "Tonight was unexpected and *fun*." He laughed softly. "Exactly what I needed."

She took a shaky breath. "I know. And it was fun." Just like every one of their dates from their brief time together. But was another night together to plan the party the best choice?

"I'll even let you buy me a drink. Or two. You are fifty bucks richer, Miss Castillo."

No, not the best choice. She also had plans on Sunday that would start at nine a.m. at her apartment. Nevertheless, she said, "*Si*. But only if you behave yourself, Mr. Lovett."

Everything would be fine.

His eyes and face brightened, followed by his delectable grin.

Jillian raised her right hand, paused for a few seconds, then placed it on his face, rough with late-in-the-day scruff. "Please tell me you're going home and *not* back to work."

As they stared at each other, the parking lot lighting became a soft glow around them.

He placed his hand on top of hers. "I'm going home."

She eased her fingers free, opened her car door, and slid inside.

"I'll text you a time and place tomorrow."

She gave him a quick smile.

Once headed in the direction of her apartment, Jillian rolled down her window and inhaled the warm, night air deep into her lungs.

Another night with Jackson for party-planning purposes? No, definitely not the best choice for *her*. But Alyson and David were worth it. There was also the unavoidable fact Jackson needed her which Jillian found more than a little okay.

Chapter Fourteen

GRACIE SQUEALED as Jackson picked her up, turned her upside down, and held her tiny, squirming body over the water.

"Uncle Jackson," she said around her breathless giggling, "*don't*."

He lowered her a fraction closer to the water.

She released an ear-piercing shriek. "Brendan dared me to do it!"

Jackson looked over his shoulder at his nephew staring at him with wide eyes. "You dared your sister to dump water on my head?" *Frigid-ass, Lake Estes water*. Despite the sun beating down on them, it had shocked the shit out of him.

"She's lying. She *always* lies," Brendan argued. "And it's not like you're really going to drop her into the lake."

He lowered Gracie a fraction more which caused another deafening shriek.

"Jackson," Savannah called out. "Would you please put her down? Everyone on this lake will think we're torturing children."

Actually, that was exactly what he was doing. But he stepped back, flipped her right side up, and carefully set her down. He then focused on his nephew. "You're right. I would never drop *her* into the lake. You on the other hand—" He stepped toward Brendan who darted to where Savannah sat with his parents under the bimini top.

Jackson laughed as Gracie hugged his left side.

"Uncle Jackson, do it again." She gave him her heart-melting, little girl smile.

He bent down and cupped his left ear. "*What*? I can't hear you. I'm deaf from all your screaming." He tickled her, and she squealed again and ran to his mom who embraced her.

Jackson straightened and caught Will watching him from where he sat.

"Who the hell are you and what have you done with my brother?"

Okay. Jackson probably deserved that when he thought about how he'd looked and sounded on Wednesday, faced off with Will in his office.

He sat across from his brother.

Will handed him a beer. "You're in a good mood."

Jackson opened the can and took a quick drink. "Today was a good idea." *Not a lie.* Cloudless blue mountain sky, perfect late summer temp, quiet lake despite the spectacular weather. But not the complete truth, either, when he recalled standing beside Jillian at her car, somehow curbing the desire to pull her into his arms and say goodnight without saying the words. "I also had a great Friday night." And he had tonight on his horizon which wouldn't come fast enough, even though he was having a much-needed fantastic time with his family.

It sounds like you miss your family. So what are you going to do about it?

He eyed his mom, sitting with her arms around Gracie now in her lap. "Mom looks really good today." She'd received a little color on her face from her moments in the sun, giving her a healthy glow. Definitely better than how pale she'd looked this time a week ago in his parents' office. She'd also been smiling and laughing almost nonstop since they'd climbed onto the boat. "Today was a good idea for Mom," he added. *Without question.*

"Yeah," Will quietly replied. "I think that all-natural stuff she's taking is helping, too."

Their dad sat near their mom. He wore a green fishing hat, a dark-blue Hawaiian shirt he'd actually bought on a Hawaiian island a handful of years ago, pale-blue shorts, and black flip flops. Savannah sat across from them, slathering sunscreen onto Brendan's back.

Jackson looked at Will. "Has Dad always dressed badly and I'm just now noticing it?"

His brother laughed. "I think it's more, *I'm retired and don't give a shit.* So, who is she?"

He frowned. "What do you mean?"

"You said you had a great Friday night. I'm guessing you were with a woman?"

Jackson's family had heard Jillian's name in the weeks they were together. His mom had admitted to seeing him stealing numerous glances of Jillian Labor Day weekend and vice versa. He could simply be honest. Tell Will what they were doing for David and Alyson. A massive part of him, however, wanted to keep it *just them* for as long as possible. He also wasn't certain how he'd explain going from checking the place out to drinking two beers each and playing three rounds of pool. Because that sounded like a date. It had felt like a date, too.

"Jackson, has the sun fried your brain?" His brother gave him a once-over. "Man, it looks like you need more sunscreen."

He glanced at his bare arms. "I need some color." His T-shirt was protecting most of his upper body. "I'll be fine."

"Only if you're going for the color of burnt to a crisp, but whatever. Are you going to tell me who you're dating or not?"

"I'm not dating anyone. Just went out with some friends after work." Apparently, Jillian wasn't the only one good at lying on the fly. "It felt good to be out in LoDo on a Friday night." That being the absolute the truth.

"Good. I'm glad you did that." Will paused, then said, "Especially after seeing how you looked when I was at your office on Wednesday."

Jackson focused on his bare feet as he recalled Jillian's statement from last night.

Everyone can see what all the pressure is doing to you.

"But whatever you did last night with your friends made a huge difference since today you're acting, looking, and sounding like my brother for a change."

Jackson definitely felt more like himself, too, and he pictured *her*, specifically last night wearing her sassy grin while she kicked his ass during their final round of pool.

"So keep going out with your friends," Will added. "That's all I'm going to say."

If not for planning the party with Jillian—her in general— Jackson would probably be the definition of a drowning man.

"Did you go to The Blues Note?" Will asked.

He shook his head. "No." But he would have if Jillian had said the word.

"How is D-Man doing? Word on the street is they're getting married here on New Year's Eve." Will grinned. "That's a big something for *all* of us to look forward to."

"Yeah." Jackson gave Will a quick smile. "I talked to him briefly on Monday. He seemed okay. I'll see him this upcoming Monday. He and Zach are going to be hiring his replacement."

Will took a swig of his beer. "You're finally hiring another architect?"

He sighed. "Will, give me a break. This current project is…" *Soul-sucking.* But he said, "It's taking up a lot of my time."

His brother held up his hands. "Okay, I'll stop. But it'd be cool if, maybe, the three of us could have lunch on Monday?"

Jackson had his meeting with Downey and Ember first thing Monday morning. A meeting that he was looking forward to for a change. Between that and Zach and David being in charge of hiring a new architect, getting the hell out of the office for lunch would be a nice break.

You miss your family. What are you going to do about it?

"Let's do that," Jackson answered. "The place in the Pavilions we like? Twelve-thirty?"

Will raised his eyebrows. "Wow. Okay. That sure as shit was easy." He laughed.

Their mom walked up and gave them affectionate smiles. "I can't tell you how much I love seeing you two like this." She pointed at Jackson, then Will. "Brothers who are *friends*? I can remember when that wasn't the case." She shook her head. "Before you left for CSU"—she gestured at Will—"I thought for *sure* one of you would kill the other in his sleep."

Jackson glanced at his brother whose eyes were wide.

"I saw the crime scene in my head," she continued, "and one of you being handcuffed and taken to jail. I could also see the trial, the orange jumpsuit, shackles, and prison van."

Jackson squinted at his mom.

What the *hell?*

"Mom," Will mumbled, "we were teenagers. Not psychopaths."

She lifted her shoulders. "One could argue those two can occasionally be the same. Anyway"—she brought back her smile —"I need to talk to your brother for a few minutes."

Will stood and eyed Jackson. "Good luck."

She sat in Will's empty spot. "You're in a delightful mood today which is why I want to have this conversation with you now."

Shit. That didn't sound good. Especially since she had yet to tell him or anyone else her big announcement. But he said, "Fine. I confess I occasionally fantasized that I didn't have an older brother…though not because I killed him in his sleep."

She laughed. "I had a feeling. And you should know he didn't get away with as much as you think he did." She clasped his free hand. "I want you to do something for me. A favor, so to speak, that came to me while I've been watching you looking incredibly relaxed and happy."

Okay. That didn't sound too bad, but obviously not her big announcement.

"At some point within the next year, but certainly sooner rather than later, I want you to take a trip. I know you haven't been on a real vacation in years."

Jackson peered at his mom.

Had she acquired the skill of mind reading in the last week?

"I recommend going somewhere you've never been and disappearing." Her smile deepened. "I also suggest taking someone special with you. How does a month sound?"

A month? Yeah, he definitely liked the sound of everything she was saying, as if she were able to read his mind, but there was no way in hell he could be gone that long. "Mom, that sounds like the vacation that never ends. Is thirty days negotiable?"

She released an exasperated sigh. "Jackson Richard Lovett, will you *please* be serious?"

He faced her. "I am being serious. A long vacation nowhere near Denver sounds *fantastic* right now." Taking a "special someone" made the mental picture that much more appealing.

Her mouth inched open. Probably because she hadn't expected his honesty.

"But with or without this current project I have going on, I can't be gone that long." Jackson doubted the "special someone" he had in mind could be gone that long either.

His mom nodded. "Then how does two weeks sound?"

He smiled. "Doable." Actually, it sounded damn near perfect.

"Does that mean we have an agreement?"

He shrugged. "Sure. We can shake on it if you want, but—"

"Jackson," she whispered, "*promise* me you'll do this."

He frowned at seeing her lower lip quivering. And it hit him.

His mom might not be here to see him take the vacation. Or more accurately, put himself—his life—before work. In fact, there were many things she wouldn't be here to see. Things he'd never really thought about having—like a family of his own—since he'd been so damn focused on his career *and* the firm's success.

The realization caused his head to become foggy as he said, "I promise you I'll do it."

"Good." She sniffed, squeezed his hand she still held, and stood. "No more serious. I have something very important to discuss with *all* of you."

Right. Her big announcement.

Jackson gave his head a hard shake and also stood.

Jillian's throaty voice saying "it could be good news" went through his mind as he followed his mom. The fact she'd just stated "no more serious" gave him hope Jillian was right. After the last few minutes, Jackson had reached his fill of gut-wrenching reality for one day. One lifetime, really. All he wanted was to continue having a great day with his family, then he could focus on meeting up with his sassy co-party planner to create a guest list.

An image that made him softly grin.

"WHERE THE *HELL* HAVE YOU BEEN?" the wedding planner hissed. "You were supposed to be here almost an hour ago. The wedding is in less than two hours!"

Jillian lifted her chin while Campbell and Hayley loaded up the carts for transporting the flowers into the venue located deep in Commerce City, a northern suburb of Denver. "There was a terrible car accident on the interstate. I called you and left a message."

Daisy's Bouquets received few jobs in the Denver suburbs, but this *lovely* wedding planner had been referred to them by another woman they frequently worked with…and liked.

The planner yanked her cell from her cross-body phone case. "I received no such—"

Jillian eyed Campbell and Hayley smirking at the woman as they pushed the carts past her on their way into the building.

The planner calmly pushed her phone back into her case, straightened, and smoothed her blonde hair. "I'll need the bouquets and boutonnières while I'm here."

Jillian went to the back of the delivery van, picked up the box that held what the planner needed, and handed it over.

"Thank you. Everything looks lovely." She turned and marched away.

Mierda. Yet another young, frazzled wedding planner who couldn't deal with the "shit happens" in life. And something she was in no mood to deal with after sitting in traffic from hell.

Moments later she joined Campbell outside to help her with the floral garland going on the arch placed just behind where the officiate would stand with the bride and groom.

The happy couple who'd planned an outdoor wedding had absolutely lucked out with today's weather. They'd also planned to say their vows as the sun set behind the mountains. It was the view from where she and Campbell stood, carefully hanging the garland of soft pink chrysanthemums and dahlias, peach carnations, and orange and white roses.

Making the fresh flower garlands happened to be one of

Jillian's favorite activities as a florist. She couldn't stop the regretful pang at missing out on making this one.

She asked, "Did Alyson make this garland? It's beautiful."

Campbell smiled. "I made this one. And I'm glad you like it, too. I'm quite proud of it."

Jillian nodded. "You should be. It's perfect."

Her face flushed before she went back to carefully hanging her end of the garland on the arch. "It's so nice to be working together today. We're missing you around the shop."

Jillian smiled sadly. "I'm missing *you* guys." More than she'd even realized. She hadn't been helping her sister's family for two whole weeks, but it already felt like two months.

"How's everything going with your family?"

She'd become her sister's servant and hormonal punching bag. "It's fine," Jillian replied. "I'm really enjoying spending time with my nephew." Still the brightest spots of the day.

Jillian's phone buzzed and went off inside her back jeans pocket. As hard as she tried, she couldn't stop the grin at knowing who it had to be. Jackson had said last night he'd text her today with a time and place for them to meet up to compile the guest list. But her grin slipped at seeing another man's name above the text.

Niall wrote, *Making sure you're not thinking too much and we're still on for tomorrow?*

She stared at his message.

Thinking too much? *Absolutamente.* Mostly about Jackson and their time together last night and seeing him again in what would be a few hours. She'd also been thinking about him quite a bit throughout the day, picturing him out on Lake Estes with his family, hopefully relaxed and enjoying the now. Allowing himself to have a good time, smiling and laughing. Just like he had with *her* nearly twenty-fours earlier in LoDo.

"Hey," Campbell murmured. "Everything okay over there?"

Jillian smiled at her and texted, *Nine sharp. Don't be late.*

Maybe spending the day with Niall, four-wheeling in the mountains, wasn't the smartest choice when she imagined her sister's head exploding if she ever found out. Nevertheless, Jillian was looking forward to getting the hell out of Denver on a beautiful Sunday. Depending on where Niall took them, maybe she'd even see some aspen trees starting to change.

Her phone went off again and lit up with another text. But this time it was Jackson.

"Someone's pretty popular," Campbell teased. "Are you seeing someone?"

If only it were that simple.

He'd texted, *I hate to do this, but can we meet at my place and do the guest list here?*

Jillian frowned as she typed, *What happened?*

Under "normal" circumstances, she wouldn't have thought twice about meeting up with Jackson at his house. For a man who spent most of his time at work, he'd created an extremely nice home for himself. She still thought it was a shame he rarely spent time there. But whatever was going on with them couldn't be called "normal," so being at his house—alone—was most definitely not the *smartest* choice.

"Jillian?"

She looked up to find Campbell peering at her. "No, I'm not seeing anyone. It's just my sister, Claudia. Wanting to know if I have plans tonight." She tried not to flinch at using her younger sister for yet another white lie.

I'll be at your place five minutes early.

Jillian smiled at Niall's message before replying, *I'll be ready.*

She was about to slide her phone back into her pocket when Jackson's response hit.

I know it's a lot to ask, but please?

Her frown deepened.

Why was he pushing this?

"I don't know about you," Campbell grumbled, "but after horrible traffic and a crabby wedding planner, I'm looking forward to a quiet night at home with a glass of wine and a book."

Jillian glanced at Campbell, her delicate features stuck in concentration while she finished hanging the garland, then back at her phone. She needed to focus on her job.

With a quick breath she texted, *Fine. I'm in Commerce City. I'll text when I'm on my way.*

Hopefully she'd made the right choice. She could also call Alyson on her way to Jackson's place so they could talk about the wedding. She wouldn't let her best friend down.

She put her phone away and continued hanging her side of the garland. "It sounds like you need a distraction in the form of a hot guy." Niall's face and impressive physique landed in her mind. Campbell had just turned twenty-eight and Niall couldn't be that far behind her in age. With Campbell's dark-blonde hair, fair complexion, and petite figure, she couldn't be certain if Campbell was Niall's type. He'd made it clear what he thought of Jillian, and she and Campbell looked *nothing* alike. Still, maybe the two would have fun together. She faced Campbell and grinned. "I know someone who would be *a lot* of fun."

Campbell's cheeks turned pink as she shook her head, which caused her ponytail to flip back and forth. "That's sweet of you, Jilly. Really. But I'm enjoying being on my own, working with you guys, and hanging out with my roommates." She smiled tightly. "Life is good."

Jillian's grin transformed into a deep frown. "I get all that. *Believe* me. But have you gone on any dates since you moved here last summer?" Also known as well over a year ago.

Even Jillian's longest mancation, which happened during the time she and Alyson were new small-business owners, hadn't lasted *that* long.

"No." Campbell stepped back. "I'm going to head inside and help Hayley." She walked around Jillian and up the white aisle runner.

Jillian watched her quick strides until she disappeared from view.

Clearly she'd said something wrong, but what? Campbell had always been on the quiet side, never talking too much about the life she'd left in Durango, outside of mentioning her mom and a younger brother. It *was* obvious she had no interest in dating, and could she really blame Campbell for feeling that way? It's not as if Jillian had been out there lately. Her reasons for singlehood, however, didn't mirror what Campbell had said.

Jillian's phone again went off, no doubt with Jackson's reply.

Thanks. And would you mind picking up some aloe vera gel? I'll pay you back.

She re-read his message, then laughed since it was now obvious what was going on with him. Right or wrong, knowing what she'd be walking into caused a wave of humor and excitement to wind through her at seeing him later...which meant she was still in *big* trouble.

Chapter Fifteen

JACKSON OPENED his front door and his eyes locked with Jillian's.

Her mouth inched open at his sunburned face, her gaze then lowering to his equally sunburned neck and arms. The cold shower he'd just taken had felt like heaven on earth. So would the aloe vera gel she held once he slathered it on his red, sensitive skin.

She burst into her throaty laughter. Which made his head buzz.

"Oh, wow. *Te ves fantástico.*"

He stepped aside to let her into his house. "Thanks. I know I look good even sunburned."

Once she was inside, he closed the door and she handed over the aloe vera.

"So I've heard," she began while wearing her sassy grin, "about this wonderful invention called sunscreen."

He grasped the bottle. "And this happens to be two layers of SPF 50 at its best."

Her grin grew. "Apparently, you should have bathed in it."

"Cute." Jackson headed into his living room. "Someone's in top form tonight."

"Only because someone has given me excellent material to work with."

He dropped to his sectional couch and set the aloe vera on the oversized ottoman.

Jillian sat one cushion away. "Why didn't you pick up the aloe vera on your way home?"

"I thought I had some." He leaned back, rested his head on a couch cushion, then flinched at the material rubbing his burned neck. "Thanks for picking it up. What do I owe you?"

"You already paid for it, Mr. Lovett. The fifty bucks from last night?"

Jackson released a quick laugh. "Right. But *not* how I'd imagined you using the money." *Total understatement, too.* He rolled his head left to find her watching him, fighting a smile. "You think I'm irresistible right now, don't you? I know I'm hot stuff." *At this moment, literally.*

Jillian removed her purse from her shoulder, placed the bag on the floor, and leaned sideways into the cushions. "I think you look a little pathetic. And much blonder than you did this time last night." She shifted forward, rested her head on a cushion, and closed her eyes.

They probably needed to get focused on compiling the guest list, but between being fried by the sun and Jillian looking tired, yet so damn good on his couch, he couldn't get there.

"Tough day out in Commerce City?"

She sighed. "That and the awful traffic to and from. But I was able to call Alyson on my way here." She grinned. "We talked about how to decorate the cabin for the wedding, and I'm feeling like a reliable maid-of-honor again."

"Jillian, you haven't done anything that's made you *unreliable*."

"I suppose. Anyway, Alyson and I are back on the same page." She rolled her head right. "Outside of looking like you set yourself on fire, how was your day with your family?"

"It was really good." And he *refused* to think about the gut-wrenching realities that had hit him after the conversation with his mom. It did, however, remind him of her announcement. "You'll never guess what my mom told us." Even he still couldn't believe what she'd said hours earlier on the boat. "She wants us to take her for a night out in LoDo." Why his mom wanted such a thing was obvious, but he refused to think about that, too.

Jillian squinted at him.

"You're looking at me the way I must've been looking at her when she said it." He laughed. "She wants to start at The Blues Note. To hear the band?"

She nodded.

"After that, she wants to be surprised by where we take her next."

Jillian's surprise transformed into a blinding smile. "I think that's so awesome." She again burst into her throaty laughter. "And 'we' meaning you, Will, Savannah, and your dad?"

"Alyson, too. Maybe even David if he can get away after they're finished playing."

Her smile slipped.

Inviting Jillian to go, as well, hit him swift and hard, and Jackson opened his mouth—

"I'm sure Becca and Matt would love to be there."

He paused before replying, "Yeah. Definitely."

She focused on the baseball game filling the T.V. hanging on the opposite wall.

His gaze went to her hair pulled up into a loose knot…striking profile…loose, black T-shirt…worn, yet snug jeans…and those black-and-white checkered Vans she refused to replace.

Jackson rolled his head forward.

With the exception of his sunburn and being hit with some harsh realities, today had been fantastic. He couldn't remember the last time—he halted that thought train. Between last night with Jillian, the awesome day with his family, and Jillian now beside him on this couch, Jackson wanted nothing more than to keep making choices that made him feel good, relaxed, and *happy*.

"You know," he casually said, "you could go out with us, too."

From the corner of his eyes, he saw her head roll right, but pretended to be focused on the baseball game while he waited for her response.

"I'll think about it," she finally replied.

He fought a smile because he'd take that over a *hell no*.

"Should we get to work on the guest list?"

Right. The real reason she'd come over to his place.

Jackson glanced at her. "Can I be honest?"

"I'm listening."

"I'm feeling pretty fried—no pun intended. It's why I didn't feel like going out tonight." He should have canceled altogether, but if he had she wouldn't be here with him on his couch.

"After my day and week," she mumbled, "I'm not feeling up for it, either."

Being mid-September, it's not like they were in a time crunch. Though Jillian had made a good point when she'd suggested doing a save-the-date with the party happening right after Christmas, what could still be considered the holiday season.

Jillian sat up. "Then I should go. Maybe we can meet after work sometime next week?"

She started to stand, but he grasped her hand.

"That'll be fine, but you don't have to leave." *Please don't leave.* Those words were now on the brink of spilling out of his mouth. But he said, "I'm not going to bite you if you stay." Their gazes caught. What the hell did he have to lose? He grinned. "Unless you ask me to."

She arched her right eyebrow. Which only amplified his desire for her *not* to leave.

"Jackson Lovett, are you really flirting with me, looking the way you do right now?"

Arched right eyebrow. Fighting her sassy smile. Not running for the door. *All good signs.*

"Jillian, I'm not dead." He inspected his sunburned arms. "I just look like I've spent the day being thoroughly screwed by the sun. And the sun got off."

She nodded. "That's an interesting visual."

"Isn't it, though?" It's about how he felt, too. He leaned forward and picked up the aloe vera gel. "If you have to leave, can you help a guy out first? Put some on my neck?"

Still fighting that smile, she took the bottle from him.

Another damn good sign.

"Turn around."

He did as she commanded, then looked over his left shoulder. "Do you want me to take my shirt off? So it's not in your way?"

"Jackson," she groaned, squirting aloe into her hand, "what are you doing?"

He released a huge sigh. From her question *and* at how good the aloe felt on his neck.

"I'm trying to use my charm to keep you from leaving." He closed his eyes, savoring her hands massaging the cool gel into his skin. "But apparently I've lost my touch."

Jackson racked his brain for *something* he could say to keep Jillian right here on this couch with him. Because regardless of that night in April, their connection was still as strong as the thickest steel cable. And no matter what she said or did, he knew she felt it, too.

She finished rubbing the aloe into his neck.

He was about to thank her when he felt her breath on his left ear.

"You haven't lost your touch," she whispered.

Jackson froze. For two seconds. Then he grinned, turned his head left, and their mouths fused. Jillian's opened easily beneath his as he shifted forward.

Every single part of him burst to life as if he'd been dormant since April.

He placed his hands on her waist and guided her onto his lap which she straddled. But when she hooked her arms behind his neck, he flinched and moaned. And not out of pleasure.

She removed her arms, tore her mouth from his, and breathlessly said, "I don't think this is a good idea. For *many* reasons."

He pressed his forehead to hers. "Jilly, maybe I'm not the only one who needs to relax and stop thinking. It would also be *fun*." He sealed his words by pressing his lips to hers.

Her body relaxed into his, sinking into the couch cushions the longer their mouths moved perfectly together. Like they had from kiss number one.

"Okay," she whispered on a breath. "You're right."

Thank God. He really hadn't lost his touch.

"But I need to do something first."

"Take your clothes off, then mine?"

She smiled against his mouth. "I need a shower." They shared another long, greedy kiss. "I feel more like an overworked, grungy florist than a woman right now."

He reached up and freed her hair from the knot. As her thick hair tumbled to her shoulders, he asked, "Want some company?"

She arched her right eyebrow. Which added to the pressure inside his basketball shorts.

"You look and smell like you just took a shower."

He grinned. "Yeah. But you weren't in there with me."

She fought a smile. "I just put aloe on your neck."

"And you can put more on my neck again later." He waggled his eyebrows. "I'll scrub your back if you scrub mine."

She stood. "Your back's not burned, too?"

He narrowed his eyes. "Keep it up, smart mouth, and payback will be a real bitch."

Jillian gripped the bottom of her T-shirt, pulled it over her head, tossed it at him, then sauntered into the hallway and went right, in the direction of his bedroom.

That was all the invitation he needed.

Jackson had no idea what would happen tomorrow. He didn't give a shit, either. Right now, the woman he wanted and couldn't stop thinking about was getting undressed and about to step into his shower. And he was going to give her his undivided attention.

The sound of running water reached him as he strolled into his bedroom. He spotted Jillian's discarded black bra on his bed and the pressure inside his shorts became uncomfortable.

He paused in the bathroom doorway to watch her as she wriggled out of her snug jeans, followed by the wisp of cloth women called underwear. His breathing then slowed while he slid his gaze over her perfect curves he knew from first-hand knowledge were soft. Smooth. *Edible*.

He'd never forgotten the fact Jillian Castillo had the body of a goddess.

She eyed him while wearing her sassy grin. "See anything you like, Mr. Lovett?"

Jackson's self-control snapped. Before he realized it, he had his mouth pressed against hers once more as he tangled his right hand into her hair. A soft moan escaped her as their kiss became deeper. Hungrier. Like their lives depended on this moment. All of this happening.

With his free hand, he opened the shower door and guided her backward, into the water.

"Jackson," she said around a laugh, "you're still dressed."

"I'm not stopping you from tearing off my clothes." But when the warm water hit his sunburned skin, he cringed. "I need cooler water." He smiled. "We'll still keep it pretty hot in here. Don't you think?"

Jillian returned his smile, turned the cold water up a fraction, and asked, "Better?"

He pressed her against the wall, the lukewarm water drenching them. "Almost." He kissed her again, followed by another…and another. As if he'd never kiss her again when tonight—right now—was over. And maybe he wouldn't, so he damn well was going to make this night count. "I think I'm still wearing too many clothes."

She grasped his now wet T-shirt, eased it over his head, balled it up, and tossed it out of the shower. His shorts encountered the same fate. A millisecond later, their arms went around each other, and his moan echoed hers as their mouths picked up where'd they left off.

Jackson slowly slid his hand down her wet back, paused to caress her firm backside—then pressed her against him and held her there.

She gasped against his mouth, her fingers gripping his wet hair. "Don't start something in here you can't finish," she murmured the second they came up for air.

"Oh, I could finish this." He placed light kisses up her neck and stopped at her ear to softly add, "I just don't want to."

She shivered, tightened her grip on his hair, and gently kissed his sunburned neck.

He smiled. "You're thinking about me finishing it in here."

Jillian leaned back, causing him to lift his head.

Her wet hair, body, and sultry gaze made him want to reconsider finishing it in here.

"Are you going to help me actually take a shower or distract me?"

The only thing stopping him was the anticipation of being inside of her.

He squeezed her butt. "Why can't I do both?"

She reached right and came back with his soap. "Wash my back?"

Jackson took the bar and made his hands as soapy as possible.

He started on her shoulders, gently massaging the soap into her skin. Her arms. Her waist. Stomach. Up to her perfectly round breasts where he massaged longer than necessary since she was backed right into and moving against him.

A round of desire shot through him and his vision blurred.

He wasn't sure how much more of this he could take without exploding.

She clasped his right hand and guided it to below her waist… and farther down.

Jackson slipped his left arm around her waist, hugged her to him, and gently slid his finger inside of her. Warm, damp, and pulsing with desire that equaled his.

She turned her head left, angled her chin up, and their mouths came together. Until he couldn't stand her moving with his finger any longer. Moving against *him* any longer.

He abruptly ended their kiss and met her gaze, a strange combination of lust and confusion. "This shower needs to be over, or I need to let you finish alone." But the pain from waiting for her to finish would probably kill him. So when she nodded and turned off the water, Jackson somehow stopped himself from groaning with relief.

Once they were in his bedroom—their bodies still wet— Jillian stretched out on his bed while he went into the top drawer of his nightstand.

His soft moan matched hers as he pressed himself inside of her seconds later.

"*Shit*," he mumbled against her mouth. "You still feel incredible."

"So do you," she breathlessly whispered, matching his slow thrusts. "Don't stop."

Stop? He wouldn't be able to stop if the world started to crumble around them. But he did pause long enough to really feel himself buried deep inside Jillian's pulsating warmth. Her bare, wet body wrapped around and joined tightly with his.

"Stay the night," he said as they continued moving together. "I don't want you to leave."

Her eyes drifted shut while she released another soft moan, then opened.

"Jilly, say you'll stay."

She clutched his hair and brought his head to hers. "Okay." They shared a quick but deep kiss. "But you'll have to do something for me."

Feeling her muscles tightening around him and fast-approaching his own edge, Jackson answered with a thrust, followed by a stronger, final one that ended with their groans.

His heavy breathing matched hers while he again buried his face into her neck that now smelled of his soap. Despite it being made for guys, he deeply inhaled the scent. *Her*.

She'd said if she stayed the night he'd need to do something for her.

If Jillian Castillo asked him to walk through a firestorm, he would. In fact, he'd say yes to anything she wanted as long it kept her right here with him for as long as humanly possible.

Chapter Sixteen

MIERDA. What the hell had she just done?

Jackson eased up, rolled off of her, and laid bedside her on his ridiculously comfortable king-sized bed.

Eso es correcto. She'd just finished thoroughly screwing the man she loved who had no idea she felt that way about him. And they'd both gotten off. Probably not the *smartest* choice.

Still, she couldn't stop herself from saying, "That felt—"

"Yeah," Jackson finished. "It sure as hell did."

Being joined together so perfectly had actually felt better than Jillian remembered. Had even missed if she continued to be honest with herself.

"What else would you like me to do for you, Miss Castillo?"

She glimpsed him giving her his mouthwatering grin.

He shifted onto his left side and propped himself up on his elbow. "I believe you said something like that a few minutes ago. But I was a *little* distracted."

She'd told Jackson the complete truth when she'd said he hadn't lost his touch. The charm. That grin. Massaging the aloe vera gel into his sunburned neck. All of that combined with loving him with every fiber she possessed, how could she not have ended up plastered against him in the shower and here in his bed?

"I need to get rid of this thing. I'll be right back."

He lifted himself from the bed and strolled into his bathroom.

Then during the most intimate, passionate moment a man and woman could share, he'd asked her to stay the night and she'd agreed. Also not the *smartest* choice.

It would, however, come with a caveat he had to go along with, or she would leave…as hard as it would be to walk away from him and out of his house.

Jillian rolled onto her right side, then winced at the damp comforter. But not taking the time to dry off after a libidinous shower is what happened when a woman wanted a man so badly she could barely see straight, much less think.

Jackson sat close to her, but on the bed's edge, and placed his hand on her bare thigh. "You're awfully quiet." He slid his warm fingers down her thigh and back up. "What's on your mind?" He paused, then added, "And please don't say the word regret."

Regret? He couldn't be serious.

Her breath caught in her throat at his fingertips barely moving up and down her skin. "Not even a little bit." Their gazes connected. "If you keep doing that, I'll have no choice but to show you how much I don't regret a thing." She'd enjoy every second of it, too.

He brought back his grin. "Oh, so you like *this*?" He continued his actions, then slid his fingers to her stomach where he drew lazy eights. "And this?"

She shivered.

"Question answered," he said around a laugh.

He slid his fingers lower.

Dammit. She needed to stop this before they ended up wrapped around each other in a round two. She had a deal to strike with him. So she grasped his hand and said, "Jackson, you still need to do something for me."

"I thought I was about to."

She sat up.

His grin doubled in size. "Between your hair and how *fantastic* you look in general right now, I don't think I'll be able to let you leave this bed tonight."

Her hands flew to her damp hair, and she smoothed the top and strands into something she hoped looked less wild. "Where's your phone?"

Jackson's grin turned into a slight frown. "My phone? Why?"

She stood. "You'll find out. Where is it?"

"Um…in the living room. On the ottoman. But—"

"I'll be right back."

Jillian headed into the hallway where she felt no shame walking by the floor-to-ceiling windows that served as the wall between the inside and out. The high fence in his backyard and trees provided total privacy. He'd told her, on her first visit to his house, replacing the wall with the windows had been his biggest change and was one of her favorite features. He'd also brought the row of windows into his bedroom that turned into double doors that opened to the backyard.

The house, the simple, but comfy furniture and decorations, the roomy backyard, the black Range Rover parked in his garage, all of it fit Jackson Lovett perfectly. He just needed to be *here* more often and without distractions when possible. On that thought, she swiped his phone off of the ottoman and lifted hers from her purse.

The caveat she was about to present would be good for her, too.

Before she left the living room, she picked up the remote and turned off his enormous T.V. They wouldn't be needing *that* anymore tonight, either.

"Here." She handed over his phone. "If you want me to stay, you need to turn off your phone for the rest of the night."

He took the device with wide eyes.

"I'll turn mine off, too." She pursed her lips. "We'll turn them back on when we wake up tomorrow morning. Deal?"

"No." He shook his head. "Jillian, I can't do that."

She released a frustrated sigh. "I promise it won't kill you." She grinned. "And if you pass out from shock, I'll be right here to wake you up."

His gaze swung between her and his phone.

"If you want me to stay, turn off your phone." *Please just turn it off.* If she had to walk out of here, she wasn't certain how they'd ever overcome it and get through party planning as the maid-of-honor and best man. As it *was,* she had no interest in thinking about tomorrow.

"Jillian, it's not that simple." He frowned. "This isn't about work, either. Believe it or not, I rarely receive work calls on the weekend. But…" His voice trailed into silence.

She suddenly realized what was stopping him and caught his gaze. "Jackson, nothing bad is going to happen to her between now and tomorrow morning."

Apprehension flashed through his eyes.

She placed her lips beside his ear and whispered, "Turn your phone off."

He sighed, and Jillian straightened.

"This is the only way I can get you to stay with me tonight?"

She lifted her shoulders. "*Si.*"

"And you'll turn yours off?"

"*Absolutamente.* It'll be good for me, too."

Silence descended…until he expelled a quick breath and pressed the two buttons. His phone went dark and he swiped right to turn it off.

But now she loved him even more for trusting and choosing her. *Them*.

The complete opposite of what he'd done in April.

"I can't believe you talked me into doing that."

Santo cielo. She couldn't—wouldn't—think about any of that right now, so she turned off her phone, and set his and hers on the nearby nightstand.

"Then again, you are standing in front of me looking like a fantasy come true." He shot her a pretend glare. "Not fair, Miss Castillo. But at the same time, well-played."

Jillian straddled his lap and gently guided them backward onto his bed. "Trust me when I say you won't miss your phone tonight, Mr. Lovett. Now, where were we?" She pressed her mouth to his, and they shared a tantalizing kiss that lasted until they needed air. "About there seems right," she breathlessly added.

He kissed the tip of her nose. "Don't hate me for saying this, but I'm suddenly feeling hungry. You?"

She rubbed against him. "I can tell."

"For food," he said around a moan. "I need to eat, or I won't make it through the night."

She sat up. "Well, we can't have that." She leisurely climbed off of *his* beautiful body and gestured at herself. "Help a girl out by giving her a T-shirt to wear instead of her grungy work clothes?" And had she really been up in Commerce City a few hours earlier with Campbell and Hayley while texting Jackson about him changing their plans?

She'd also been texting another man who she had plans with at nine tomorrow morning. Something else she couldn't—wouldn't—think about at this moment.

Jackson smiled as he stood. "Maybe I want to eat naked with you."

She arched her right eyebrow.

He placed his head beside hers. "That eyebrow thing you do makes me crazy." He straightened and winked. "The good kind of crazy." He walked around her, toward his dresser.

That was certainly new and unexpected information.

Jillian watched as he pulled a red T-shirt from a middle drawer. "You never told me that."

His smiled slipped while he handed her the shirt. "Never got the chance to."

Not having anything to say to that, she slipped into his T-shirt while he pulled on shorts.

"So," he said, standing in front of his fridge, "the best I can offer you is leftover pizza and beer. Or we can order something."

From her seat at his island counter, Jillian had a perfect view of his mussed, blonder-than-usual hair, sharp profile, and long, toned physique.

Even sunburned, Jackson Lovett looked like the god of wearing basketball shorts.

He glanced at her. "Thoughts?"

"Pizza and beer sound perfect."

As they sat together quietly eating, an overwhelming sense of déjà vu surrounded Jillian.

Her in one of his T-shirts, him shirtless and wearing basketball shorts, and them sitting at an island counter, eating and drinking. *Their weekend together in March.*

It was as if history was repeating itself, but in a different location, different time of year, and now they were no longer new to each other when it came to physical intimacy.

That was also the weekend she'd realized she was headed for the point of no return, in spite of the conversation they'd had about love while sitting at the counter.

Still, his parents had been lucky. His brother. Alyson and David. Alyson's parents. David's parents. Brynn and Marcos. Why couldn't she—they—be lucky like them? Yes, she'd witnessed her parents' travesty of a marriage and would rather be alone than end up in a miserable relationship. But Jackson had only ever been around love involving soul mates.

Everything between her and Jackson had snapped into place from the moment they'd met. Everything had been so easy. So natural. Dating him, being together in general, had never felt like work, even at the very beginning. And the physical intimacy? *Beyond unbelievable*.

On the surface, it was hard to understand why they weren't together. Even now, sitting together in companionable silence while eating, felt right and comfortable and perfect. Just like it had in March while they'd been at his family's cabin.

Why couldn't they figure this out?

Her breathing slowed when the answer landed in her mind with a thud.

She hadn't given Jackson Lovett a chance.

Had he been ready to hear declarations of love in April? *No, en absoluto.* But what if she'd reacted to *that project* differently? Kept her anger in check, no matter how much it pissed her off he'd chosen to align himself and his firm with the soulless Keith Marsden. Since then, he'd allowed *that project* to take over his life. He hadn't said those words, but she wasn't stupid.

Jillian eyed Jackson, finishing his piece of pizza, and she couldn't stop from frowning. At this very moment, he was the man she'd fallen in love with in the spring, but come Monday—

"You're staring, Miss Castillo." He wiped his mouth and sat back. "Was I eating like a high school kid who'd been given his last meal?" He picked up his beer. "I was pretty hungry."

Come Monday, he'd probably be back to unrecognizable, not just because of work. He was also doing a remarkable job of keeping other, much harder realities from his mind.

But these burdens meant he was *no closer* to hearing how she truly felt about him than he'd been in April.

All she could do was be in this blissful moment with him, continue helping him plan the party for their best friends, and…be there as a friend like she'd done the last two Friday nights.

She inhaled a shaky breath, then said, "Thank you for turning off your phone. I know it was hard for you because of everything that's going on with your mom."

He looked at his beer before taking a drink. "You were right, Jillian. Nothing bad is going to happen between now and tomorrow morning." He cracked a smile. "My mom looked and sounded really damn good today." He laughed. "She was so… animated…while telling us we had to take her out for a night in LoDo. I mean, I know—we all do—why she wants a night out like that, but I still can't believe it." He shook his head. "Bar hopping with my parents in LoDo? Never imagined *that* ever happening."

Jillian swiveled in his direction. "It's a fabulous idea. It'll be fun for all of you."

He kept his gaze trained on her. "My invite for you to go with us wasn't an empty one."

She tipped the beer bottle to her mouth as she said, "I know." And, dammit, if she didn't want to go. But that wouldn't be the best, *smartest* choice for her.

He set his beer on the counter, slid off the stool, and gently spread her bare legs to stand between them. "What can I do to convince you to go with us?" He grasped her beer and set it beside his. "To be my date that night?"

Oh, no.

Jackson lowered his head and nuzzled the spot where her shoulder curved into her neck.

The soft groan escaped before she could stop it.

How did he make her yield so easily?

"Tell me what to do," he murmured, followed by placing a

series of airy kisses up and down her neck. "I promise I'm listening."

She breathed him—them—into her heart. Her mind. Her soul.

"*Jillian*," he whispered into her ear as she wrapped her legs around his thighs.

She moaned his name before their mouths came together.

In a blur of breathless kisses and rapid movement, they were back on his bed, minus their clothing, and she was straddling him once again. Only this time, with him pulsing inside of her.

As they moved together in perfect unison, she said, "Dance with me that night."

He leaned slightly back and gave her his scrumptious grin. He then opened his mouth, but she silenced him with a kiss and lost herself in him. *Them.*

Chapter Seventeen

JACKSON STRETCHED, rolled right, and reached for Jillian. At his arm curling around a thick pillow, he opened his eyes. He blinked until the fog cleared, realizing Jillian wasn't even in bed.

He sat up and looked around his room. Early morning light filtering through the windows caused him to glance at his alarm clock. It wasn't quite seven-thirty.

Had last night been a dream? Between the early hour, empty right side of his bed, and silent room, he couldn't escape the feeling he'd just awakened and emerged from his version of paradise. Where he and Jillian had been the only ones who'd existed.

He glanced at his deep pink arms and flinched. Which made his face hurt for a second. Unfortunately, getting fried by the sun yesterday had been real. *Shit.* He'd be peeling for days once the red, soreness part went away.

"Hi." Jillian—and completely dressed—strolled into his room while piling her hair on her head. "I'm glad you're awake. It would've felt wrong leaving without saying goodbye."

Goodbye? It was early in the morning on a Sunday and it's not like they'd gotten a whole lot of sleep during the night. "You're leaving?"

She stopped at his nightstand and picked up their phones. "I have to." She handed his over. "Congratulations, Mr. Lovett, for being off the grid for nearly ten hours."

He watched as she turned hers back on, then frowned. "Why do you have to leave?" He wasn't anywhere near ready for her to walk out of here. They also still had a guest list to compile. "Do you have a wedding?" During their way-too-quick time together, she'd worked a few Sundays due to weddings. Jillian having to rush out of here for work hadn't crossed his mind when he'd asked her to stay while their bodies had been one. In fact, it hadn't occurred to him at any point she'd have to leave this early. "I guess I should've asked that last night."

She set her phone down and went into his bathroom.

No reply to his question. What the hell was going on here? With her?

Jackson turned his phone on and flung the blankets aside. As he pulled on his shorts, his phone lit up and dinged with text messages, as did Jillian's. He was reading his mom's message about going up to Longmont for family dinner and to watch the Broncos game when Jillian's phone continued to ding. Or more like blow up.

Unable to stop his curiosity, and fueled by confusion at her rush to leave, he peered at her phone still lit up from all her missed messages. A couple were from her sister Claudia, one was from Alyson, and two from—he narrowed his eyes at seeing an unfamiliar guy's name.

The screen went dark.

Jackson focused on his bed, thoroughly rumpled from their night together.

No way could they have shared what they had if she was seeing someone. It wasn't possible. It had been like *that night* had never happened. She'd even agreed to be his date for LoDo night with his family. And David had made it a point to tell Jackson she was single that Saturday of Labor Day weekend. It felt like two months ago, but only two weeks had passed.

He eyed her phone, still dark.

There was only one way to know for sure, so he picked up her phone.

Jackson stopped in the doorway of his bathroom and leaned against the frame.

She stood at the sink, in front of the mirror, wiping under her eyes.

"Jillian, who's Niall Donnelly?"

She halted before looking at him.

He held out her phone which she grasped. "I didn't mean to look at the screen, but it was blowing up with texts…including a couple from him."

She smiled, but it seemed forced. "He's a new friend and is friends with Brynn and Marcos. It's how I met him."

Jackson slowly nodded. "And what kind of friend would he be?"

Jillian slid her phone into her back jeans pocket. "Is that really any of your business?"

He raised his eyebrows. "After last night? Yeah. I think it is."

Her phone dinged with what had to be another text.

"He's just a friend, and I have to go." She skirted past Jackson, into his bedroom.

And the reason why she was in a hurry to leave hit him swift and hard. To the point his breath stalled in his chest. "Is *he* the reason you're in such a rush to get out of here?"

"Jackson, we're absolutely not doing this."

That meant he was right. Another, more powerful emotion swept through him and obliterated his shock while he slowly followed her path from his room into the living room.

He filled his lungs with air in an attempt to eradicate the jealousy. Maybe he had no business feeling this way, but that sure as hell wasn't going to change anything. Especially after their night together. "What about the guest list we didn't work on?" he quietly asked. "If memory serves, we decided to take the evening in a…different direction."

Jillian picked up her purse and faced him. "You can't be standing there now complaining about that different direction."

He crossed his arms. "No. But now I *am* going to complain about the fact that after our phenomenal night, you're running off to go meet up with another guy." Saying the words out loud only fueled a second round of breath-stealing jealousy.

Jackson focused on the floor as he struggled to pull more air into his lungs.

"For the third time," she enunciated, "Niall is a friend. You're not this guy, Jackson."

He raised his head, and their eyes locked.

"You have several women friends."

He leaned forward. "You're right. But I'm not the one running out of here, early on a Sunday morning, to go meet up with one of them." What exactly did she and this guy have planned—he ceased that thought, then squashed it.

She lifted her chin. "When I made plans with Niall on *Thursday*, my crystal ball wasn't working so there was no way for me to know Saturday night would go the way it did."

She and this guy had made plans on Thursday? That info made all of this even better.

"*Por favor,* Jackson. Don't do this." She sighed. "Don't make me regret what happened."

Okay. He sounded like a jealous asshole. But he wanted her to stay with him. Go back to bed and fall asleep with her curled in his arms. Wake up a few hours later and have breakfast. Sit outside—in the shade—and work on the guest list. Talk. Really get caught up on what they'd missed in each other's lives the past several months. Maybe even talk about giving their relationship a second chance since that shitty night in April couldn't be their end.

No, not after yesterday and their last two Fridays together.

Jillian dropped her phone into her purse and shrugged into the strap.

Jackson couldn't be alone in feeling that way and he suddenly needed the truth. "Jillian, why did you really end things between us?" Yeah, she'd been pissed about the Downey Project, but he knew there'd been something more going on than his business decision.

She squinted at him. "Where'd *that* come from? And you know why."

"No," he persisted. "I know that's not the real reason. All I want is the truth."

Her dark eyes widened with what appeared to be…fear? But she lowered her gaze and stepped backward.

Fear. Not a good sign since, from what he'd seen and knew, nothing scared Jillian Castillo.

"I saw that." He closed the gap between them. "You're not telling me something."

"I have no idea what you're talking about. I have to go."

He followed her to the door. "Jillian, if I said or did something in April—outside of taking the Downey Project—that put me into the category of dickhead, I want you to tell me."

She flung the door open and said over her shoulder, "Let's plan on touching base about the guest list in a couple days."

Jackson stood in his doorway, watching her nearly sprint to her car parked in his driveway. Seconds later, she was gone.

He muttered a choice swear word under his breath, then slammed the door shut.

What the hell was she not telling him? If he had done or said something in the realm of asshole back in April, didn't he deserve to know what it was? He had no desire to see or be with any woman but Jillian, despite her baffling behavior. But considering how *stupendous* everything had gone between them this morning, it seemed she may never again get to the same place as him. Which meant he'd eventually have to move on to another woman. Someday.

In the meantime, there was absolutely no way he could stay in his house with his thoughts. His vivid imagination would be focused on her, spending time with—

Jackson gritted his teeth and shook his head.

He needed to get out of here. When was the last time he'd taken off with his mountain bike and subjected his body to a long, grueling ride? *Of course he couldn't remember.*

He marched into his room, keeping his eyes off of his thoroughly rumpled bed.

After the ride, he'd head up to Longmont where he'd continue to *not* think about Jillian. Or the fact it was Sunday and he had a meeting first thing tomorrow morning with Nelson Downey and Ember Leventhal.

▭

JILLIAN LET herself into her apartment and closed the door where she paused.

Santo cielo. This morning had not gone the way she'd planned. She'd probably never forget Jackson staring at her with so much confusion and shock and *hurt.*

"Where have *you* been all night?"

Jillian shrieked and jolted, which caused Claudia to laugh.

Her sister stood at the end of the hallway where it ended at the living room. Claudia wore a black-and-white exercise bra, skintight matching leggings, and her Nikes. She also had her chin-length hair pulled back into a tiny ponytail.

Jillian placed her hand on her chest. "What the hell are you doing here?"

Claudia lifted a spoon, heaping with peanut butter, to her mouth. "I live here?" She stuck the dollop into her mouth. "I didn't mean to scare the shit out of you," she said around the bite. "Your door's closed. I figured you got in after me last night and were still asleep."

Jillian arched her right eyebrow. "You live here? Since when?"

"Ha, ha." Another spoonful of peanut butter went into Claudia's mouth. "Afton and I have been bitchier than usual with each other. And the deal we made is if that happened, we needed breathing space." She pointed the empty spoon at Jillian. "Your turn."

It had never crossed Jillian's mind that her sister would be home at this early hour on a Sunday morning. What the hell could she say? Certainly not the truth. It would take too long to explain how she'd ended up staying the night with Jackson—more like wrapped around him—and she had to get ready before another guy showed up.

"You don't know him, Claude." She'd become way too good at lying on the fly. "I'm getting in the shower." While in there, she would not think about the delectable one she'd taken yesterday evening. "Do you need in there?" At least, she would try hard not to think about it.

"Ooh, a random dude." Claudia released a wicked laugh. "Aren't we living dangerously? But it's about time. Was he as good-looking as Jackson? Better? I hope he was, since I know Jackson was the last guy behind you sneaking into the apartment like this on a Sunday morning."

Yes. He had been. *Mierda*. Last night had not gone the way

she'd initially thought it would, either. "I wasn't sneaking," Jillian shot back. "Do you need in the bathroom or not?"

Claudia lowered the peanut butter jar and spoon. "I don't get details? Really?"

"I don't have time for this." Jillian turned left, in the direction of her bedroom. "I have somewhere to be today."

"So I guess that means you don't want to go to the gym with me?"

"No!" She dearly loved her younger sister, but at this moment Jillian wanted to be alone.

Minutes later, she stepped under the hot spray and took a deep breath.

Niall's texts this morning had caused an unnecessary problem with Jackson she'd never seen coming, but thank *God* he, too, was running late. Also known as the reason for all his texts.

She closed her eyes and angled her head back into the water.

Dammit. Why had Jackson looked at her screen? She'd heard her phone going off while in the bathroom but hadn't felt the need to rush out to read the texts. Clearly, she should have done just that when she again recalled the range of emotions on Jackson's face. She'd rightfully defended herself and Niall, but while driving home she hadn't been able to ignore a simple fact: If Jackson had been the one "running off" to meet up with another woman—friend or not—after their *phenomenal night* together, Jillian would have reacted the same way.

Not one part of her had wanted to leave, but staying wouldn't have been the smartest choice for either of them. Since going in a different direction yesterday evening with barely a second thought, things between them were officially confusing. Staying this morning would have only added to it, as well. There was also the fact he'd asked her that question.

Jillian grabbed the shampoo, squeezed some into her hand, and lathered it into her hair.

All I want is the truth.

If only telling Jackson the truth was that simple. He'd also assumed he'd unintentionally done or said something to cause what happened and wanted that truth, too.

It's not as if she was trying to be deceitful. He just wasn't ready for the truth. Jackson Lovett had enough going on in his life. It wouldn't be fair to add to his burdens. Jillian knew him well enough that he'd feel terrible—guilty—for not feeling the same way about her…and what she'd accidentally overheard him say about them in April while on the phone with his brother.

It was the reason she'd known he'd been nowhere near ready for a *real* relationship.

Based on what Jackson had told her Friday night while they walked to her car, he was already battling guilt involving his family and friendship with David. She couldn't add to it and sure as hell couldn't put herself through such heartache. *Absolutamente no.* So leaving this morning had been the best choice she'd made since walking into his house.

Jillian buried the vivid memories of the previous evening deep into her mind while she finished getting ready for her four-wheeling day with Niall. Still, as she climbed into Niall's forest-green Jeep Wrangler she couldn't help but wish it was Jackson's Range Rover.

"Morning." Niall pointed at a coffee cup in the holder. "For you, per your order."

His final text to come through had been asking her if he should pick up coffee on his way.

Jillian grasped the cup. "Thank you. It's been a rough morning." *Without a doubt.*

He drove away from her building. "Sounds like someone else had a really late night."

"Yes," she murmured, settling into the passenger seat.

Jillian slid her gaze to her new friend, wearing his aviator sunglasses. Today was the first time she'd seen Niall without a baseball hat. He had dirty blond hair cut stylishly short. She also couldn't help but notice he looked really good in his khaki shorts, a navy-blue T-shirt, and dark tennis shoes. He hadn't shaved that morning, but the dark-blond scruff suited his angular face.

Maybe she could change Campbell's mind about dating? The two would be cute together.

"Are you checking me out?" he asked, keeping his eyes on the road.

"Yes."

He glanced sharply in her direction.

"I think you'd be a good match with a friend of mine."

Niall braked at a stoplight, lowered his sunglasses enough to catch her eyes, and grinned. "Does she look like you?"

She arched her right eyebrow. "No, she doesn't look like me."

His grin deepened. "Well, I like women who look like you. *Estás caliente.*"

That was a first—a kid with Irish ancestry flirting with her in Spanish.

"Niall, please don't flirt with me." Definitely amusing, but Jillian wasn't in the mood.

He sighed. "Okay. You're right. You made yourself clear last week."

"Thank you. How is it you're fluent in Spanish?"

"Four years in high school and four more in college. I studied Spanish and international business. Now I'm working on my MBA at CU."

Her eyes widened. "Wow." She cringed. Maybe referring to Niall as a kid hadn't been terribly fair to him. "So the landscaping job is…?"

"Paying the bills for now. A good buddy's dad owns the company. Eventually, I'll have to get an internship." He looked at her and back at the road. "What's your *real* job?"

She placed her head against the headrest. "Florist. I co-own a shop in Denver with my best friend. We had a wedding yesterday."

He nodded. "Small-business owner. Very cool."

Jillian sipped her coffee.

In spite of Niall's flirtatious comment about liking women who looked like her, she couldn't help but feel he'd be good for Campbell. Maybe not in the sphere of *forever*—

"So what's the guy's name?"

She whipped her head in his direction. "Excuse me?"

"The reason for your '*mancation*' and the sad eyes?"

Dammit. Niall Donnelly was awfully perceptive for a kid—guy—who couldn't be more than twenty-five, twenty-six years old. "I don't know what you're talking about."

"Yeah, you do. Is he also the reason for your '*rough morning*'?"

She faced him. "That's an awfully personal question."

"That means yes." He laughed. "I wasn't the only one who got lucky last night."

Heat engulfed her face as she replied, "I'm not talking about this with a stranger."

Niall's humor faded. "If you really thought of me as a stranger, you wouldn't be sitting in the passenger seat of my Jeep right now. And if you don't want to talk about it, that's fine. But we've got about an hour-long drive ahead of us. It would suck to sit in silence the entire time."

"*Fino.*" She pointed at him. "Why can't we talk about you?"

He looked left, out his window, as they merged onto the interstate. "I had a terrific night. Thanks for asking. But I don't kiss and tell."

She released an exasperated sigh. "That's not what I meant." *And he knew it, too.*

"Oh." He flashed her a sly grin. "Sorry." He wriggled into the driver's seat as if making himself comfortable for a long drive *and* chat. "Her name was Amy."

Jillian peered at him. "What are you talking about?"

"The girl who broke *my* heart." Niall eyed her. "That's what happened with his guy, right? He broke your heart?" He frowned. "But then, why would you spend the night with—"

"He didn't break my heart." *Not exactly, anyway.* "And neither of us are going to talk about how we spent the evening."

She went back to sipping her coffee as Niall moved into the fast lane of I-70; the interstate that led to the mountains when headed west.

"I'll go first, then you can go?" Niall quietly asked.

In that moment, Jillian realized she'd never told anyone the story. The *truth*. Not Alyson, not Claudia, not one soul knew she'd fallen in love with Jackson Lovett. And so damn quickly. She'd been too mortified and wanted to protect the truth. Maybe she did need to unload everything this one time? She softly said, "I'm listening." She had nothing to lose and might relieve some of the weight from her own shoulders.

"Amy and I were high school sweethearts," Niall began. "But after we graduated, she went to Austin, Texas, for school and I stayed here."

Jillian gave him a sad smile. "Long distance is tough. Especially at that age."

"Yeah," he mumbled. "She met someone new. From what she said, not too long after school started." He shook his head. "She told me she didn't like the thought of breaking up over the phone, so I had no idea. I didn't see the break-up coming when she was home for Thanksgiving." His gaze briefly met Jillian's. "We had an ugly, epic end. The kind of ending that involves shouting and way too many rotten things being said."

She frowned. "I've never been through a break-up like that, but it sounds awful." Yes, her parents' marriage had *definitely* ended in such a way. But that night in April with Jackson had been the closest she'd ever come to a relationship imploding. "I'm sorry you went through that."

He shrugged. "Thanks, but it was a long time ago. What about you and your guy? It doesn't sound like things ended too badly." He fought a smile. "It actually sounds like you've become friends with benefits."

"No, it's not like that!" she snapped.

Niall's smile vanished.

Jillian closed her eyes and slowly inhaled. "I'm sorry." She exhaled, paused long enough to gather her thoughts, and allowed the entire story to pour out of her.

From her beginning with Jackson in February; to falling in love with him during their weekend together in Estes Park, though she kept out the other details; the two weeks they had together after that weekend; and then to the night in April.

Jackson had told her about taking *that project* while they'd walked to her car. In a flash of anger at him and at herself for falling for him, she'd lost her temper. She'd told him they weren't right for each other and that it was over. Then she'd driven off, leaving him standing in the rain.

It wasn't until she'd stepped into her bedroom that she'd freed her frustration and sorrow.

"Whoa," Niall murmured once she'd finished taking him to last night, minus the details.

Reliving and sharing her break-up with Jackson had made it sound like a different kind of epic, ugly end.

"I have a feeling you're going to make me turn around and head back to Denver for saying this," Niall slowly began, "but it sounds like you may have broken *his* heart."

Jillian gaped at him. "What the hell are you talking about?"

Niall held up his right hand. "Just hear me out for a sec."

She lifted her chin. "*Fino.*"

"You admitted the real reason you dumped him was because you didn't—don't—think he feels the same way about you. But you never gave the guy a chance."

She froze since she'd come to that same conclusion last night. But there was that conversation Jackson had with his brother she hadn't shared because of how much it still stung.

"From what you've said," Niall continued, "it sounds like he really likes you." He smirked. "I do have to stop flirting with you because I *don't* have a chance in hell."

Jillian faced forward. "Niall, this isn't about him *liking* me." She knew that much since she wasn't clueless.

"Okay, you're right. But I think you should be honest with him."

All I want is the truth.

Jackson wanted honesty and maybe Niall was right, but genuine like did *not* equal love. Telling him the truth wasn't that easy right now. Not even a little bit. She, of course, hadn't shared Jackson's family situation with Niall. So she quietly said, "Thanks for listening. And the advice." Under completely different circumstances, she might have considered it, too.

"Jillian, seriously. Give the guy a break. He might surprise you."

Surprise her? Not when it came to something like this. She had to protect herself, and Jackson didn't need any more surprises in *his* life.

The truth would stay right where it belonged, locked inside of her heart, mind, and soul.

Chapter Eighteen

JACKSON STOOD at the white projector screen where he had the designs displayed. Once Downey and Ember were seated at the conference room table, he tried not to smile about what he was going to tell them. "Miss Leventhal, you need to make a choice." He pointed at the spot she'd bulldozed her way into. "You can keep this spacious location that belonged to Diana *or* you can choose one of the slightly smaller spots that do face west. I can't give you both."

Ember narrowed her black, soulless eyes. "What do you mean I can't have both?"

Jackson somehow kept a straight face.

"Lovett, get to the damn problem." Downey crossed his bulky arms.

"Miss Leventhal said she'd consider taking a location that already faced west if I could make it bigger, but I only have so much space to work with." Jackson used his index finger to circle the entire design. "No matter how I tried redesigning the buildings, expansion in the west facing section"—he pointed to that area—"will cut into fire truck access." He fought a smile and added, "The Fire Marshall will never sign off on it."

Ember dramatically rolled her eyes and went back to her phone.

Downey's body and jaw became rigid.

The dark side of Jackson's psyche wanted to laugh from the satisfaction of professionally telling Nelson Downey—and by extension Keith Marsden—and the so-called great Ember Leventhal, *hell no*. Hopefully he'd be able to control himself until they left the building.

"But Ember can have her two stories?" Downey practically snarled.

"That won't be a problem. However"—Jackson tapped the area of the designs located opposite Ember's space—"it would be best if we could turn this building into two stories, as well. From a design standpoint." Though he still felt it would be a huge waste of his time.

Marsden looked at the area Jackson had indicated. "Some Asian-fusion restaurant wants that spot. I doubt they need two stories."

Jackson stayed silent while trying not to smirk. As successful as he'd been yesterday keeping this meeting far from his mind, it was going exactly the way he'd hoped it would.

"Then again," Downey added, giving Jackson the condescending smile he now despised, "I have ways of persuading people to change their minds, and we officially have an empty spot."

Downey and Ember exchanged triumphant glances.

Dread crawled up Jackson's spine as to what his foul client was about to say.

"Diane-what's-her-name decided to pull out altogether," Downey continued. "Right choice for everyone."

If Diana Shepherd had been standing next to Jackson, he would have congratulated her on getting the hell away from Nelson Downey and, ultimately, Keith Marsden.

"We already have someone interested, but not in the spot that Diane gave up."

Jackson frowned.

Diana. How hard was that name to remember?

"Keith Marsden's eldest daughter has her own, successful line of purses, shoes, and accessories." Downey smiled at Ember. "We're putting her store next to Ember's."

The clothing designer grinned at Jackson. "We're very good friends and colleagues, and I expect you to give her anything she wants done with that space."

"Everyone expects that from you, Lovett," Downey echoed.

Jackson's jaw tightened as he raised his chin.

Now he'd have Keith Marsden, by way of his daughter, breathing down his neck until God knew when. The way all of this was going, he'd never be free of this soul-sucking project.

That he never should have taken.

Downey came to his feet. "I need to get back to my office and get on the phone with some business owners." He brought back his condescending smile. "There will be some shuffling around and if the owners don't like it, they can get out like that Diane-what's-her-name. We won't have any problems filling the spots should they choose to leave."

Jackson walked stiffly to the table where his laptop was plugged into the projector.

"Thank you, Nelson." Ember stood and flounced out of the conference room.

"As for you," Downey said, "I'm not telling you again, you *will* take my phone calls, as well as Ember's and Keith's daughter when she's ready to talk to you. No more getting the run around from your receptionist."

Jackson slid his hands into his pockets. "So just to be clear, I'm to answer your calls and theirs even when I'm taking a leak?"

A tense silence crackled between them.

"You have a real smart mouth, Lovett."

Jackson glared at his loathsome client.

"Not sure talking to me like that is a real smart move for you or your firm."

He was also beyond fed up with hearing that threat.

Downey stepped backward. "Don't make me regret choosing you and your firm." The squat man turned and waddled out of the conference room.

Jackson yanked the projector cords from his laptop. "*Shit!*"

He hadn't been entirely looking forward to the damn meeting, but he'd still walked in here feeling in complete control. But Downey—the dirty sonofabitch—kept throwing fast curves Jackson couldn't dodge. And always followed by threats to his career and firm.

He gripped his phone inside his pocket; the fury racing through him making him feel he could crush the device into a pile of electronic pieces.

"Hey."

Jackson glanced up to find David, dressed in a suit and tie, leaning against the frame.

"You look like you're ready to tear someone's head off," David added.

He nodded. "Yeah. One guess who." Jackson pulled out the nearest chair and sat, then held out his hands. "I'm so pissed off right now I'm shaking." He sighed. "I can't remember the last time—" He stopped, so sick of saying and thinking those words.

David strolled toward the table where he sat on the edge. "While I was waiting for your meeting to end, Zach and Cruz told me how hellish this project has gotten on top of everything else you're dealing with around here." He frowned. "Which explains why you're wound up tighter than a corkscrew and that's not the guy I've been friends with for twenty-plus years."

No, it sure as hell wasn't.

Jackson breathed deeply through his nose to settle his still racing pulse. "You and Zach taking over hiring another architect is a huge help." *Total understatement, too.* He cracked a smile. "Thanks for stepping in."

David lifted his shoulders. "No thanks required."

Jackson sat back and pointed at David. "It's weird seeing you in a suit and tie. I've gotten used to seeing you dressed like a poor, starving musician."

He laughed. "Al said something similar, but in a much nicer way. And you saying that reminds me, what the hell were you doing Saturday night? You didn't text back until yesterday."

Jillian and her alluring, addictive *everything* flashed through Jackson's mind. Someone else he'd tried to keep far from his thoughts yesterday but hadn't been terribly successful.

"I think you would've liked the band we had that night." David grinned and gestured at Jackson. "That deep shade of pink is a great color on you, by the way."

"Isn't it, though?" But the sunburn from hell provided him with a great white lie. "I crashed and burned early Saturday night —no pun intended. I spent the day up in Estes on the boat with my parents, Will, Savannah, and the kids." At least that part was the truth.

"It's cool you did that." David paused, then asked, "How's your mom?"

Jackson gave him a half smile. "Really good." He laughed. "She announced she wants us to take her bar hopping in LoDo, not this Friday, but next. We're starting at The Blues Note since she wants to hear you guys play."

His friend squinted at him. "Bar hopping. In LoDo?"

"Yeah, and you and Alyson are going with us." The bigger question, though, was if Jillian still wanted to go with them. To be his date that night. He had agreed, during their second time joined as one, to *her* request. But then Sunday morning had happened.

"You've got to be shitting me." David laughed. "I'll bet Becs and Matt would love to go."

Jillian had said the same thing, and that's when Jackson, feeling no fear, had suggested she also come with them. That feeling of no fear had ultimately led to the night going in a different direction. But then Sunday morning had happened.

"You should invite them." And it hit him. If Jillian's new friend *Niall* really was more than a friend, Alyson would know… possibly David. What Jackson was about to do probably made him worse than pond scum, but he couldn't stop himself. "Hey, can I ask you a question?" He hesitated before saying, "It has to do with Jillian."

David's humor slowly transitioned into a frown. "Okay."

Jackson released a quick breath and asked, "Has Alyson mentioned Jillian seeing a guy named *Niall*?" She'd insisted before racing out of his house that the guy was just a new friend. She'd been so adamant there was no reason not to believe her. But it didn't jive. Her having somewhat early plans on a Sunday morning with a new friend that happened to be a guy?

Yeah, Jackson was still nursing his jealous, wounded pride she'd left him following their unexpected, spectacular night together. Yet, he would have felt that way had she left him Saturday night after compiling a guest list. What guy *wouldn't* have reacted the way he had?

"I…can't say I've heard that name. But Al hasn't seen much of Jillian lately. She's up in Boulder during the week. Her sister's pregnancy became difficult."

Jackson nodded. "I know."

His friend angled his head back. "How do you know that? Have you talked to Al?"

Oh, *shit*. He wasn't supposed to know. As far as David and Alyson knew, the last time Jackson and Jillian had spoken, even seen each other, was at the cabin Labor Day weekend.

Unless Jillian had told Alyson about him going to see her after he found out about his mom?

"Jackson, how do you—" David's stare became piercing. "Wait a sec. I texted you late on Saturday and you didn't answer. Al texted Jillian late on Saturday and she didn't answer."

Jackson remained silent.

"The last time you two ignored our texts was when you were *together*."

Jackson stood. "I'm up to my eyeballs in bullshit that isn't going away anytime soon, so I'm going to get some work done. But don't make plans for lunch. We're meeting up with Will." He grabbed his laptop.

David shook his head. "Oh, no…You just asked if she's seeing someone new *and* know the guy's name. Now you're avoiding my observation." David followed him from the conference room. "What the hell's going on, Jackson?"

"Your imagination is working overtime," he tossed over his shoulder. "Go hire your replacement." Jackson walked into his office and shut the door.

Great. He'd inadvertently opened a can of worms because of his curiosity. On the bright side, he had the rest of the morning to concoct a lie to save the surprise bachelor-bachelorette party. He honestly didn't give a crap if anyone found out about him and Jillian since he wanted to be with her again. Unfortunately, the party and them were welded together.

Jackson sat at his desk, set his laptop aside, and moved his wireless mouse to wake up his desktop computer. Per the usual, he had a slew of e-mails, but an invitation from Laura caught his attention and he promptly opened it.

He grinned at Laura and Josh's "Save-the-Date-for-Our-Wedding-in-Aruba Party" invite for this Saturday night at their loft.

Aruba. God, did that sound perfect. In fact, any place but right here would suffice. Not a typical feeling for him, though, because before he'd decided to go forward with the Downey Project, architecture had been his number one passion. Now he felt passionately inclined to grab a special someone and go far away from where he sat.

His mom's request from Saturday reappeared in his mind.

I want you to take a trip.

Jackson sat back and stared at the invite.

If he wanted to take Jillian Castillo anywhere again, he had to let go of what happened yesterday and accept what she'd said about Niall simply being a "new friend." She'd agreed to be Jackson's date for the night out in LoDo with his family, and he wouldn't blow it. But it was well over a week away. There was no way in hell he could wait that long to go on a date with her.

Maybe if he could get back to the guy he'd been Saturday night—the real him—she'd go with him to Laura and Josh's party?

Jackson pulled his phone from his pocket and went into the texting thread with Jillian. His thumbs hovered over the screen until he thought of what to say.

He finally settled on, *Hey. I think we should talk and not just about the guest list. Wednesday, same place and time?*

He set his phone down and responded "yes" to the invitation. Even if Jillian didn't go with him, he would be there for Laura and Josh. Because of Saturday night, and regardless of how yesterday morning went, he still felt pretty good about what Jillian's answer would be.

JILLIAN TOSSED the freshly laundered pillows *and* pillow cases onto Brynn and Marcos's bed with freshly laundered bedding, then reached into her back jeans pocket to grab her phone.

She paused at seeing Jackson's name before reading his text. That was surprisingly…polite…when she remembered how she'd left him yesterday morning. A reaction she couldn't blame him for, either. So she couldn't help but grin at his message that seemed to be saying "truce" without mentioning the word. Before she could respond, though, her phone started to buzz and burst into song because Niall was calling her. *Santo cielo*. Too weird.

She eyed the master bathroom doorway. Brynn had gone in there to take a bath while Jillian, being her sister's *servant*, stripped the bed to put on freshly laundered everything.

"Hi," she quietly answered, turning from the bathroom. "What's up?"

"Can you talk right now?" Niall just as quietly asked. "You answered like we have to do this all secret-mission style."

"I told you yesterday Brynn's pregnant-with-twins hormones have stolen her sanity." Being stuck in this house all day, every day, couldn't be helping, either. Still, there was only so much leeway Jillian was willing to give her sister after stripping the king-sized bed, having to wash the pillows and blankets, and put the bed back together.

"I had a great time with you yesterday."

Jillian moaned. "Niall, we talked about this—"

"Easy there, double-oh-seven. I'm not flirting. Just being honest. I'm calling to invite you to the Broncos game on Sunday."

She sighed. "Niall, I had fun yesterday, too." Completely the truth since the last time she'd gone four-wheeling was in college. "But a Broncos game sounds like a date." Though she hadn't been to a game in a few years. Going to one had been something she and Jackson had—

Jillian shook her head in an attempt to focus.

"It won't even be close to a date," Niall argued. "I've taken many friends—even *female* friends—to games. You also said how much you love the Broncos."

She remained silent.

"We'll be around seventy thousand people. Some friends—even *female*—will be there. We'll get there early and tailgate with them. You can also tell me about that friend of yours."

Dammit, if she didn't want to go, but how would she explain going to the game with Niall to *everyone* in her circle…including Jackson? The person she'd prefer to be with at a Broncos game. But if she changed Campbell's mind about dating before Sunday, maybe Niall could make plans with her before he and Jillian left the stadium?

"I was going to ask a good buddy of mine, but you could definitely use the distraction."

Her *yes* was on the verge of release, but she rightly said, "I'll think about it."

Niall sighed. "Not the answer I was hoping for, but better than no. I guess," he grumbled. "Be prepared to get a text from me everyday until you give me your real answer. I'll also be there on Thursday to bug you about this in person."

"I'm hanging up now," Jillian said as she turned. And her eyes locked with Brynn's.

Mierda. From the blood-chilling glare her sister was giving her, Jillian had a feeling Brynn had overheard most of her conversation with Niall.

"Don't work too hard this week. You'll need to be at your best come Sunday."

Jillian hung up and put her phone back into her jeans pocket.

Smirking, Brynn removed the towel from her head, releasing her long, wet hair. "I can't believe you, Jillian. I told you to stay away from Niall. What did you two do yesterday?"

She crossed her arms. "It's none of your business!"

"Stop saying that!" her sister snapped back. "Niall is a good guy. He's working hard on his MBA and works full time. He doesn't need to get caught up in your heartache."

Jillian frowned. "*Heartache*? What the hell are you talking about?"

Brynn walked the few steps to the bed and eased onto the edge. "It's obvious that Jackson guy did something to you. He was around one day and gone the next, and you refuse to talk about it. Or him. You also haven't dated anyone since him." Her eyes rolled upward. "Until now, and I'm telling you Niall's too young and good—" Brynn looked away.

Jillian clenched her hands into fists so tight she felt her nails digging into her palms. "By all means, finish what you were about to say. That Niall's too young and good for me?" She stepped forward. "Go ahead, Brynn. Finish your sentence."

Her sister lifted her chin. "That's not what I was going to say."

"Of course it was. And FYI, I ended things with Jackson. It's no one's business why." Yes, Niall knew the real reason, but that fact had nothing to do with this conversation.

Squaring off with Brynn reminded Jillian of how they'd been as teenagers sharing a bedroom before Brynn left for college. Arguing over everything and nothing, specifically when it came to wanting the bedroom to themselves, especially if a boy was involved. Though that had been more Jillian's desire than—oh, my God. *That's* what this was about.

As much as Jillian hated it, their mother had been right to be concerned about Jillian and Brynn coming to blows. This time because of Brynn's hormonal and pregnant insanity.

Jillian released a humorless laugh while shaking her head. "I can't believe it. You're jealous." Actually, when she thought about their teenage years, she could believe it.

Brynn, though striking, had not had the same kind of social life as Jillian or even Claudia.

Her sister's eyes became slits. "*Estas loca.*"

"No, that would be you." Jillian stared at Brynn. "You've

been treating me like your servant with your mile-long to-do lists for almost two weeks."

"You agreed to help me—us—out, Jillian."

"Help you," she enunciated. "Not become your servant. And why, exactly, can't Marcos do some of the stuff you've thrown at me? Like doing *all the damn laundry*?" She gestured at the bed for emphasis. "Is he allergic to doing laundry?"

"I told you," Brynn calmly said, "he's working on a tough case right now and his hours are longer than usual."

"Well, so are mine since I agreed to *help you*. And when you haven't been treating me like your servant, you've been bitching at me about my personal life and Niall who's a friend." Jillian leaned forward. "Just like he's your friend."

Brynn returned her glare.

As a taut silence fell, Jillian knew this was the last place she wanted to be or belonged. Yes, she'd thoroughly enjoyed spending quality aunt time with Sebastian, but she'd already had more than enough of her older sister's hormonal craziness. There was no way in hell she'd make it until Brynn gave birth. It was time to relent, though what she was about to say would probably cause more damage. But at least she'd be back at Daisy's Bouquets where she belonged with Alyson, Campbell, and Hayley.

"I'm done."

Brynn's eyes widened.

"Go ahead and call Mom." Jillian managed not to flinch at the words. "I'm sure she's waiting by the phone and will love hearing she was right." *Because Eva Castillo was never wrong.* She headed for the bedroom doorway. "I'll continue to help you guys out until she gets here. But I'm also done with your ridiculous to-do lists *and* your laundry."

"Jilly, wait a sec!"

Jillian fled down the stairs, into the kitchen, and out the French doors onto the deck.

She paced its length, shaking out the tension from her hands that had been tightly clenched during most of that wonderful exchange with her fabulous older sister.

Dammit. She really, really hated the fact their mother had been right. Still, Jillian had thought she'd made the right choice by stepping in to help Brynn and Marcos. Her sister had been the one to ask for her help. Brynn was pregnant with Jillian's nephews. How could she have said no? And saying no had meant keeping their mother in Hawaii. *But not anymore.*

Jillian stopped her pacing to stare into the perfectly landscaped yard.

Niall had invited her to the Broncos game and she really wanted to go, so she took out her phone. But first she needed to return Jackson's text.

I'll be there. To Niall she typed, *I've thought about it and I'm in.*

She and Niall were friends, and she was well within her right to go to the game with him.

Chapter Nineteen

JACKSON WALKED into the coffee shop and was greeted with the sound of chatter above the barista steaming milk.

He removed his sunglasses, glanced left, right, and his gaze locked with Jillian's. She sat at a table by the window, gave him a soft smile, and raised a cup.

As he approached her, he couldn't help but notice how good she looked. A different kind of good than Saturday night. More tired, too. But he'd always liked it when she wore her thick hair loose, bouncing around her shoulders.

"Hi." He lowered himself to the chair as she slid the cup toward him. "Thanks."

"Sure. It was my turn to buy." Jillian sipped her coffee.

He took a drink before saying, "You doing okay? You look like I feel." *And it was only Wednesday.* But Jillian's obvious fatigue wasn't normal for her.

"It's already been a long week."

"Welcome to my world," he mumbled. "I'm guessing yours has to do with your sister's recent transformation into the Wicked Witch of the West?"

"You could say that. We had a huge fight on Monday." Jillian set her cup down and turned it back and forth. "Our mother will be here on Friday huge." She smirked. "She'd be here by now, but she has a closing tomorrow."

He nodded, remembering Jillian mentioning her mom was a successful real estate agent. And he only knew enough to understand Jillian's mom being here for the next several weeks was not what she and her sisters would choose unless absolutely necessary.

"You two must have had some fight."

"Brynn pushed me too far and I lost my temper." She looked out the window. "I get that from our dad."

Jackson sat back. "Do you want to talk about it?" He had a shitload of work waiting for him at the office, but right now he didn't want to rush their time together. Especially after what happened Sunday morning that he planned on apologizing for as soon as he could.

"Do you really want to know?"

He tilted his head left. "I wouldn't have asked if I didn't want to know what happened."

She drank more coffee and said, "Niall."

Jackson froze.

"And the fact she turned me into her *servant,*" Jillian muttered under her breath. "But you're not the only one having trouble believing Niall and I are just friends."

His shoulders slumped as he shook his head. At the same time, she'd given him the opening he needed to say, "Jillian, I'm sorry. Really." Their gazes connected once more. "I was caught off guard by you rushing off and I...didn't want you to leave. So I was a dick." Every word he'd said was the truth, too.

Surprisingly, she gave him a warm smile. "I know you didn't want me to leave. And I don't blame you for reacting the way you did." She lifted her shoulders. "If it had been *you* rushing off to go meet another woman—even a friend—I would've reacted the same way."

He straightened.

Shit. That had been an unexpected confession on her part. An unexpected confession that caused hope to surge through his bloodstream that maybe they were on the same page.

"It's been awful being up in Boulder since Monday," she continued. "It's like walking into a house made by Elsa the Snow Queen." She frowned. "Sorry. I've been watching a lot of Disney movies lately."

Jackson grinned. "Believe it or not, I understood the reference. Gracie loves that movie."

She laughed quietly. "I'm sure she does. Anyway, it's been so awful up there I told Claude last night I couldn't wait for our mother to get here on Friday."

He took a drink. "What'd she say to that?"

"Because *I'm* the one who said it, she offered to check me into the psych ward of the closest hospital. Our mother will be better for Brynn, but"—she sighed—"I don't know how my sister and I will come back from this." She stared at her cup as she moved it in a complete circle.

Jackson wanted to pull her into his arms, the feeling so strong he gripped his coffee cup with both hands. He hated seeing her like this. So serious. Of the two of them, she wasn't the serious one. Jillian Castillo was the one full of passion and excitement, and sassy smiles and laughter. Even during the time when she and Alyson had no idea where their flower shop would go after being kicked out of their spot in the Highlands by *Marsden* Enterprises, she'd managed to stay positive and open-minded about the shop's uncertain future.

"Jilly, it sounds like you have a complicated relationship with your older sister."

Her gaze met his and she slowly nodded.

"On Saturday, my mom told Will and me—right after complimenting the close relationship he and I *now* have—she thought for sure when we were teenagers one of us would kill the other."

She laughed. Which made his head buzz.

"She was completely serious, too," he added. "Said she'd been able to picture the crime scene and aftermath and trial, then one of us being hauled off to prison."

She continued to laugh.

"But I get what she was really saying. That she never thought we'd ever get along as well as we do now." He paused before saying, "Come to think of it, I'm not sure I ever thought we would, but now I can also call him a best friend."

Her smile slipped.

"My point is, you and Brynn are sisters—family—and you'll get past what happened on Monday. Maybe it'll even make you closer." Jackson remembered almost this time last week facing off with his brother, then their time together on the boat, talking easily about life *and* how good their mom looked—something that wouldn't last.

He released a slow breath.

Watching their mom's health *really* decline was a harsh reality they'd be facing later.

"I thought Brynn and I had moved past our long ago, sibling drama," she softly said, "but I guess that is *not* the case." She sat up and grinned. "Thanks for the funny story. And encouraging words. We're really here to talk about the guest list, though."

Not true at all. But he said, "I have something for you." He reached into his pants pocket and withdrew the piece of paper. "To save time, I went ahead and made a list of people who David would want at the party." He slid the paper across the table. "Even managed to track down e-mail addresses for people not in my contact list."

Jillian's grin became a blinding smile. Which was an incredibly good sign.

"This is amazing." She opened the paper. "When did you find time to do this?"

He swallowed some coffee before answering, "During down time at work. Eileen helped a bit which means she knows what we're up to. But she and Hugh have been sworn to secrecy."

Jillian arched her right eyebrow. An even better sign.

"You have down time at work? Since when?"

Jackson shot her a pretend glare. "Since I decided to make some time, smart mouth." Compiling the list had also been a welcome break from the Downey Project, other projects the firm had going, and from being *the boss* in general.

Jillian folded the paper and placed it inside her purse. "Okay. I'll put together my list and then we'll send out a save-the-date with a huge emphasis on the party being a surprise."

"Sounds good."

They stared at one another.

He still needed to invite her to Laura and Josh's party. To be his date.

She pointed at his face. "Your sunburn is looking a bit better."

They continued to stare at one another, but Jackson strongly suspected she, too, was now thinking about their phenomenal Saturday night. Something he wanted to experience with Jillian again and again, and so much more than even that, which meant they had to start somewhere.

"I need to ask you something."

That same flicker of fear from Sunday flashed across her face, but Jackson forced himself to curb the desire to once again point it out. *One thing at a time.*

"Do you remember me talking about Laura, our lead interior designer, and her boyfriend, Josh?"

Jillian nodded.

"Actually," he amended, "Josh is her fiancé now. They got engaged while on vacation in Indonesia a few weeks ago."

Her eyes widened. "Indonesia? *Santo cielo*. That sounds like an incredible vacation."

Total understatement. "They're avid travelers," he continued, "and have already decided to have a destination wedding in Aruba."

She laughed. "Must be nice."

"Yeah"—he cleared his throat—"anyway, they're having a save-the-date-for-their-wedding party this Saturday night. David told me he and Alyson are going, too."

They went back to staring at one another as women at a nearby table burst into laughter.

Jackson scooted forward on his chair and placed his left hand beside hers on the table. "Will you go with me?" He caressed the back of her hand with his thumb. "Be my date?" *Please.*

Her eyes went to their hands and back to him. "What about the night out in LoDo?"

"That's not happening until next Friday." He sighed. "Jillian, I don't fully understand why you ended things between us that night." And maybe if he hadn't taken *that project*, she wouldn't have said and done what she did. Maybe. "But I've really liked reconnecting with you the last couple of weeks." He paused before adding, "I also can't help but think you feel the same way." He drew lazy circles on her hand. "Or am I *loco*?"

She remained silent, and Jackson held his breath. Waiting. And waiting some more.

Shit. There was no way in hell he was alone in feeling this way.

"*No estas loco.*" She met his gaze. "*Si.* I'll be your date this Saturday night."

Jackson smiled, released a quick breath, then laughed. That had actually gone better than he'd imagined. The best sign yet.

"To be honest," she added, "I'm going to need a night out with friends after this week."

Friends. Yeah, David and Alyson would be there. Jackson still felt the need to say, "I'll make it my mission to help you forget all about the week and make it a night you won't regret." He followed his words up with a grin.

She responded with her sassy smile. "I'm going to hold you to that, Mr. Lovett."

When they were outside, standing to the right of the coffee shop's door, Jackson grasped her hands and tugged her toward him. "If you need to talk, vent, scream…cover up a crime… between now and Saturday, I'm here. I promise."

Jillian laughed. "Good to know. And thank you."

Feeling that same rush of no fear from Saturday, he lowered his head enough to place a soft kiss on her forehead. And three little words landed in his mind with enough force he froze.

"We're going to shock the hell out of Alyson and David. And a few others. We'll need a story. You know that, right?"

Jackson absently nodded. "Yeah. Definitely." He squeezed her hands. "I'll see you later."

They exchanged quick smiles before he turned and headed in the direction of his SUV.

As he walked, the street, buildings, people, and cars blurred together while one question filled his head—when exactly had he fallen in love with smart, stunning, sassy Jillian Castillo?

▭

JILLIAN ANGLED her head left as she gave her reflection in the mirror a long once-over.

Little black, long-sleeved A-line dress with skirt length that stopped *about* mid-thigh. Black, closed-toe stiletto heels that added *about* three inches to her height. Hair she'd taken the time to flatiron. A little more makeup around her eyes than usual.

She had every intention of Jackson Lovett fulfilling his promise from Wednesday. She'd agreed to the date with little hesitation and she was going to have a damn good time from beginning to end. That reminded her, however, she needed to text Niall about bowing out of the Broncos game tomorrow. He'd be disappointed, but she wanted this night—and a much better morning after with Jackson —way more than going to a Broncos game with her new friend.

She absolutely wasn't going to think about her feelings for Jackson or whether doing this was the *smartest* choice. Or how surprised Alyson and David, and maybe some other people would be, when she and Jackson showed up together at Laura and Josh's place.

No serious thinking whatsoever. Just being in the moment.

She smiled at her reflection. Her phone then burst to life.

At seeing the caller, her smile instantly became a deep frown. She'd been dreading this call for the last twenty-four hours or so and was about to tap ignore when she decided to just get it over with.

"Hi, Mom."

"Jillian, you need to call your sister," Eva Castillo stated. "Brynn is still extremely upset about what happened on Monday and it's the last thing she needs."

She clenched her teeth. "I don't know what Brynn has told you, but that argument was not my fault. She should be the one calling *me*."

"Are you the one pregnant with twins and stuck at home in bed?"

Jillian shook her head as she gripped her phone. "I'm not calling her." If her sister really wanted to make it right, she would have to call Jillian without their mother being involved.

"She admitted she may have been a little hard on you," her mother quietly added. "But you know she's not herself right now. What woman would be in her situation? Jillian, *por favor.* Call your sister."

The buzzer exploding from the hallway made Jillian say, "My date is here, and I have to go." She hung up and tossed her phone onto her bed.

She should have let the call go to voicemail.

Jillian breathed deeply while carefully walking into the hallway. She hadn't worn these heels since…Halloween last year? As part of her naughty French maid costume?

She pressed the button to allow Jackson into the building, then calmly smoothed her hair and short, flared skirt. When she heard his footsteps stop at the door, she smiled and opened it.

Jackson gave her his mind-melting grin…looking pretty mind-melting in snug jeans and a dark-blue, quarter-zip sweater that fit him *perfectly.* But his grin vanished as he slid his gaze up and down her body, where they lingered on her heels.

"Holy shit." He released a quick laugh as he walked inside. "This is going to make me sound like a Neanderthal, but I'm not sure I can let you leave looking like you do."

Jillian smiled and carefully walked back to her bedroom. "Why's that, Mr. Lovett?" She stopped at her dresser to put on earrings.

"Because you're clearly trying to kill me with those come-and-get-me heels." Jackson leaned against the doorframe. "Not fair, Miss Castillo."

Jillian glanced at him. "You look pretty damn good yourself." As always and even with the remnants of his sunburn. *That* wasn't fair.

"No Claudia?" he asked.

She finished putting on her earrings and faced him. "No. She and Afton had their brief break and are back to being inseparable."

He peered at her. "Everything okay? You seem a little…off."

"Just my mother." Jillian sighed. "She called right before you arrived downstairs to tell me *I* need to call my sister and—you know what? It doesn't matter." She smiled. "I don't want to think or talk about my mother or sister tonight."

He nodded. "Fair enough."

"Are you ready? I just need to grab my coat." The Denver area, and not unusual for this time of year, had been hit with a cold front and some rain.

Jackson straightened. "I'm not quite ready to leave." He walked toward her. "I have a great idea on how to help you clear your head." He stopped when they were toe-to-toe.

Jillian's breath slowed at his hypnotizing eyes radiating a combo of mischief and naughtiness that his grin only amplified. "Jackson, I just finished getting ready." Though the thought of tearing his clothes off, then hers, wasn't a terrible image.

He backed her up until she was against the wall. "Only one thing will come off of you." His grin deepened. "I swore I'd make it my mission to make this a night you wouldn't regret."

She opened her mouth, but was silenced by his warm, yummy lips.

Jackson placed his hands on her thighs and leisurely slid his fingers up and under her skirt which made her tremble.

"What are you doing?" she asked between a breathless kiss.

He quietly shushed her and whispered into her ear, "Just relax."

Their mouths became one as she locked her arms behind his neck. Seconds later, he hooked his fingers under her lacy, thong panties and eased them down until they fell to the floor.

White-hot desire wound its way through Jillian, blurring

everything around them, and she opened her legs just enough for him to—

She moaned as he slipped a finger inside of her, now hot *and* wet.

Jackson brought their kiss to an end and pressed his forehead to hers. "Do what you did in the shower last Saturday."

She slowly moved with his finger.

He buried his face between her neck and hair, keeping his finger deep inside of her as she started to move a bit quicker. Breathe a bit quicker. And the only thing she could feel was him while the pressure between her thighs intensified…made her mind go blank…until her release replaced the silence while her entire body shuddered.

Jillian kept her arms tightly wound behind his neck. "*Mierda,*" she breathlessly said and felt the warm breath from his laugh on her neck. "Aren't you full of surprises, Mr. Lovett."

Jackson lifted his head. "So are you, Miss Castillo." He gave her a long once-over. "This is what happens when you dress like you are right now. And smell as good as you look." Keeping his gaze on her, he slowly removed his finger which made her sigh. "But now I need an ice-cold shower." He straightened and glanced around her bedroom.

She smiled. "Well, if you're looking for the shower, you'll find it in the bathroom."

"Cute."

"Or do you need a tissue?"

He focused on her, then his left hand. He stepped back and with *his* grin slid his middle finger into his mouth and back out, followed by a wink. "No, I'm all good. You?"

Her mouth inched open at everything Jackson had just done because it had been so unbelievably *hot*. "I'm…" She shook her head, hoping the right word would appear.

He bent down, grasped her panties, and carefully pulled them up. "You might want these tonight. Fall is definitely here."

Jillian shimmied back into them and smoothed her skirt.

She'd vowed not to think about her feelings for Jackson and be in the present. But she couldn't do that.

"Where's your coat?" he asked. "Because I need cold air *ASAP*."

"In the hallway closet."

Her gaze followed him until he disappeared from view.

Jillian wanted every part of Jackson Lovett to be all hers from now until parted by death…as the wedding vow sometimes went. That meant she had no choice but to take a huge risk when the time was right and hope Jackson *would* surprise her.

That realization reminded her she still needed to cancel her Broncos plans with Niall.

While eyeing the doorway, she scooped her phone off of the bed.

Once in their messaging thread, she swiftly typed, *Change of plans. Not going with you tomorrow after all. Have fun!*

Jackson walked back into her room. "You ready?" As he helped her into her coat, he murmured, "If we don't leave now, we'll never make it to the party."

She laughed while shoving her phone into her coat's right pocket.

"Those shoes are the definition of *damn* hot, but do you need me to carry you?" Jackson asked in response to her slow, deliberate steps down the building's stairs. "I won't mind."

Jillian opened the downstairs door and a blast of cool air hit her bare legs which caused her to shiver. "How gallant of you, but I'm fine. I just haven't worn them in a while."

"So, Miss Castillo," Jackson began when they were settled into his SUV, "I was hoping we could end the night at your place. Or mine." He shot her a naughty grin. "I'm not picky."

She returned his grin. "My place. It's way closer to where we'll be tonight."

"Done." He pulled away from the curb. "I was also hoping that we could…spend tomorrow together?" He paused before saying, "And, maybe, talk about *us*?"

Jillian stared at Jackson.

Had she heard him correctly? He actually wanted to talk about *them*?

She had no idea what could be on his mind. Considering everything he'd said *and* done since walking into her apartment, it couldn't be awful. And spending tomorrow together would absolutely give her the opportunity to finally be honest with him.

Jillian hesitated, then said, "I think that's—" Her phone went off inside her pocket.

It had to be Niall.

Her phone dinged a second time.

She withdrew it and eyed the screen.

"Everything okay over there?" Jackson asked.

Niall had texted, *You're thinking too much.* His second message was, *Am I going to have to call you so we can talk about this?* He'd also added the winking emoji.

"Dammit," she muttered.

Why did Niall Donnelly have to be so persistent?

She tapped out, *Please don't call. I now have plans with Jackson tomorrow.* She added a smiley face and hit send.

Jackson stopped at a red light. "Jillian, what's going on?"

She looked up and caught his inquisitive gaze.

Tell him the truth or lie? Those were her only options.

Her phone dinged for the third time.

Mierda.

She took a deep breath and said, "It's Niall." There was no reason to lie to him.

Jackson frowned.

Still, why wasn't Niall letting this go? She clearly should have texted him way earlier, but she'd been busy getting ready. Then her mother had called. Then Jackson had arrived and…been the *Jackson* she'd fallen in love with in March.

At his continued bewildered expression, Jillian added, "I was supposed to go to the Broncos game with him tomorrow, but I changed my mind." For *them*.

Her phone went off for the fourth time.

"Niall can be really persistent." Right now, he was being downright obnoxious.

Jackson faced forward.

The light turned green, and they accelerated into the intersection.

"It's just who he is and I know he'll…" Blinding headlights and screeching tires caused her to stop. Metal then smashed into metal as glass exploded around her, followed by darkness.

Chapter Twenty

DEEP, quiet voices penetrated Jackson's foggy, achy head and he forced his eyes open.

He squinted into the harsh, florescent lights and blinked several times.

"Hey, David," a familiar voice said, "he's waking up again."

Jackson swallowed as Will appeared at his right side; David on his left.

"You're in the ER and have been drifting in and out for a while," Will said, his eyes wide with concern. "How's your head?"

Jackson cleared his throat. "It hurts. What are you two—" The sound of crushing metal and glass shattering broke through his head's thick fog and achiness.

He sat up. Which made him feel as if he were on that tilt-a-whirl ride. "Where's Jillian?"

"Jackson, slow down." David gripped his upper arm. "You have a severe concussion."

"I'm fine. Where's Jillian?" He focused on David, whose eyes were also wide with worry, then his brother.

"She's in the ICU," David quietly answered.

The Intensive Care Unit.

"The light was green," Jackson said more to himself than them.

"Yeah, it was," Will assured. "A woman in a pickup truck ran the red light and hit you guys on the passenger side."

But he'd hit the gas pedal because—

Jackson swung his legs off of the bed…and waited for the room to stop spinning. He then stood with David still grasping his upper arm.

Will appeared at his other side. "You need to go slow. You shouldn't even be up."

"I *need* to see Jillian."

David hesitated before releasing Jackson's arm.

Jackson walked from the room, paused long enough to find the "Exit" signs, turned, and almost collided with a young nurse.

She held up her hands. "Sir, you shouldn't be up like this."

Will and David stood beside him as he asked, "Where's the ICU?"

She gave him a patient smile. "I really need you to go back into the room."

"I'm fine. I just need you to tell me where the ICU is." The sound of the smashing metal and glass became deafening in his throbbing head as he pictured *his* Jillian in the Intensive Care Unit. "I need to know where to go."

The light had been green, but he'd hit the gas pedal because of what she'd said seconds—

"Sir, it would be best—"

"I'll find it myself." Jackson walked around her.

When they emerged from the ER, he halted at the sight of Savannah in the waiting room. His eyes then went to a sign indicating where the ICU was located, also on the main floor.

Savannah stood and rushed toward them.

Jackson started to walk in the direction of the ICU, but was stopped by his sister-in-law.

"They released you?" She glanced at Will and David, and back at Jackson.

"No," Will stated. "He released himself."

"Because I'm *fine*." But Jillian *wasn't* fine and Jackson needed to get to her. "You guys should go home." He frowned as a question hit his hazy, jumbled head. "Who called you? And where are the kids?"

Will sighed. "The police called Mom and Dad who are babysitting for us, and they called me."

Jackson muttered a choice swear word under his breath.

His parents—his mom—didn't need this. Especially now.

"Your parents called me, too," David added. "Alyson and I were already at Laura and Josh's place. Al's actually in the ICU waiting room with Jillian's family."

Jackson looked at Will, Savannah, and David, their faces tight with dismay.

To his brother and Savannah, he said, "Thanks for coming here. Really. But you should pick up the kids and go home." *He needed to get to Jillian.* "I'll call you guys later." He stepped back. "Tell Mom and Dad the same thing."

His brother and Savannah slowly nodded.

Jackson and David walked around them.

Ever since Will's skateboarding accident years ago, Jackson had never liked hospitals. Particularly the way they looked and smelled. Like death was also in the waiting room. And he and David were headed toward the *ICU* waiting room.

Intensive Care Unit. Where *his* Jillian would be.

Between hearing the accident in his head—the sound of how hard they'd been hit—and the fact Jillian was in the ICU meant her condition had to be serious. That realization became amplified when he and David entered the quiet waiting area.

Alyson, seated next to Claudia with Afton right beside her, sprung from her chair when she saw them. All three women's faces were stuck in a combination of shock and grief and fear. Across from them sat a man with a beard streaked with gray and older woman.

They turned to look at him, their expressions mirror images of everyone else's.

Alyson frowned. "Jackson, you shouldn't be here like this." She focused on David. "There's no way they released him."

Jackson started to respond, but Claudia stood, followed by the man and older woman.

As they approached, he noticed the guy looked to be around Will's age. The petite older woman's short, dark hair and familiar eyes told him she had to be Jillian and Claudia's mom.

"*Mamá*," Claudia said, "this is Jackson. Jilly's boyfriend."

Boyfriend? Could he call himself Jillian's boyfriend? They weren't officially back together. But he'd hoped to be by the end of this weekend.

He cleared his throat. "I'm not sure boyfriend is the right word."

"Yes, it is," Claudia stated. "Jackson, this is our mom, Eva, and brother-in-law, Marcos."

He and Marcos shook hands, though if felt insane to be doing such a thing. *Surreal.*

Claudia subjected Jackson to a long, hard stare. "It's really good to see you right now, but as an ER nurse I feel I *have* to say—"

"I know," he interjected. "But I'm telling everyone here that I'm *fine*. I need to know what's going on with Jillian." He also needed to see her. That couldn't happen soon enough.

Eva pressed her lips together before saying, "They brought her in…unconscious…and took her to get a CT scan to find out the extent of the head injury, but that was some time ago."

Unconscious. Head injury.

"She's breathing on her own," Eva continued, "which they said was a good sign. That's all we know."

Breathing on her own.

A stiff, lengthy silence descended on their tight huddle.

"My daughter and I were on the phone when you showed up," Eva softly said. "She said her date was here and she had to go. Then she hung up."

Jackson knew that was the last time mom and daughter had spoken. He also knew the conversation had not been a good one. Had even helped Jillian forget all about it.

He'd sworn to make it a night she wouldn't regret.

How the hell could they be here like this? In an ICU waiting room?

"I didn't know she was seeing someone seriously, but your name sounds familiar." Eva glanced at Claudia. "Did I hear his name from you and Brynn?"

Claudia nodded and shrugged. "Probably. But that was months ago. They just got back together." She eyed Jackson. "That's how it sounded to me and Afton." She released a sad laugh. "My sister was so excited about going to that party with you tonight."

Jackson stared blankly into the waiting room.

The light had been green…but what if—

"Maybe you should call Brynn again?" Eva said to Marcos. "We need to keep her as calm as possible."

Because she was having a difficult pregnancy with twins. The reason Jillian had been helping her sister and family. But they, too, had also been on the outs. Fighting.

Marcos nodded and excused himself.

"I need to call Dad." Claudia went into her purse.

"Please don't do that until we know what's going on with your sister," Eva replied.

She, Claudia, and Afton went back toward the chairs and sat. Faces still stuck in shock and grief and fear. Like Alyson's and David's.

And his now that he knew the extent of Jillian's injury.

"I'll go home and let Thatcher out," David said. "I'll be back as soon as I can. Are you two going to be okay?"

Going to be okay? Not until Jillian opened her eyes. *And she* would *open her eyes.*

He ran a hand through his hair. Which instantly reminded him of his aching head.

"We'll be fine." Alyson reached out and grasped Jackson's hand. "Claudia and I will keep a close eye on him while you're gone."

David nodded, gave Alyson a quick kiss, then left.

Jackson probably needed to track down a nurse to get something for his head, but he refused to leave this room. So he followed Alyson to the chairs and sat beside her. He was about to ask if any of them—specifically the women—had something he could take when an older man with dark, graying hair, wearing glasses and a white coat, walked into the waiting room.

Jackson stood, followed by everyone else, and again waited for the spinning to stop.

Alyson clutched his hand, and he squeezed hers in gratitude.

"All of you must be here for Miss Jillian Castillo?" the man asked when he reached them.

He'd said Castillo like Jillian did. With that hint of an accent Jackson loved hearing from her throaty voice.

Eva stepped forward. "Yes. I'm her mother. *Please* tell me you're here to tell us what's going on with my daughter."

The man gave her a warm smile. "I'm Dr. Vargas, the neurologist."

"Is she awake? I want to see my daughter."

"*Mamá*," Claudia murmured, "let him talk."

"It's fine," the doctor assured Claudia. "And I'm here with some good and bad news."

Alyson's grip on Jackson's hand tightened.

"The bad news," the doctor continued, "is I'm afraid Jillian is still unconscious."

Shit. Why wasn't she waking up? *She had to wake up.*

Eva cleared her throat. "And the good news?"

"There's no skull fracture or bleeding. We're treating the swelling with medication."

Jackson glanced at Alyson, her eyes wide with relief. As were Claudia's and Afton's.

"Jillian is also still breathing on her own. These are very good signs." He focused on Eva. "I'm hopeful that the medication will treat the swelling so surgery won't be required."

That statement settled into their tight space near the doctor.

Jackson looked at the floor as the sounds of the accident again invaded his mind. Horrific sounds he was certain he wouldn't forget. Like hearing his brother slamming into the concrete years ago. He'd also never been in a car accident as bad as this one.

And what if he *hadn't* hit the gas pedal?

"Can I see her now?" Eva asked again.

"Yes. But only two visitors are allowed in the room at a time."

Eva eyed Claudia. "Are you coming with me?"

"You go ahead," Claudia answered, though she was focused on Jackson.

Eva followed the doctor from the waiting room.

"Can I talk to you over there?" Claudia pointed at a corner, steps away from them.

Jackson absently nodded.

The light had been green, but he shouldn't have hit the gas pedal like he did.

When they were alone, she looked up at him, her dark eyes—like Jillian's and their mom's—wide, but relief seemed to have replaced some shock.

"The nurse in me firmly believes you should have stayed in the ER."

He sighed and opened his mouth to again defend himself, but she held up her hands.

"The *sister* in me understands and is happy you're here," she continued. "This is going to sound weird, but out of all of us I think you're the one who really needs to be in there with her."

Yeah, Jackson sure as shit wanted to see her. To be as close to her as possible. But he wasn't her family. *He'd also hit the gas pedal.* "Claudia, I appreciate you saying that, but—"

"I meant every word." She sniffed. "I don't know what happened between you two in the spring. Jilly wouldn't talk about it. But I *know* she was crazy about you, and you obviously feel the same way about her."

He raised his eyebrows.

Crazy about him? The statement didn't fit Jillian's words and actions that night in April.

"So you go in there." Claudia stepped back. "Alyson, Afton, and I will get our chance. We can all take turns until Jilly wakes up. Because she will." She walked toward the chairs.

Jackson rubbed his dry eyes.

Focus on one thing at a time. That was all he could do. All he could manage.

He headed in the direction Eva and the doctor had gone. When he reached the quiet nurse's station, he said, "I'm here for Jillian Castillo."

The nurse sitting at the desk gave him a soft smile. "Last room on your right."

Jackson's steps became slower the closer he got to her room. To her. But he forced himself to keep going because he had to see her. However, he halted in the doorway at the sight of her. Eyes closed. Not moving. Hooked up to machines.

The last time he'd seen her she'd been sitting in the passenger seat of his SUV, holding her phone while telling him who she'd been texting.

Then, in his shock and frustration, he'd faced forward, the light had turned green, and—

He shook the accident sounds from his head and stepped into the room.

Okay. They'd been hit by someone who ran a red light.

Eva, standing beside Jillian's bed, wiped her cheeks. "*Santo cielo*. It's too much for the heart." She looked over at him, her eyes shiny. "Seeing your child like this?"

Jackson stayed silent as guilt shrouded him. *Because he wasn't blameless.*

She stepped backward. "I'm afraid I'm going to need some air. I'm…having a little trouble breathing in here."

He walked toward her. "Do you need me to get Claudia?"

"No, I…simply wasn't prepared to see my daughter like this." She continued to stare at Jillian. "I just arrived in Denver yesterday to help Brynn and Marcos. But I'm sure you already knew that. I haven't seen Jillian—my daughters—in a while. I live in Hawaii. The Big Island." She faced him. "Will you excuse me? I think it's also time to call her father." Eva walked around him with her hand over her mouth. Then she was gone.

Jackson approached the bed, keeping his gaze trained on Jillian's eerily tranquil face that, upon closer scrutiny, was colorless. She also had some cuts on her face. A thin bandage on her forehead. All of it had to be from the shattered glass. He probably had some, too.

But his worse injury was only a concussion.

He slid his eyes over her still form and stopped on the I.V. hooked into her left hand. He then clasped her icy fingers and whispered, "Jilly, I'm *so sorry*." He gently squeezed the four fingers he held. "I love you and you need to wake up." He then eased onto the bed's edge.

Jackson wasn't going anywhere until Jillian opened her eyes.

Chapter Twenty-One

"JACKSON?"

The raspy voice barely penetrated Jackson's semi-conscious mind that he'd been keeping awake with cup after cup of coffee.

He squeezed his gritty eyes shut for a few seconds, opened them, rolled his head slightly right—and froze. At catching Jillian's groggy gaze.

"Are you really here?" she asked, scarcely above a whisper.

He blinked numerous times while he sat up, removing his feet from the chair he'd been using as a footrest. He then gave Alyson a quick glance. She was on the other side of the bed, stretched out on two chairs like he'd been, burrowed under David's jacket with her eyes closed.

He again concentrated on Jillian.

She swallowed while forcing her foggy gaze to stay on him.

Jackson couldn't stop from releasing a quick, breathless laugh as he stood.

Holy shit. She was awake.

He gave her a soft smile and lowered himself to the bed. "Yeah, baby," he murmured, gently clasping her right fingers. "I'm really here."

Her lids drifted shut and came back up. "I can't…stay awake. Please don't leave me."

He leaned forward and lightly kissed her forehead. "I won't. I promise."

While Jillian's breathing steadied, he looked at Alyson and said her name.

Her head snapped up. "What's wrong?"

He smiled for the first time in…he had no idea what time it was. It also didn't matter because Jillian had opened her eyes. And spoke. "Jillian just woke up. She recognized me, too." Which had to be another damn good sign after a *serious* head injury.

Alyson returned his smile, removed David's jacket, and went right to Jillian's left side. She, too, sat on the bed. "Jilly?" she softly said. "It's Alyson. Can you open your eyes for me?" Her voice hitched on the last few words.

Jillian's lids fluttered open.

Alyson grinned. "Hi there. Do you recognize me?"

She barely nodded before drifting off once more.

"Oh, my God." Alyson straightened. "She's awake." Her bleary gaze locked with Jackson's. "I don't know whether to burst into laughter or tears."

He nodded while releasing a shaky breath.

She eased off of the bed. "I need to go tell everyone. And the nurse."

Jackson went back to focusing on Jillian as Alyson darted from the room.

He needed to go to the bathroom for what had to be the umpteenth time in the last several hours. But he couldn't—didn't want to—leave her side. Not now. Because she'd opened her eyes and spoke. And recognized him and Alyson.

He'd also promised her he wouldn't leave her.

A nurse, the same one from hours earlier who'd told him where to find Jillian, entered the room with a bright smile. "I hear our Sleeping Beauty has awakened." She pointed at him. "I'm going to need to wake her up and give her a quick check."

Jackson reluctantly released Jillian's fingers, stood, and backed away from the bed.

Eva swooped in at that moment and went right to her daughter's other side. "Jillian? Honey? *Es Mamá.*"

"Miss Jillian?" the nurse asked while checking her I.V. "Can you hear my voice? Your mom's here. And your boyfriend."

Boyfriend. Jackson sure as hell liked the sound of that word. One thing at a time, though.

Thank God she'd woken up.

Jillian's hazy gaze flitted from the nurse, to him, and to her mom. "*Mamá?*" She squinted. "What…are you doing here?" Before Eva could answer, Jillian was again drifting off.

"She'll be in and out of consciousness for a while," the nurse explained. "Completely normal with head injuries. Dr. Vargas has been notified and should be here shortly." The nurse grinned at Eva, then him. "From what I've seen, I feel optimistic." Her grin grew. "Miss Jillian is very lucky. I've seen so much love in here all night."

Jackson managed a half smile. Between him, Eva, Claudia, Afton, and Alyson, Jillian had never been alone in the room.

The nursed stepped back. "My shift is coming to an end, but I will be back tonight."

He frowned. "What time is it?" He didn't have his phone and hadn't missed it one bit.

"It's almost six in the morning," the nurse answered. "If you can, I recommend all of you getting real rest at some point today. Like I said, Miss Jillian will be in and out for a while. Perhaps you can also take turns staying and going home?"

Jackson had no plans to leave this hospital any time soon.

Eva, on the other hand, nodded. "Thank you. For everything. I'm sure you'll see all of us tonight when you return."

The nurse smiled warmly at them and left.

Eva moved the chair Alyson had been using closer to the bed and sat. She glanced over at him. "Claudia's ready to take over for you if you'd like a little break?"

The last thing Jackson wanted to do was leave Jillian's side. He'd promised her he wouldn't leave. But he still needed the bathroom. He really needed to call his parents, too. David had to still be in the waiting room, so he could use his friend's phone.

"I don't want to, but I should take a short break," he finally said. "I'll send Claudia in."

He turned to leave, but was stopped by, "Thank you for loving my daughter."

Jackson looked over his shoulder at Eva, smiling at him.

"I have no idea who you are," she continued. "But since it's clear how much you love her, I'm hoping that we'll get a chance to know one another after…" She sniffed and cleared her throat. "Before I go back to Hawaii." She focused on Jillian.

He quietly left the room.

Jackson had no idea what the friction was between Jillian and her mom, but all he'd seen for the last several hours was a grief-stricken mother scared for her daughter's life.

He headed into the waiting room.

Claudia sprang from her seat between Afton and Alyson, flashed him a smile, and nearly sprinted in the direction from which he came.

David, looking as bleary-eyed as Jackson felt—all of them, for that matter—gently untangled himself from Alyson's arms and stood. "I need to talk to you for a sec."

Jackson followed him to the same corner where Claudia had talked to him hours before.

When Jillian had still been unconscious.

"Your parents and Will called me," David said. "They really need to hear from you. Especially now that Jillian's awake?"

"I know, but I need to use your phone. Mine has to still be in my car." *His car that had to be totaled.* "At some point, I'm going to have to track down where it was towed."

"We'll figure it out. How are you feeling?"

He shrugged. "The stuff the nurse gave me a while ago helped. I'm fine." More than fine now that Jillian was awake. But the memory of the accident—that had also been heavy on his mind—made him say, "David, I *know* the light was green when I went, but…" He sighed, unable to say the words out loud.

"It wasn't your fault." He stared at Jackson. "The woman ran the red light." He unlocked his phone and handed it over. "Stop thinking that way, okay?"

Jackson nodded. "Yeah," he said on a breath. "Thanks." He shoved his thoughts aside and went to stand just outside the waiting area.

His parents' landline rang twice, then, "Jackson?" his mom answered. Sounding no better than Jillian had during her brief, lucid moment.

"Hi, Mom. I woke you up."

"Hardly." She cleared her throat. "Don?" It came through as muffled before, "It's Jackson." To him she asked, "How are you? How's Jillian? Is she awake? We've been so worried about her *and* you. When the police officer called us last night—" Her voice cracked.

"Mom, I'm okay. And Jilly did wake up. Just now." *Thank God.*

"It's such a relief hearing your voice. And good news, too." She paused, followed by, "Do you know anything else?"

He leaned against the wall. "She's speaking clearly. And recognized everyone she's seen. The nurse left her room feeling optimistic. The doctor should be here soon, too." Which was when they'd really get the information they wanted and needed.

"Have you been able to get any rest? Will said you have a severe concussion."

"I'm fine." In truth, he'd been fighting to keep his eyes open for a while, despite his determination and the coffee; the reason he'd been frequently in and out of the bathroom, and why he needed to go at this moment. "I'm not leaving her or this hospital. Not until I know what's happening. And that she's really going to be okay." Even then he wasn't sure he'd leave.

He'd promised her he wouldn't.

"I understand that, but *please* don't forget to take care of yourself?"

Jackson straightened. "Mom, try not to worry." *She didn't need it.* "I promise I'll call you guys when I know more. Can you give Will a call for me?"

Silence fell, followed by, "Yes. And we'll keep this phone, and our cell phones, close by."

Yeah, all of them needed what the nurse had suggested. But Jackson strongly suspected *no one* would be leaving until they really felt confident with Jillian's condition.

He was walking back into the waiting room, after finally using the bathroom, when he caught from the corner of his eyes a nurse rushing into Jillian's room.

Jackson's breath stalled and before he realized it he was jogging toward her room. He came to a halt as her shrill, panicked voice reached him.

"I don't understand why I'm here. Why won't anyone tell me what happened?"

He moved to stand just outside the doorway.

Dr. Vargas, the nurse, and Eva were hovered around her bed, and Jillian was pulling away from them. Claudia, her eyes round, stood behind her mom.

Jillian's agitated actions snapped Jackson from his fog and he ended up at the foot of the bed. He didn't give a rat's ass if there were too many people in her room.

Jillian glared at him. "Where were you? You promised you wouldn't leave me!"

Her surprisingly clear and strongly spoken words might as well have been a bowling bowl hitting Jackson's gut, but he managed to hold her hard stare.

"Jillian," Eva firmly, yet softly said. "*Necesitas calmarte.*"

As Jillian's eyes became wet, Jackson tightened his hands to stop himself from going right to her side. To wrap her in his arms and not let go until someone pried them apart.

"*Mamá.*" Jillian's lower lip trembled. "I can't…remember what happened."

"I know you're a little confused right now," Dr. Vargas said, speaking as quietly as her mom had. "It's completely normal, considering you were in a bad car accident last night."

Jillian peered at the man but stayed silent.

Another round of guilt surrounded Jackson. *Because he knew what had* really *happened.*

"You're in the hospital, and your family and friends have been here all night."

She looked at Jackson, then her mom and sister, and the tension in her face slowly lifted followed by her lids again closing.

Dr. Vargas faced Eva and Claudia. "Based on the way she was struggling with us just now, it doesn't appear anything is broken. But I will need to give her a more thorough examination to check for other injuries."

Jackson glanced at Jillian, her eyes still closed. As the nurse skirted from the room, he said, "She doesn't remember what happened." Which was actually a good thing when the sounds of the accident once again filled his—no. He wasn't going to go there.

"It's common for patients with severe head injuries to not remember what happened to them." The doctor slid his hands into his pockets. "The memory may come back over time or she may never remember. The fact the medication is working, that she knows her family members and friends, and is speaking clearly, is what we need to concentrate on. She also appears to have good function of her arms and legs. These are all really good signs."

Jackson exchanged quick looks with Eva and Claudia, their faces relaxed from relief.

The same relief rushing through him.

"I'm going to schedule some tests for this afternoon," the doctor added. "But I'm extremely encouraged by what I'm seeing so far." He gave them a warm smile. "I know all of you are relieved and excited Jillian woke up, but only two visitors in the room, please." After a quick nod, he swiftly left the room.

Jackson stepped back. "I only came in here because I saw the nurse rush in. I'll go."

"No." Claudia shook her head. "Afton and I were talking about going to the apartment since it's closer than Afton's place." She rubbed her eyes. "We were going to eat, take a nap, shower, then come back." She focused on Eva. "*Mamá,* will you be okay?"

Eva nodded. "*Sí.* I'll call your sister and Marcos. And your father?"

"I called him after you left to come in here." The two embraced. "I know all your stuff is in Boulder, but you could come with us. Jilly and I have everything you'd need. Except clothes."

"No, I need to stay." Eva released Claudia. "But I'll call if I need anything."

As Claudia passed by Jackson, she grabbed his hand and gave it a hard squeeze.

"*Santo cielo*," Eva said around a deep breath. "I'm going to need a few glasses of good red wine before all of this is over."

Jackson nodded. "Yeah." In fact, he'd go with something ten times stronger.

"Since Jillian is asleep again, I need to go call Brynn and Marcos." She smoothed the blanket covering Jillian. "Jillian and Brynn may say and do awful things to one another, but their love for each other is fierce and always will be." She faced him. "Do you have siblings?"

He cracked a smile. "An older brother."

"Are you close?"

"Now we are. But when we were kids—" Jackson suddenly remembered what his mom had told him on the boat. And Jillian's throaty laughter when he'd told her what she'd said. "My mom thought one of us would kill the other before my brother left for college."

Eva walked toward him. "Please tell your mom I can relate to that sentiment." She then wrapped her thin, short arms around him for a quick hug that he returned. "I'll be back shortly."

Once he was alone with Jillian, he again lowered himself to the bed.

Her expression was back to serene as her chest moved steadily up and down.

All he—they—had wanted the last several hours was for Jillian to wake up. But he hadn't considered what her emotional and mental state would be after that. Her panicked voice filled his mind. Panic from not remembering the accident. The accusatory stare she'd given him followed that memory, then her harsh words. Because he'd promised her he wouldn't leave.

He ran a hand through his hair and released a slow breath.

"You don't seem real."

He whipped his head in the direction of Jillian's drowsy voice.

She stared at him through narrow eyelids. "But if you are, lie down with me."

Jackson smiled as she fell back asleep.

There was just enough room for his head on Jillian's pillow and next to her on the narrow bed, so he eased down, facing her. He stretched his legs out while resting his head close to hers. Which made her mumble something incoherent and sigh.

He gazed at the way her long lashes rested on the skin under her eyes. Her small nose. Full lips. Peaceful expression as she slept. Eventually color would return to her face and the cuts from all the glass would be long gone.

Thank God she'd woken up.

Jackson watched her until his eyelids became heavy from the emotional, mental, and physical exhaustion of the last several hours. So heavy, he could no longer fight.

Chapter Twenty-Two

JILLIAN SQUINTED at Jackson lying beside her, his breathing steady with deep sleep.

So this wasn't a dream. But this wasn't her bed or his.

She blinked until he became more in focus, stretched out next to her on a narrow bed with white sheets and blankets. That's when she noticed and felt the I.V. in her left hand, resting between them. Her head—her entire body—ached. She ached so much she was afraid to move and make it worse.

Jillian lifted her head just enough to glance at her surroundings. A soothing male voice—not Jackson's—floated through her murky mind.

You're in the hospital. Bad car accident. Family and friends have been here all night.

She laid her throbbing head back down, trying to remember what the hell had happened. Her body definitely felt like she'd been in a terrible car accident.

Jackson shifted beside her but remained asleep.

Jillian gently placed her right hand on his cheek rough with scruff that she saw on his jawline and chin. He was in fact real and warm and wearing clothes that appeared vaguely familiar. But she frowned when she spotted small cuts on his forehead and cheeks.

They must have been in the car accident together.

Why couldn't she remember?

She slid her fingers through his soft, familiar, rumpled sandy-blond hair and remembered doing that not too long ago. Maybe even Saturday?

Jackson stirred, then his hand covered hers. He opened his eyes which locked on Jillian. His mouth curved into a sleepy grin. "Hi."

She swallowed and said, "Hi." But it came out gurgled and she cleared her throat.

He kept his hand over hers and asked around a yawn, "How long have you been awake?"

"Not long." She stared at him. "I thought you were a dream." She slid her gaze around their sterile surroundings. "I thought all of this was a dream. Not really a bad one," she absently added. "Like being in a…cold, gray watercolor painting."

He slowly nodded.

"Jackson, what happened? And what day is it?"

"It's Sunday," he murmured. "I don't know what time it is. Afternoon? It could be later."

"So I've been here since…when?"

He hesitated, then said, "Last night."

"And my mom and Claudia and Alyson?"

He gently folded his fingers around hers. "Also not a dream. They've been here all night, too. And Afton. And David, but he stayed in the waiting room. Marcos was here for a while—brought your mom here—but he had to go home for your sister and nephew."

Brynn. Their huge fight. Their mom coming to Denver.

The memories returned, flashing through Jillian's mind as if a rapid slideshow. But the biggest thing she needed to remember remained black.

"Jilly"—Jackson lightly squeezed her fingers—"what's the last thing you remember?"

She peered at him and shook her head. "I'm trying to find the memory, but I can't." She focused on his shoulder. "Except being briefly cold." Tears hit her eyes, and he softly shushed her. Then another memory appeared. Them together in her bedroom, and Jackson's breath on her ear as he shushed her and whispered something. "We were in my room. Am I right?" If not, it had to be a dream that had mixed with reality.

His grin came back. "Yeah. Early last night. Before we left for the party."

She frowned. "Party?" What the hell was he talking about?

"Jillian, don't worry about that. Not now." He leaned forward and placed a soft kiss on her forehead. "Tell me how you're feeling. That's what's important."

She released a deep sigh, then winced. "I'm sore. All over. And my head is throbbing."

Jackson sat up. "I'll go get the nurse on duty so they can give you something."

"No, don't leave!"

He stopped at her sharp command.

His face became a watery blur. "I'm sorry. Just…stay with me. I'm okay right now."

"Are you sure?" His forehead formed a deep V. "I'm not surprised you're feeling the way you are because of how hard we were hit on your side—" He broke their eye contact.

On her side…of the car?

"So we were together," she quietly stated. "In *your* car?"

Jackson's gaze found hers once more. "Yeah, but we don't need to focus on that now."

"I can see the cuts on your face," she persisted. "Were you

hurt anywhere else?" Outside of the cuts and clear exhaustion around his eyes, he looked okay, but—

"Jillian, I'm fine. I promise."

She nodded, but felt the need to say, "I'm sorry. I wish I could remember—" Her voice broke on the words.

"No, you don't," Jackson muttered, lying beside her once again. He placed his hand on her cheek, then tucked some hair behind her ear. "Don't apologize, either. You're awake. And talking. And remember us. Your family and friends. Jilly, that's all that matters. *Trust me*. Okay?"

Awake. Talking. Remembering family and friends. Bad car accident. Aching head and body. Maybe Jackson was right. Maybe she didn't need to know what had happened. At least, not at this moment in time.

"*Si*." She grasped his hand. "*Confío en ti*."

He smiled. "Spanish. That's good. It's also *you*." He released a quick laugh. "And your mom and Claudia."

Jillian nestled her head into the pillow. "You've met my mom." Something she'd never imagined happening.

"Yeah." He softly rubbed her lower lip with his thumb. "You and Claudia have her eyes."

"So does Brynn."

"Your mom and Claudia are going to be so relieved to see you like this." His eyes scanned her face. "And Alyson and Afton. I should probably go out to the waiting room—"

"*Please* don't," she moaned. "For some reason, you still don't seem real." Yet another memory appeared. Or had it been a dream? *Dammit*, why was this so hard? Trying to make sense of everything in her achy head? "Did we hold hands for a long time last night?"

Jackson's mouth inched open.

A nurse, who was an older woman, suddenly appeared at the

foot of the bed and gave them a sappy smile. "I'm glad you're awake and hate to interrupt, but it's time for your tests."

He slowly straightened.

"No." Jillian snatched his hand. "I don't want this to end."

"I know." He pressed her fingers to his lips. "But I need to see who's still here. Let them know how you're doing." He glanced at the nurse. "What time is it?"

"Just after one in the afternoon. You two were asleep for a while." She focused on Jillian. "Your mom came in several times to check on you, as did a friend of yours. All of us decided it would be best to let you two sleep."

Jackson released Jillian's hand and eased off of the bed.

"You'll be back later?" Jillian asked. "Right?"

"I promise." He followed that up with his perfect grin and left the room.

The nurse laughed. "He is what me and my fellow old ladies call a tall drink of water." She gave Jillian a warm smile. "You're an *extremely* lucky lady."

Jillian somehow sensed the nurse wasn't only referring to Jackson.

She couldn't remember anything about last night except the vague memory of being with him in her bedroom. But she could clearly remember being crazy in love with Jackson and him having no idea she felt that way.

"We're going to get you ready for those tests, alrighty?"

Jillian absently nodded. That's when she again became acutely aware of her aching head and body. "Everything hurts. Especially my head."

The nurse came to the side of the bed still warm from Jackson. "We'll get you something for that as soon as possible."

Jillian closed her eyes, ready for more sleep.

Maybe the next time she woke up, she'd really be in her bed

or Jackson's, curled into his strong, warm arms as if nothing bad had *ever* happened.

━━

JACKSON'S STEPS faltered as he and David reached his friend's SUV.

He stopped at the rear and breathed the dreary, brisk fall air deeply into his chest in an attempt to clear his head. One reason they'd left the hospital.

"Hey, are you going to make it?"

He leaned against the SUV. "David, I feel like my insides were blown apart last night and only two pieces are back together."

"And I get it. Believe me."

Of course he did. David had been through worse times twenty over ten years ago when he lost his parents and almost lost Becca…in a horrible car accident.

Jackson stared at David. "Are *you* doing okay?"

He sighed. "All of this has definitely brought back *a lot* of rough memories, but I'm good. And none of this is about me."

In that moment, Jackson truly understood how his best friend had ended up in an unhealthy relationship with alcohol as a way to numb everything.

"I'm sorry," Jackson mumbled.

David frowned.

"About that night in the apartment years ago. After Alyson left?" Or more like David had all but thrown her out and told her to never come back. "I was so pissed at you for shutting down like you did and all the damn drinking. But I get it now. Why you did that."

David fought a grin. "Your fist in my face didn't hurt as much as you'd like to think it did." He shrugged. "I also deserved it."

Jackson cracked a smile. "Speaking of Alyson, how's she doing?" He hadn't seen her since early this morning in the waiting room, after Jillian had woken up and remembered them.

David also leaned against his SUV. "When you and Jillian had been asleep for about an hour, I *strongly* suggested that she and I take a break. Al wasn't comfortable with leaving, but after we got home, walked Thatcher, ate, and showered I think we were asleep before our heads hit the pillow." He rubbed his eyes. "She was still sound asleep when I got up and left to come back here to give you what I need to right now."

That being the second reason David had convinced him to leave the hospital.

"This is the first thing." He handed Jackson his key fob. "You can borrow my car until you can get into a rental."

Jackson nodded. "Thanks, Man. I appreciate it." But David loaning Jackson his SUV reminded *him* of two things. "I still need to track down my car so I can get my phone."

David withdrew a piece of paper from his back jeans pocket. "Which leads me to thing number two." He held up the paper, then handed it to Jackson. "Your dad found out where they towed your car and left the info with me when he couldn't reach you on your cell." He cringed. "It sounds like your car's totaled."

"I figured. But it's cool my dad did that. I'll call them once I have my phone." Hopefully it would have a charge. All of this, however, was reminding him of his second thing. "It's Sunday afternoon." Meaning tomorrow was *Monday*. "David, I can't deal with work tomorrow." He stared at the hospital looming straight ahead from where they stood. "I can't go to work in the morning with Jillian still here. I don't want to leave right now," he added. "I don't want to leave this hospital without her." Because he loved Jillian and couldn't stand the thought of not staying with her after last night.

And no matter the facts, Jackson couldn't shake the guilt from hitting the gas pedal because of her admitting she'd been texting Niall about not going to the Broncos game today.

Niall. Who hadn't been taking no for an answer.

Jackson caught David carefully watching him and pushed the thoughts aside.

At this moment, he needed to focus on getting his phone and figuring out tomorrow.

"Then don't go back to work until Jillian is home," David replied.

Jackson ran a hand through his hair. "But that puts the firm down *the boss* and two architects. Zach's already on overload and has a wife and baby at home. Cruz isn't ready—"

"I'll be in there tomorrow morning for a few more interviews," David interjected. "Tell me what you need."

He stared at his friend as the words filled his exhausted, jumbled head. "Honestly?"

"Yeah. Of course."

Jackson hesitated. What he was about to say to his best buddy, who'd left architecture behind without a backward glance, would be a lot to ask. But *shit*, Jillian needed him more than the firm until she was at home where she belonged.

"Jackson, what do you want me to do?"

He straightened. "I need you to be me. Just until—"

"Okay. Done." David released a quick laugh. "I may even be better at it."

Jackson frowned. "Shouldn't you talk to Randy first?" It's not like David didn't have his own business obligations. He did co-own a popular jazz and blues nightclub. "And Alyson?"

David lifted his shoulders. "If Jillian keeps improving—and I'm sure she will—she'll be home this week. Randy and I can figure something out so I'm not at the firm during the day and the club at night." He grinned. "Al will understand. She loves Jillian *and* you."

Jackson expelled a long, slow breath as the one-hundred pound weight lifted from his shoulders. "Thanks, David. I mean it." *Total understatement, too.*

"No thanks required. But what about the Downey Project?"

Right. The soul-sucking project Jackson never should have taken for many reasons.

"Have Marjorie send the bastard's calls to me and I'll deal with him." *Somehow.* But he couldn't and wouldn't think about Nelson Downey until he had to. "And if you and Zach like an architect from this week or last, hire the person."

David angled his head back. "You don't want to—"

"No." Jackson had to start letting go of some of his managing partner responsibilities and *now* was the time. "We need another architect in there, and I trust you two completely." He managed a half grin. "That doesn't mean I think you'll be better at being *me* the next few days."

"Sure I will." David paused before adding, "With Marjorie's help."

"I wouldn't count on too much help from her. She's still pissed about that damn stapler."

David shook with laughter.

Jackson couldn't help but smile at standing with his best friend, feeling lighter at letting go of work responsibilities that he'd handed over to two men he trusted not only with the firm, but with his life. If it ever came to that.

He rested his gaze on the hospital.

David had been right. If Jillian kept improving, and there was no reason to believe she wouldn't, she probably would be released sometime this week. He'd be the one to take her home, too. Then not leave her side until she kicked him out. Or had Claudia kick him out. Beyond that, Jackson had no idea what would happen between them. They still needed to talk about many things if they wanted another chance. Based on how Jillian had been with him only moments ago and what she did remember from last night, he couldn't help but feel even lighter about being a *them* and everything that little word would include.

She'd also, by way of some strange, inexplicable force, remembered him holding her hand while he sat with her last night. That had to mean something significant.

"Hey." David nudged him. "Al's up. She sent me a text she's on her way here. Go do what you need to do. I'd even go home for a bit if I were you. Everything will be fine."

Eva was still inside, and Claudia and Afton would soon be here again. By the time Jackson came back from getting his phone, and stopping at home long enough to shower and eat, Jillian would be in her room, tests completed—hopefully with results. But based on the way Jackson had just been interacting with her, she sure as shit had seemed like she would walk away from this without any permanent injuries.

The entire aftermath of the accident being the definition of a miracle.

"Okay. I'll be back soon." Jackson went to the driver's side.

As anxious as he was to really talk to Jillian, tell her how he felt about her and them, it would have to wait indefinitely. Making sure she was in fact okay and getting her home as soon as possible was what mattered most. That's all he would focus on for now.

Chapter Twenty-Three

EVA TUCKED the blankets around Jillian's body.

Jillian couldn't remember when her mom looked as haggard as she did at this moment. Tension had settled around her eyes and mouth, as had clear fatigue. Her face had also lost color, despite the tan she'd acquired not long after moving to Hawaii.

She returned to the bed's right side and sat on the edge. "I really wish that doctor would let us know how your tests went."

So would Jillian. The pain medication the nurse had given her earlier was beginning to wear off, as well; pain she felt *everywhere* in her body. She was also ready for more sleep, but she'd really been hoping Jackson would be back before she gave in to her dry, tired eyes. Maybe he'd even stretch out beside her again since no one had seemed to care he'd done just that earlier in the day. Thinking of her sleepiness, however, caused her to focus on her weary mom.

"*Mamá,*" she murmured. "You need rest."

"Your sisters have been saying the same thing." She clasped Jillian's right hand. "Marcos will be back this evening. By then, Dr. Vargas will have shared your test results." She squeezed

Jillian's hand. "I'm not leaving you until then. I'll go back to Boulder with Marcos tonight."

She nodded, but said, "You should've gone back to Boulder last night with him. It couldn't have been comfortable sleeping in the—"

"*Sleep?*" Her mom's eyes became round. "You think I, or anyone else, slept last night?"

Jillian pressed her lips together.

That probably hadn't been the best assumption. Still, she hated the thought of people she loved consumed with worry and fear and staying with her every second because of a car accident she couldn't even remember. Though a potent memory from Saturday night had returned while she'd been dozing in between tests.

Being in her bedroom with Jackson, him looking perfect in jeans and a sweater that he'd still been wearing today, and she in a little black dress and shoes with high stiletto heels. She now remembered him gently shushing her and *everything* that had followed, including walking down the stairs in her apartment building with Jackson behind her. They'd been talking, she'd opened the downstairs door, and a cool breeze had hit her bare legs.

She glanced at her right hand her mom held.

After that, all she remembered was her right hand being incredibly warm. It's why she'd asked Jackson the random question about them holding hands last night.

"*Mi hija,*" her mom slowly began, "getting a call from your scared younger sister who could barely tell me you were on your way to the hospital and unconscious from a car accident was a frightening reality check."

Their eyes met, but Eva's were wet, matching the emotion in her voice.

For the first time in forever, Jillian's heart split for her mom.

"And seeing you like you were last night," she quietly continued, "after they finally let us into the room, is something I sincerely hope you, Brynn, and even Claudia, if parenthood is a path she chooses, never experience with your own children."

All Jillian could do was nod while blinking her eyes clear.

There were no words that *could* follow her mom's honesty.

"So no, *mi hija,* not one of us actually slept last night." She shook her head. "Brynn was determined to come to the hospital with us, too, but Marcos and I convinced her she had to stay home and take care of herself and Sebastian."

Jillian picked at the blanket with what was left of her thumb nail. "I guess that means I should call her." She'd also remembered, after the Jackson memory had landed in her mind, the tense conversation with her mom before he'd arrived at her building.

"I know she'd love to hear your voice, as would your father, but that can wait until later." She paused, then added, "Not one of us wanted to leave your side all night."

Jillian managed a slight smile, though she'd always despise the thought of her family and friends having to go through what they did.

"Jackson really didn't want to leave your side."

She looked up, and her mom gave her an affectionate smile. An action Jillian couldn't recall seeing in years due to their... tense relationship.

"He's the man you dated in the spring?"

Jillian nodded and shrugged.

"And now you're back together."

She continued to pick at the blanket. "I don't know what we are." Not a lie, in spite of their reconnection over planning the party for Alyson and David, and his mom's health.

"That can't be true. You didn't see what I saw all night and this morning."

"*Mamá,*" Jillian almost groaned, "he was worried. Just like all of you."

"Claudia did introduce him as your boyfriend and he really didn't argue." Her mom's warm smile came back. "I know my opinion probably doesn't matter, but I like him. Quite a bit."

Jillian's mouth eased into a soft grin. "Actually, that's nice to hear." Eva hadn't been a part of Jillian's private life since high school, something she hadn't been at all concerned about throughout her adult dating life. Her mom had also been living hundreds of miles away for years which had been a relief. But that caused guilt to surge through Jillian while she focused on Eva, and her fatigue, concern, and tension. So she added, "Thank you for saying that. I like him, too. Quite a bit." Still, it felt absurd saying those words considering how she truly felt about Jackson.

"Since it's clear he's *extremely* fond of you, I'm hoping I'll be able to get to know him while I'm here the next several weeks?" Her mom's eyes turned shiny once more. "I'd love to spend time with you, Jillian. And get to know Jackson."

Jillian squeezed her mom's hand.

She had no idea what would happen beyond the walls of this hospital when she was released. But something about spending time with her mom and Jackson, and the two getting to know each other, made her suddenly feel as if shrouded by a soft, fluffy blanket.

It was in that moment, with her mom sitting beside her and holding her hand, that the truth landed in Jillian's achy head. Maybe it was due to feeling vulnerable from the accident. Maybe it was seeing Eva Castillo in a whole new light—as a scared and worried parent. Maybe it was the fact they were quietly and easily talking for a change. But she missed her *mom.*

So what was she going to do about it?

"Jillian, *por favor.*" Her mom wiped under her eyes with her free hand. "I know you and your sisters think I'm controlling and overbearing and pushy and a list of other things. It's why none of you wanted me here to help Brynn."

She shifted into a more upright position. "Mom—"

"I am who I am," she continued, "and though your sisters don't like those qualities about me either, I'm not their enemy." Her stare became piercing. "I can't keep being your enemy." She gestured at Jillian and their surroundings. "Not after hearing the fear in Claudia's voice while telling me about the car accident. And the endless drive into Denver from Boulder. And waiting and waiting for the doctor to tell us what was going on. And seeing you like you were—" She cleared her throat. "Whether you believe me or not, I want to be a part of your life. I want to hear from *you* about how well your business is doing, and about your friends and personal life."

Jillian focused on the blanket that had become hazy.

"I promise I'm not saying all of this to upset you, *mi hija.* But I love you as much as Brynn and Claudia and always will." She paused before adding, "Whether you like it not."

A couple tears slid from Jillian's eyes and she swiped her cheeks. "It's just…it can be really hard to talk to and be around you most of the time because—" She sniffed.

"Because of all those lovely qualities of mine I listed?"

Jillian nodded.

Her mom turned and inched backward on the bed until she was beside Jillian. She then put her left arm around Jillian's shoulders and gently hugged her close. "I've been wanting to do this since you woke up." She released a quiet laugh. "But Jackson beat me to it, more or less."

Jillian sank into Eva's warm arm and realized how much she'd missed being held by her *mom.* She had to have been a young teenager the last time she'd been this physically close to Eva due to all the tension—from being unable to understand her, even like her, most days because of her personality. Jillian had also witnessed so much darkness in her parents' marriage, but not all of that had been Eva's fault.

Her dad did have a temper that Jillian herself had inherited… which had never helped her relationship with her mom or older sister.

It also hadn't helped that night in April with Jackson.

"How about if I promise to try *very hard* to be less controlling, overbearing, and pushy with you and your sisters, if you'll get me caught up on your life and let me stay caught up?"

Her mom gave her a long squeeze which caused Jillian to snuggle closer.

"*Si*," she whispered. "*Lo siento, Mamá.* It'll be better. I promise." *And it would be.* But thinking about her parents' ugly marriage, and feeling close to her mom for the first time in years, made her ask, "How did you and Dad end up so miserable?" What Jillian really wanted to know was how had their love turned into excruciating pain, then death.

Why hadn't they been soul mates?

She shook her head. "Our expectations of each other became unreasonable. In hindsight, we had little in common…until we had you girls." She frowned. "The qualities about me that you and your sisters find *challenging* your father learned to despise. And I ended up having no patience for his temper. Though Brynn once told me it's gotten better over the years."

Jillian absently nodded before asking, "Why did you stay together for so long?"

Her mom sighed. "We foolishly thought it would be easier on everyone—especially you girls—if we hung in there until Claudia left for college. But it was a terrible mistake, and I've often wondered if that's the reason you and Claudia…" Her damp eyes met Jillian's. "If that's the reason you and your sister are still *alone*. For lack of a better word." She sniffed, then gave

Jillian a quick smile. "Though Claudia seems quite taken with Afton."

Jillian managed a small grin.

"And *you* seem quite taken with Jackson."

Jillian remained silent since she couldn't deny the truth.

"If you are, it's okay, *mi hija*," she softly continued, "because you are not me, and Jackson is not your father."

Jillian's lower lip trembled as her mom squeezed her tight. "Thank you, *Mamá*." And maybe—just maybe—that's what she'd been needing to hear, especially the last few weeks.

"Don't thank me. Just tell me all about Jackson."

She sighed, then winced at the sharp pain in her side because *everything* hurt.

It was time to tell someone in her close, immediate circle about her feelings for Jackson. She'd never imagined that person would be her mom. But at that moment, while being held by her and after everything she'd said, she was the only person Jillian wanted to tell…besides Jackson. "I'm in love with him and have been since March, but he has no idea I feel that way."

Eva peered at her, opened her mouth, but then the doctor strolled into the room, wearing his warm smile.

"Excellent. You're awake and Mom's with you."

Her mom sat up, keeping her arm around Jillian's shoulders.

"The swelling has decreased significantly." His smile grew. "There also doesn't appear to be any permanent damage to your skull or what it's protecting."

Jillian winced at those last several words.

Maybe not remembering the car accident *was* for the best.

"Dear God, *gracias*," Eva murmured.

"Amazingly, no broken bones. A cracked rib and bruising for sure, which I'm sure you're feeling."

Among everything else that ached.

"The memory loss you're experiencing is completely normal,

but have you, by chance, remembered anything else from Saturday night since we last spoke?"

Sandwiched between Jackson and her bedroom wall while getting lost in *them* was probably not a memory she needed to share with her mom beside her. "I now remember walking down the stairs in my apartment building with Jackson, then cold air, then…nothing."

He nodded. "You remembering that is actually a very good sign. And the memories from last night may keep appearing exactly in that way. Flashes and feelings. Anything could trigger the memories, too. Or what you remember right now may be it."

Jillian couldn't help but feel grateful for her current last memory of Saturday night being with Jackson, incredibly happy and feeling so close to the man she loved.

"I'd like to keep you here for another night, possibly two, for observation," the doctor said. "We'll get you into a real room once a bed opens up. In the meantime, pain level?"

"It's very high," she answered. "What the nurse gave me earlier is wearing off."

"Okay." He stepped back. "I'll get someone in here to take care of that. Do you have any questions or concerns you'd like addressed before I leave?"

Jillian looked at her mom who smiled at the doctor.

"No, Dr. Vargas. You've told us everything we wanted and needed to hear." Eva's smile deepened. "Thank you for taking such good care of my daughter."

"Of course." He focused on Jillian. "I know you may not feel this way right now because of the pain, but you're very lucky. I've seen car accidents like the one you and your boyfriend were in end much differently."

His words dangled in the air before he brought back his warm smile and left.

Very lucky.

Jillian rested her head on her mom's shoulder.

More than lucky. Miraculous seemed to better describe Jillian's experience.

She also really liked the word boyfriend going with Jackson Lovett.

"Very good news," Eva said on a breath. "Maybe tonight all of us will get some rest." She focused on Jillian. "And while we're still alone, I'd love to know why you haven't told Jackson how you feel. I know I said this earlier," she swiftly added, "but you didn't see him in here all night with you, almost refusing to leave your side when Claudia or Alyson or I tried to give him a break. Just to go stretch his legs and get some fresh air."

Jillian softly grinned.

Things did seem different with them, and not only because of the accident. She could remember the strong feeling that something had shifted between her and Jackson.

"I think if you were to tell him how you feel, he might pleasantly surprise you."

She suddenly remembered Niall saying the same thing to her a week ago—Niall. Had they made plans to do something this weekend? *Dammit*, that seemed familiar. But why would she have made plans with him when she and Jackson were dating again? She and Niall were just friends, but it still didn't make sense.

Her mom wiggled deeper into the bed beside Jillian. "I'm sure Jackson or Alyson or Claudia will be walking into this room any second so is there anything else you'd like to tell me? Like about how well the business is doing? Or even about being Alyson's maid-of-honor and the wedding? I'd love to hear all about that, too."

Jillian cleared her mind of Niall.

She didn't need to be thinking of him or if they'd had plans. She only wanted to concentrate on being here like this with her mom, telling her about the business, Alyson and David's wedding, and the surprise bachelor-bachelorette party she and Jackson were planning. As they talked, though, she would be keeping an eye out for Jackson, the man who deserved to hear how she felt about him. Between the car accident, what her mom had said about him, and how he'd been before he left the room, Jillian could no longer contain the truth.

Chapter Twenty-Four

"SWEETHEART," Jackson's mom said as he pulled into a parking spot at the hospital, "I think it's wonderful that you're having David help you out at work the next few days. I have a feeling Jillian won't mind you being around for her."

Jackson heard the smile in his mom's voice while he put David's SUV into park.

"Thank you for calling to tell us how you're doing and Jillian's prognosis," she added. "It sounds like she'll be home before we know it and that's remarkable."

The prognosis Jackson had received via a voicemail from David. But he said, "Yeah, she's really going to be okay." As relieved as he still felt at what David had said, Jackson hated like hell he hadn't been with Jillian when the doctor came back with her test results.

After showering and putting on a different pair of jeans and fleece sweatshirt, he'd made the huge mistake of eating on his couch with the Broncos game on in the background. He'd then sat back and closed his eyes. Which had turned into an almost two-hour nap. He'd been so sound asleep he'd missed calls and texts from not only David, but from his parents and brother.

"I'm about to head back into the hospital now." He turned off the engine and opened the door. "Are you doing okay?" He also hated like hell how much worry this had brought his mom. His family in general.

"Jackson, please stop asking me that. You have enough going on, and I'm not going to drop dead tomorrow."

His steps wavered at her strongly spoken words. "Mom, don't say it like that." *Shit.* He didn't need or want that image in his head on top of everything else.

"It's the truth and you know it. I want you to do something else for me," she threw in.

Jackson continued to head for the hospital. "The last time you said that, I ended up promising you I'd take a long vacation as soon as I could." After the last twenty-fours or so, that long vacation was looking and sounding better and better.

"You also have to take someone special with you," she reminded him, and Jackson again heard the smile behind her words which made him grin. "Anyway, when Jillian is feeling up to it, all of us would love to *really* meet her."

His grin deepened. "You want me to bring her up to Longmont to watch the Broncos game and for Sunday family dinner." Something he'd already been picturing as soon as Jillian did feel better. But he wasn't about to confess that to the all-knowing Nancy Lovett.

She laughed which came out on the hoarse side. "That would be perfect."

He paused, steps from the hospital's entrance. "Actually, Jillian was supposed to go out with all of us this Friday…" Had it only been just over a week ago that she'd agreed to be his date for LoDo night? Something she'd agreed to while they'd been joined as one on his bed.

Jackson observed his surroundings. Twilight sky. Big, sterile hospital. People, including staff, walking in and out of the building.

How could life change like that? Go from on its way to being better than fine to *this*.

"We'll reschedule it for when Jillian is one-hundred percent. Or close to it."

His mom's words invaded his thoughts and he said, "That would be great. I know she was excited about going."

Dance with me that night.

It was all Jillian had asked of him and he'd been more than agreeable, not just because they'd been joined as one. He'd loved the idea of dancing with smart, beautiful, sassy Jillian Castillo. And taking *them* on a long vacation, far from Denver, was an idea he loved even more.

"Please let Jillian know all of us are thinking about her and call tomorrow?"

"Yeah. I'll do that." He hung up and entered the building.

During his moment with Jillian, after he woke up due to her fingers moving through his hair, it felt as if they could have been in his bed or hers. Or the bed in the cabin where they'd slept late Saturday and Sunday during their weekend together.

Thinking about their fantastic time with no work, no family, no friends, just the two of them, Jackson couldn't escape the thought he'd fallen for her that weekend but had been too stupid and caught up in work to realize it. Then he and Jillian had made questionable choices.

But he didn't need or want to think about any of that right now. He only wanted to get to her room and stay with her, maybe right beside her on the bed, until someone told him he had to leave. If that even happened.

Jackson rounded the corner, but his steps slowed at seeing Marcos right outside the waiting area, in deep conversation with some tall, lanky guy with dark-blond hair. Marcos also held a bouquet of what looked like store-bought pink roses that couldn't be for Jillian from *him*.

As he passed the two men, Jackson caught Marcos's nod and tight smile. The other guy gave him a long, hard stare before focusing on Marcos.

David stood when Jackson reached where he'd been sitting.

"Is Alyson with Jillian?" he asked while glancing over his left shoulder.

Marcos and the guy were still locked in a conversation that seemed serious, based on their frowns, and something about it gnawed at Jackson's instincts.

"Yeah, she's in there with Eva. Claudia and Afton left to go get some food."

Jackson casually angled his head left. "What's going on over there?"

David's gaze flitted between Jackson, and Marcos and the stranger. "I don't know."

"Who's the guy?" Jackson persisted. "A friend of the family?"

"I think so." David hesitated, then mumbled, "I'm pretty sure Marcos called him *Niall*."

Jackson froze.

"Marcos seemed surprised to see him here, too," David quietly continued. "The kid got here not too long ago. Marcos pulled him over there and they've been talking like that."

Jackson turned, squinted at the guy whose eyes went to him and back, and faced David once more. "No, that can't be right."

There was no way in hell that was Niall. The guy Jillian had rushed off to meet a week ago today? Though the kid wasn't repulsive, he looked barely old enough to legally drink.

Jackson narrowed his eyes, remembering Jillian's phone blowing up last night as she'd told him who she'd been texting. *Niall.* Because she'd chosen not to go to the Broncos game with him. And Jackson could only hope the reason had been choosing *them*.

Okay. Jillian had been adamant she and Niall were just friends. Once Jackson had let go of his adolescent jealousy, he'd accepted what she'd said and apologized. But those pink roses Marcos held had to be from Niall. Which seemed like an intimate gift from one *friend* to another, considering Jillian and Niall had only recently become friends through her sister and Marcos.

This was the guy—kid—who hadn't been taking no for an answer?

His jaw tightened as he turned and marched over to Marcos and *Niall*.

"Jackson," David softly enunciated, "wait a minute."

When Jackson reached the pair, he felt Marcos's gaze on him but stayed focused on his friend as he crossed his arms. "You're Niall?"

The kid lifted his chin. "Yeah, I'm friends with Jillian." He glanced at Marcos, then back at Jackson. "We were texting last night. About the Broncos game today. It's why I'm here. I wanted to see for myself she was okay." He sighed. "She was supposed to go with me."

"But she changed her mind," Marcos swiftly inserted. "It's why they were texting."

"I know all of that because I was in the car with her." Jackson leaned toward the kid. "You need to learn how to take no for an answer."

The kid frowned at Jackson. "You must be Mr. Architect."

He straightened as his arms fell to his sides while he processed the fact Jillian had talked about him with this kid. That knowledge then collided with the fear, shock, and worry of the last twenty-four hours—the last few weeks in general—with the force of fighter jets going Mach 3.

Before Jackson realized it, he was smashing his right fist into the kid's face. He then grabbed his shirt and slammed him into the nearest wall. With his hard gaze locked on Niall's stunned expression, he said, "Call me that one more time, you little shit." Someone was trying to yank Jackson backward as he made himself almost nose-to-nose with the kid. "I dare you."

"Sir!" a female voice said as someone succeeded in pulling him away. "If you don't calm down, I'll have to call security."

Marcos, staring at Jackson with clear judgment and mortification, edged his way between him and the still stunned kid, now rubbing his cheek. Marcos placed his hand on Jackson's chest and gave him a solid nudge as he was jerked backward a few more steps.

Marcos grabbed Niall's upper arm and practically dragged him away.

While taking a deep breath, Jackson watched them until they disappeared from view.

"I can't have behavior like that in here."

He focused on the friendly nurse from last night and early this morning. But now she was looking at him the same way Marcos had as he'd hauled his friend away.

She leaned forward. "If I have any more problems with you, I'll have to keep you from visiting your girlfriend."

David stepped up from behind Jackson. "I'm sorry. I promise that won't happen again." He glanced at Jackson. *"Right?"*

He nodded before walking back into the waiting area. The adrenaline, fueled by rage, coursed through his body and he stared at his shaking right hand, his knuckles red from the force of the punch. *"Shit."* David stood beside him. "The last time I hit someone like that was—"

"Me," his friend finished. "What the hell was that all about?"

Jackson dropped to a chair and clenched his hands in an attempt to stop the trembling. He then told David what had been happening seconds before the accident...and hitting the gas pedal right after the light had turned green. "The little shit wasn't taking no for an answer, and I—"

"Jackson, it *wasn't* your fault." David sat next to him. "You're not the first person to hit the accelerator right after a light turns green."

"I know that. But I did it because I got pissed off at the situation." David didn't need to know what Jackson and Jillian had been doing not too long before her texting with Niall had started. Because she'd chosen not to go to the Broncos game with the little punk.

"It doesn't change the fact," David countered, "a woman made the shitty choice to run a red light." He sighed. "Jackson, give yourself a break and let it go. *All* of it. There are more important things going on here. And it sounds like Jillian and that guy really are just friends."

Jackson sat back.

"I'm not condoning you trying to knock the kid's teeth out," David quietly added, "but you have to feel a little better?"

He rested his head against the wall. "No." He then eyed David, staring at him with raised eyebrows. "Okay, maybe a *little* better." Not a lie, either.

David also sat back. "Is that what I looked like after you clocked *me* all those years ago?"

He looked at him. "No, it pissed you off even more. But if memory serves, I apologized for that hit earlier today."

His friend grinned. "All of this is reminding me that you and Jillian are going to owe me and Alyson a long story as soon as Jillian's feeling better."

Jackson slowly nodded. He then recalled how he'd been feeling when he'd walked into the hospital only moments ago. Relieved about Jillian's prognosis and excited to see her. To be within touching distance of her, hopefully for the entire night.

"You're right," he admitted. "We will owe you guys a story.

And there are definitely more important things going on here." Which meant he would bury the *Niall* shit into the deepest parts of his mind…But after he told Jillian the truth about last night.

It was the only way he'd really be able to let all of it go and face forward, in the direction of the future. He and Jillian deserved that, if not more.

▭

JILLIAN'S EYES fluttered open at warm fingers lightly brushing hair off of her face.

"Sorry," Jackson murmured. "I wasn't trying to wake you up."

She blinked the fog away, then smiled at the sight of him near her on the pillow just like he had been the last time she'd woken up like this. Although his hair was adorably rumpled, which was normal for him, he had less scruff and wore different clothing. But her smile faded when she remembered waiting and waiting for him while her mom, Alyson, and Claudia and Afton had kept her company.

"What took you so long to come back?" She yawned. "What time is it?" What day was it seemed like the more necessary question.

He softly brushed his thumb against her lower lip. "I have no idea what time it is. And I'm sorry about last night. It took me longer than I planned to get back here. Then you fell asleep while your mom and Alyson were with you." He clasped her right fingers. "I wanted to be here when the doctor shared your test results but David told me in a voicemail."

She pointed at her head. "Still the same." *Thank God.* And still felt like a miracle, too.

Jackson's perfect mouth eased into his irresistible grin. "Excellent. I like your head exactly the way it is."

Jillian pulled her hand from his and placed it on his face.

That's when she spotted something pink behind him. She raised her head and stared at the roses in a clear vase sitting on the counter. "Are those from you?" She loved flowers, but roses were her least favorite.

"No." Their gazes locked. "I asked you on our first date, since you're a florist, if you have a favorite flower or like all of them." He covered her hand with his. "You said you love lilies because of how they look and smell."

She laughed quietly. "I can't believe you remember that."

"Jillian, it wasn't that long ago."

She nodded, though it truly surprised her Jackson had remembered something they'd talked about in passing on their first date back in *February*.

"I know I should've brought you a dozen lilies by now," he added, "but I've been focused on you and that beautiful head of yours."

"Then I guess I'll forgive you." She glanced at the roses. "Who are they from?"

His grin slipped. "Those are from your new friend, Niall."

She frowned. "Niall? He was here?" That same powerful feeling from yesterday, that she'd had plans with him, rushed through her head that wasn't quite as achy.

"He brought them by last night because he was worried about you but couldn't stay."

She squinted at Jackson. "You saw him?"

He lifted his shoulders. "Only for a minute or two."

Jillian stared at the flowers. "I don't understand why he'd bring me roses. We only hung out that one—" She pressed her lips together since that Sunday morning with Jackson was a crystal-clear memory. "It's strange. That's all. I'm hoping to set him up with Campbell," she added, just in case Jackson was still nursing some jealousy because of last Sunday.

"I'd wait a couple weeks to set them up. Something tells me he'll need it."

Her frown deepened. She was about to ask him why, but he pressed her hand to his cheek.

"Jilly, I have to be honest with you about a couple of things that can't wait anymore."

Too weird. She also needed to be honest with *him* about a couple of things.

"I know you don't remember the accident or what happened before we were hit."

That wasn't entirely true, but she stayed silent due to his serious expression and tone.

"But I do."

He paused for several seconds. It seemed as if he were searching for the right words.

"Your phone was blowing up with texts from Niall because you'd decided not to go to the Broncos game with him today."

So she had *made plans with him.*

Her mouth inched open before she whispered, "I knew I wasn't remembering something when it came to him." The memory of agreeing to go with Niall to the game, following her fight with Brynn, filled her mind. She winced. "He invited me, and I hadn't been to a game in so long I agreed to go with him."

"Jillian, you don't owe me an explanation. I promise it's fine." He released a heavy sigh. "I asked you what was going on and you were honest with me. But we were on our first real date since April, he wasn't giving up, and it…pissed me off. So as soon as the light turned green, I—"

She covered his mouth with her hand. "I asked Alyson yesterday what happened. She told me a woman in a pickup truck ran the red light."

He tried to move her hand, but she pressed harder.

"It was a terrible accident," she continued. "I'm okay, you're okay, and that's all that matters…though you did lie to me when I asked if you were hurt anywhere else." She arched her right eyebrow. "Alyson and Claudia told me all about you walking out of the ER with a severe concussion without being released. And that's *not* okay, Mr. Lovett."

He narrowed his eyes.

"We're not talking about the accident anymore. Or Niall. Nod if you promise to agree to this, and I'll take my hand off your mouth."

He nodded.

She then pushed aside thoughts of Niall. When she was back home, she'd shoot him a quick thank-you text for the flowers. But she'd need her phone before she could do that.

"I heard your SUV is totaled, and I'm so sorry. But my phone and purse have to be inside of it."

Jackson pointed at her fingers still over his mouth.

Jillian fought a grin as she removed her hand.

"I found both in my car when I went to get my phone. I gave them to Claudia before she and Afton left last night." He gently clasped her fingers once more. "The second thing I need to tell you is that I want to be with you. And only you."

Jillian's breath slowed while they stared at one another.

Had Jackson Lovett really just said that to her? Her head was still on the hazy side.

"And it's not because of the accident. It's from reconnecting with you the last few weeks." He scanned her face and blanketed body. "I knew I wanted only you *before* Saturday."

All Jillian could do was continue staring at him.

A dream. A very real, vivid dream. That's what this had to be, brought on by her injury.

"I'm in love with you," he softly added, "and want to be with you as much as possible."

She leaned forward and pressed her lips to his. Familiar. Warm. Yummy. Incredibly real.

They shared a slow, soft, chaste kiss before Jackson angled his head back.

"So does that mean I'm not sounding like a complete jackass right now?"

"No," she breathed. "I was checking to make sure this wasn't a dream." Though it still felt like one. But now it was undeniably her turn. "I have to be honest with *you*."

He raised his eyebrows. "Okay."

Jillian closed her eyes, inhaled, opened them, and said, "I'm in love with you, too."

Mierda. Her everything felt a million times lighter at finally saying those words to him. Knowing Jackson felt the same way about her made her feel as if she may start to levitate.

He brought back *his* grin.

There was only one more thing she needed to confess. "And have been since March."

His grin slowly vanished. "Since *March*?"

She nodded, not knowing what else to do since it was only a matter of time before he'd put the pieces—

"Is *that* the real reason you dumped me in April?"

She cringed. "*That* word seems a little strong."

He frowned. "It's exactly what you did. In the cold, pouring rain."

"Jackson, do we really need to rehash that night? It also wasn't the only reason."

"Right. The Downey Project."

"And the fact you were nowhere near ready for that kind of commitment," she tossed at him, remembering yet another moment with him in April. "I overheard you on the phone with your brother one night at your place, right after our weekend in Estes Park."

He peered at her. "What are you talking—" He stopped and took a deep breath. "Now isn't the time for this conversation. You're still recovering from the accident and need rest."

"Jackson, I'm sick of resting." She stared at him. "I know you weren't ready because I overheard you tell your brother—who I guess asked about us—that I was *'great but you didn't need anything serious right now'*." Unfortunately, she'd overhead the words at the wrong time and it had hurt way more than it should have. "Hearing you say that not long after realizing I was in love with you, and you taking that project, were the reasons I ended things."

He released her hand, rolled onto his back, and rubbed his eyes.

Yes, the truth was out, but did it even matter anymore? Except that she and Jackson felt the same way about each other. A truth she was still trying to wrap her weary mind around.

"I remember that. He did ask about us." He turned his head right. "It was the wrong thing to say. But we were still so new and my brother was being nosy. I was also trying to get off the phone with him. Where were you?"

"I was coming from your room, about to walk into the kitchen, but stopped when I heard you on the phone." Then caught the wrong part of the conversation.

"Jillian, I'm sorry I said that. And no, I wasn't ready to hear words of love then." He paused before adding, "But even though I didn't say it to my brother—because it was none of his business— I really was *committed* to seeing where we could go."

She focused on the blanket as regret settled around her. "*Fino.* I was angry about you taking the project, feeling frustrated with you and myself, and acted hastily." It was a thought she'd been zeroing in on since the Saturday night with him. "I also realized while talking to my mom yesterday I need to work on keeping my temper in check." *And she absolutely would.*

If she didn't, she'd continue to unintentionally sabotage her relationships with people she loved dearly. What if she *had* reacted differently to Brynn's hormonal behavior that really wasn't her fault? And her mom's determination to be right all the time? And Jackson taking that project?

"Deep breathing helps me," he mumbled. "*Most* of the time."

She nodded. "I promise I'll try it, too."

He sighed. "I know taking the Downey Project didn't earn me any points. In fact, I'm sure I lost all of them that night."

She smiled softly. "Not all of them."

"I guess that's something." He shifted back onto his right side. "If it'll make you feel better, I know now I never should have taken that damn project and regret it. But I honestly thought it was the smartest business move for *everyone* in the firm."

"I know," she whispered. "The project won't last forever."

"It also won't be finished soon enough." He grinned. "What I don't regret is falling for you that weekend in March. I was just too stupid and distracted with work to realize it."

She carefully scooted closer to him. "I do like hearing that." *Extremely ironic, too.* But that confession would never top hearing he was in love with her.

"If you liked that, you're going to love what I have to say next."

How could he possibly have more to tell her? He'd said all she wanted to hear from him.

Jackson opened his mouth, but somewhere nearby a phone started to ring.

"That would be me." He reached into his jeans pocket and withdrew his phone. He glanced at the screen and back at her. "It's Monday morning."

Her eyes widened since it was Monday morning and he was here with her in the hospital, after obviously spending another night by her side.

The realization stole her breath.

He silenced the call and eased upward. "It's work, and I have to return the call."

Air left her lungs in a frustrated huff as he stood. "Jackson Lovett, you can't be serious."

He held up his right hand. "Jilly, trust me. This won't take long and then I'll be back so I can I tell you what I need to."

She cautiously eyed him. "You're *not* going to work today?"

"Hold that question. Please?" He then turned and left.

Jillian rolled onto her back and surveyed the hospital room she wanted to be out of now. When her gaze settled on the warm spot Jackson had just left, every single thing he'd said inundated her head until she managed to focus on the most important thing he'd confessed.

I'm in love with you and want to be with you as much as possible.

His words that she'd echoed. It also seemed he'd chosen *her* over work today.

She continued to stare at what had become his spot on the bed.

Santo cielo. Was she still sound asleep?

Chapter Twenty-Five

JILLIAN CASTILLO WAS *in love with him and had been since* March.

Jackson had not seen that one coming. At the same time, her feelings for him explained so damn much, including Claudia's "she was crazy about you" comment. He could also now pinpoint his conversation with Will when Jillian had started to become a little distant. It was the only word that fit. A week or so later the firm had been "awarded" the Downey Project.

He walked outside into the brisk, morning air, veered left, and squinted into the sunlight.

All these months Jillian had been in love with him, and he'd been absolutely clueless while missing and wanting *her*. Yeah, he'd been a little confused and pissed and hurt by her actions for a while, but once he'd let all of it go, he'd ended up where he'd been before that dismal night in April—crazy for Jillian. He'd been completely honest with her, too, when he told her about being committed to seeing where they could go. No, he hadn't been ready to make professions of love back then. Maybe he would have been if not for his stupidity and drowning in work?

But, dammit, he would have gotten there because that's exactly where he was *now*.

He stopped to pull air into his lungs.

That's what mattered most, too. The now. Getting Jillian out of this place, and back home and into her life where she belonged. Then they could start to focus on them. Which was all he wanted to do at this precise moment, but he had to take it one step at a time.

Jackson stared at his phone.

He'd already taken step number one, telling Jillian he was in love with her. He'd been lucky enough to hear her say the same thing to him. That's what mattered. Not what happened in April. Not anymore. It was also time to take step two.

"Hey, it's me," he said when Marjorie answered. "Is every-thing alright?"

"Jackson, are you okay?" she asked. "David told me—when he arrived right after I did—that you and a close friend were in a terrible car accident Saturday night and you'd be out of the office today and tomorrow. And maybe Wednesday? You haven't missed a day of work since the firm opened over three years ago."

Shit. That made him sound like the definition of a workaholic in need of an intervention.

"Slow down, Marjorie. I promise everyone's fine." *More than fine, really.*

Silence fell on her end before, "This person must be more than a close friend."

Jackson smiled remembering Jillian's softly spoken words.

I'm in love with you, too.

"She's definitely more than a close friend."

Marjorie again fell silent.

"So I need you to play nice with David while he's there trying to be me."

"I can do that," Marjorie replied. "He did bring me a very

nice, new electric stapler. It was even wrapped in beautiful paper Alyson must have given him."

Jackson laughed while shaking his head.

"The other reason I needed to talk to you," she continued, "is that Nelson Downey called right at eight a.m. He and Marsden's daughter want a meeting with you as soon as possible. I didn't know what to tell him beyond I'd give you the message."

Jackson's mirth vanished.

Of course that sonofabitch wanted him to drop everything for yet another damn meeting, but now with the daughter of the devil instead of the so-called great Ember Leventhal.

"They're going to have to wait until I'm back in the office," he stated. "But I don't expect you to tell him that, so I'll call him next. Anything else?"

Silence.

"Marjorie, are you there?"

"Yes, but I have nothing else for you. Except that I hope you and your more than close friend are really okay. And that you're able to spend some nice time together."

The line went dead, and even more weight lifted off of Jackson's shoulders.

Between Marjorie, David, and Zach, the firm would be more than fine without him. Maybe by the time he was back in the office David and Zach will have hired another architect. Which would only add to the lightness he was now experiencing for the first time since starting the firm. That thought fueled his next step.

"Lovett, I'm in the middle of something," Downey answered. "I'll call you back. Are you finally in the office?"

His jaw turned to steel. On the bright side, his client's nastiness would only make this easier. "No. And I won't be in the office the next few days." David had told Marjorie that Jackson would possibly be gone through Wednesday, and Jillian needed him more. "The meeting with you and Keith Marsden's daughter will have to wait until then." He held his breath. It also sounded like Downey was excusing himself from a group of people.

"Lovett, have you lost your mind?" Downey asked around a heavy breath. "I don't wait for people, they wait for me. I want that meeting today. Tomorrow at the latest and you will make it happen."

Jackson gripped his phone. "Someone very close to me needs me and I won't let her down. The meeting will have to wait until Thursday," he articulated, then again held his breath.

"And you should know I don't give a rat's piss about your damn personal life."

Which was why there was no point in telling Downey about the car accident.

Jackson stared at the sidewalk.

He'd known Nelson Downey would react like the soulless dickhead he seemed to enjoy being, but this was the first time in their months of interaction Jackson wanted to hit him harder than he'd hit Niall. Despite the fistfight with David years ago, and occasional, childhood scuffles with Will, he'd never considered himself a violent guy. But after everything he'd endured since Saturday night, Jackson's tolerance level for dealing with pompous shit heads had hit zero.

"I'll be back in the office on Thursday," he managed to calmly repeat, "and we can meet first thing that morning. I also won't be available by phone the next few days." Because he'd be giving Jillian—them—his undivided attention. "But if you need anything, Marjorie will make damn sure to get you to someone who will be able to assist you." The weight that lifted from Jackson's shoulders was so extreme he wanted to laugh long and hard.

"What the hell is this?" his client practically snarled. "You're the architect on this project. We chose you. Not someone else in your damn office! Now if I were you, I'd hang up and have that receptionist get me and Keith's daughter on your calendar for a meeting—"

"Actually, you chose my firm for this project," Jackson interjected. "Everyone in the office works as a team. We trust each other implicitly. If there's anything you might need with this project while I'm gone, they'll be more than capable of helping you. If you don't trust them, that means you don't trust me, and I'm not used to doing business like that."

Miraculously, his client fell silent.

Jackson could only assume it was out of shock because someone in Nelson Downey's immediate business sphere had unleashed the guts to challenge him. Since he was on a roll and also done with his career and firm being threatened by this asshole, he said, "The way I see it you have two choices. You and Marsden's daughter can wait until first thing Thursday morning to meet with me so the project can keep moving forward *or*"—he took a quick breath—"you can waste valuable time and money firing my ass and, by extension, my firm." He paused before adding, "I'll need your decision now so I can let my staff know what the hell's going on."

Holy shit. He'd just gambled everything he'd worked for and achieved since graduating from CU with a degree in a profession he typically loved. But he couldn't keep letting his work and firm—or this bastard of a client—control him. Not anymore.

"You must have gone somewhere to reclaim your balls. Congratulations, Lovett."

Jackson closed his eyes and breathed deeply through his nose.

"We'll be in your office at eight a.m. sharp Thursday morning. I highly recommend you be there, too." Downey hung up.

Jackson released the laughter he'd barely held onto earlier and opened his eyes. To find an older couple walking by while staring him down.

"I just found out I didn't lose my job." Or career or firm or everything else he'd worked *insanely* hard to get.

The couple gave him cautious smiles and hurried toward the hospital's entrance.

As light as he felt at this moment, step four wouldn't be quite so simple.

Jillian had basically commanded they weren't going to talk about the accident or Niall from this day forward. Jackson would keep his promise, too. But letting go of the *what if he'd reacted differently when the light turned green* would take time. His next step—telling the woman he loved he was all hers for the next few days and being by her side until she told him to leave—would definitely put him on the path to letting *all* of it go. Someday.

Jackson headed for the entrance, but an idea stopped him.

Yeah, it would postpone going back inside and being with her like he'd said he would. But he needed and wanted to surprise her, and it's not like Jillian was alone. Though everyone but him had left last night to get better rest, Eva had come back at some point while he and Jillian had been asleep in the room. He'd caught a glimpse of her, alone, as he left to return Marjorie's call. Marcos, who Jackson wasn't certain would ever speak to him again after last night, must have decided to stay in Boulder.

Giving Jillian more time with her mom seemed like the right thing to do, considering the last thirty-six or so hours. On that thought, Jackson turned and walked to where he'd parked. He also couldn't help but notice the slight bounce in his step that made him smile, then laugh.

THE NURSE WALKED into Jillian's room and smiled. "I have good news."

Jillian sat up and glanced at her mom.

Were they going to let her go home?

"Beds will be opening up later this morning and we'll *finally* get you out of this room." The young woman gestured at the gray, ICU room with no windows. "I'm so sorry they couldn't get you moved yesterday. Weekends can be quite unpredictable around here."

Jillian gave her a tight smile. "It's okay. But I was really hoping you were going to say something else." She'd been entertaining vivid fantasies of Jackson getting her home, taking the longest, hottest shower of her life, then curling up on the couch— or her bed—with him and falling asleep in each other's arms. He had indirectly admitted he wasn't going to work today…after making a few other amazing statements that still didn't seem real.

"I know." The nurse's smile dipped. "Dr. Vargas wants to do another CT scan at some point today and keep you one more night for observation."

Jillian released a tiny moan.

"*Mi hija*," her mom murmured, "it's for the best and is only one more day and night."

She sighed. "*Sí.*" Though she *was* right, it didn't change the fact all Jillian wanted was a shower, her own bed, and Jackson… and to hear him again say he loved her.

"How's your pain level this morning?" the nurse asked.

She pushed the images aside and answered, "Not as bad, but still achy all over."

"I'll be back soon to take care of that."

When the young woman left, Jillian rolled her head left and caught her mom's dark eyes that contained considerably less fatigue and concern than yesterday. "You look better today."

She laughed. "I definitely feel better after a shower, real food, and a long nap."

Jillian frowned. "*Mamá*, you should've rested longer. Everything's been fine here."

Actually, that was a terrible word to describe waking up with Jackson again stretched out beside her on this bed and every amazing word that he'd spoken before he left to go deal with work. Her frown deepened, though, when she realized he should have been back by now.

"I understand that, but this is where I want and need to be." Her mom stood and sat on the bed's edge. "Afton went to work today, but Claudia should be here later this morning." She paused, then asked, "Did Jackson rush off earlier to go to work?"

Jillian softly grinned. "No. He had to return a call but said he'd be right back."

"It sounds like we should have enough time for something that can't wait any longer." She leaned right and down, then straightened while holding her purse. "There's someone who absolutely needs to talk to you. Well, two people really," she hastily added. "But your father will have to wait until your sister gets here since I don't have his phone number."

Jillian pressed her lips together and slowly nodded.

No, her parents had not been lucky in love. At least not with each other. Maybe, hopefully, that would change for them someday. But real love and passion and friendship had found Jillian in the perfect, yummy shape of Jackson Lovett. Just like real love, passion, and friendship had found her best friend, older sister, and Jackson's brother and his parents. Thinking of Jackson's parents, however, made her picture his mom.

At some point, Nancy Lovett's unfair reality would take a heart-wrenching turn and all any of them would be able to do was watch while keeping her as comfortable as possible.

When that time came, it would be so incredibly hard and painful. Still, that day wasn't today or tomorrow or next month. Jillian firmly believed that, too. She felt in her heart, mind, and soul Nancy would not miss Alyson and David's wedding and make it far beyond then.

"Brynn needs to hear your voice, so I'm calling her."

Her mom's statement broke apart Jillian's thoughts and she blinked several times.

Eva held out her phone which Jillian grasped, and she cleared her mind to focus on her older sister. "Brynn?"

Silence, followed by, "Jilly, I'm so, so sorry." Her sister's voice broke and she burst into tears. "I've been acting crazy," she said around her choppy breathing. "I wish…I was there to say it in person…but Marcos and Mom won't let me come to the hospital…to see you."

Tears burned Jillian's eyes at hearing her sister's obvious remorse. "It's okay. I know you're not yourself."

"It's not okay." Brynn sniffed twice. "You were right. I was jealous and acting *estúpida*. And *loca*. I love my life. Even though I'm bigger than a blue whale and stuck at home."

"I know you do," Jillian softly replied. "And I'm sorry, too."

"No. Don't apologize. I can't believe I was acting like that."

"Let's just blame hormones, okay?"

Her sister sighed. "*Fino*. I'll also be apologizing to you until we're senile."

Jillian managed a slight grin. "Probably longer, if I have anything to say about it."

No matter how difficult and hurtful Brynn's behavior had been, and Jillian's fiery, terrible reaction to all of it, her bond with her sisters would always be unbreakable.

"Alright. Longer. I'm okay with that." Brynn sniffed again. "Claude and Mom told me how awesome Jackson has been. Even Marcos seems to like him so when do I get to meet him? You should bring him up here while Mom's in town. Maybe even a few times?"

Jillian glanced at their mom, examining a broken fingernail a little too closely. "I'd love that and will as soon as I can." She had a strong feeling Jackson would love that, as well.

"Good," Brynn breathed. "I love you. You, me, *and* Claude will talk tonight."

They hung up, and she returned her mom's phone.

In that instant, every single moment Jillian had felt, experienced, seen, and heard since waking up early yesterday morning engulfed her as if caught in a monstrous ocean wave. Her breath became lodged in her throat. Seconds later her dam disintegrated.

Her mom scooted closer and wrapped her arms around Jillian.

She sobbed into her shoulder while shaking from the force of her emotions.

Relief that she'd be okay from the accident she still couldn't remember. Grateful for the same reasons, and the fact she had incredible family and friends who'd refused to leave her side until she woke up. Feeling all their love, too, and loving them just as much.

She tightened her arms around her mom who squeezed her back.

"*Está bien, mi hija*," Eva whispered. "Everything will be fine."

All Jillian could do was continue unleashing everything she felt in that instance which lasted until she heard, "What happened?"

She pulled slightly away from her mom and looked up to find Jackson—now a wet blur—standing just inside her room and holding a vase overflowing with what looked like perfect white and pink lilies. But that only made her laugh, then continue crying.

He walked past the bed to set the vase beside the pink roses and faced them. "Please tell me you didn't get bad news. I wasn't gone that long."

"She's okay," her mom answered. "I think everything she's been through has caught up with her. Would you mind asking the nurse for a box of tissues?"

"Yeah, I'll be right back."

Her mom smiled. "I really do like him, Jillian. He's a keeper. You must do whatever it takes to keep that man—"

"*Mamá*," she groaned, "stop." Still, she did love hearing how much her mom liked Jackson since her plan was for him to be around until death parted them.

He reappeared beside the bed and handed over the box, all while watching her with wide eyes. "So this isn't about bad news?"

Jillian pulled a tissue from the box and swiped her nose and cheeks.

"The only bad news we've received," her mom replied, "is that Dr. Vargas wants to keep her here another day and night for observation. He also wants to do another CT scan today."

Jackson's shoulders relaxed.

Her mom stood. "Since you're here, I'm going to take this time to check in with Brynn and Claudia." She grinned at Jillian. "I know I'm again leaving you in quite capable hands."

Once she and Jackson were alone, he sat in his spot on the bed. "I wanted to surprise you with the lilies, but for a few seconds there I thought you'd received bad news." He ran a hand though his hair, rumpling it even more. "It does suck that you have to stay another day and night. I don't know about you, but I hate hospitals."

She nodded and sniffed.

"But do you feel better?"

Jillian sat back and cleared her throat. "*Sí.*" In actuality, she felt like an entirely different woman and hoped *this* Jillian never went away long after she left this hospital. She pointed at her flowers. "The lilies are absolutely beautiful and clearly came from Daisy's Bouquets."

"Yeah. But Alyson made it clear that they're also from her and Campbell and Hayley...who wasn't even there."

She giggled. "They're perfect and kind of put the roses to shame. Don't they?"

He looked right, grinned, and focused on her once more. "To be honest, I've never liked roses. I think they're boring, no matter what color they are."

"I agree." She patted the spot right beside her.

He repositioned himself and stretched out next to her.

Jillian rolled onto her left side. "I'm afraid your social calendar will be very busy when I'm feeling better because Brynn and my mom want to get to know you better."

Jackson rolled onto his right side. "I'm glad you and your mom and Brynn made up."

She nestled her head into the pillow. "Me, too."

"And my mom told me the same thing about you last night, so I guess both of our social calendars will be busy."

She stared into his eyes that were back to bright, hypnotizing blue. "How is your mom?"

They must have talked about Nancy recently, but it felt like weeks had passed since Jillian's last memory of Saturday.

"She's been worried about you and me which I don't like. It's not good for her," he softly added. "But she'll be ready to hit LoDo on a Friday night when you're feeling up to it."

Jillian laughed. "I can't wait."

"Your laugh," he murmured. "It makes me the good kind of crazy. Like that eyebrow thing you do." Their gazes locked. "The first time I heard it was while we were standing at the makeshift bar at Becca's birthday party. I don't remember what I said. Probably because I was so distracted by the sound of your laughter. Which made *me* laugh."

"Well, I *do* remember." She grinned. "You asked me if I liked red or white wine. I said I liked red better. Then you said you do, too, but called it 'headache in a bottle'."

"That's all I said to earn your laughter?" He scooted closer. "You must have already been hot for me, Miss Castillo."

"I was. And it was the way you said it." She slid her fingers through his hair, then remembered something he'd said before he left. "You're back. What were you going to tell me?"

He unleashed his mind-melting grin. "That I'm all yours until Wednesday night."

Her mouth inched open.

"David offered to be me at work—or at least try—the next few days because I need and want to be with you as much as I can."

Santo cielo. Her life had actually turned into a fantasy come true.

"Unfortunately," Jackson continued, "the Downey Project will still be there first thing Thursday morning. But until then, it doesn't exist." He laughed. "Feel like joining me in that temporary, yet perfect place?"

She laughed with him. *"Absolutamente."*

He leaned forward and placed a long, soft kiss on her forehead.

In the gray, ICU hospital room with no windows it suddenly became just them, as if they were the only two people on the planet.

Soul mates.

Epilogue

JACKSON GENTLY TUGGED Jillian onto his lap and picked up his beer that he held up. "We are, hands down, the best surprise bachelor-bachelorette party planners ever."

They lightly tapped their glasses and drank.

He scanned the second-level bar area from their spot in the corner that gave them a full view of the massive space filled with the people David and Alyson loved most in the world. Some were playing pool, some ping-pong. Several guests, including his parents, were simply seated at one of the many tables, talking and laughing with others.

"So," Jillian began, "your mom's having a *great* night."

He nodded, knowing what she really meant by that statement since Nancy Lovett had been proving to everyone in her life she was not going to lie around and wait for death. But Jackson cringed at the memory of saying such a rotten thing to his mom in September.

"In fact, she's having such a great night," Jillian continued, "that I heard her trying to talk your dad into being her pool partner because she wants to take on the bride-and-groom-to-be."

He forced his mind into the present because that's what mattered most. The now.

"Yeah." He laughed. "David and Alyson are definitely the hustlers tonight."

"I didn't hustle you that night, Mr. Lovett. But do you think *we* can take them?"

"Hell yeah, Miss Castillo. But there's something I need to do first." He started to reach into his back pocket when two guests clearing the top of the stairs stopped him.

"Campbell and Niall are finally here," Jillian said, smiling and waving at them.

His eyes caught Niall's for a second before the kid nodded and led Campbell to the bar.

"I'm so glad she decided to give Niall a chance. Aren't they cute together?"

Jackson swallowed some beer and said, "Absolutely adorable." She elbowed his chest which made him almost spill his beer. "Anyway, I have something for you." He reached into his back pocket and withdrew the three slips of folded paper. "A belated Christmas present."

She arched her right eyebrow. "Ooh, paper. How sweet of you."

"Keep it up, smart mouth, and I won't tell you what's written on the papers." He held them out. "I made a promise to my mom. That day I spent with them on the boat?"

She shot him her sassy grin which Jackson returned.

"I promised her that I'd go on a long vacation and take someone special with me."

Her grin slowly faded.

"We'll go for two weeks and leave when David and Alyson come back from their honeymoon. I narrowed it down to visiting your dad in Argentina, exploring islands of Indonesia, or taking a Caribbean cruise." He smiled. "I came up with the last two for the purely selfish reasons of seeing you in nothing but skimpy clothing the entire time we're gone…or naked."

She covered her mouth with her free hand.

"You get to choose, but we won't know what you chose until you open the paper."

Jillian burst into her throaty laughter, and Jackson's head buzzed. She then stared at the papers, reached for one, hesitated, and pulled the middle one from his fingers.

He watched her closely.

She brought back her sassy grin. "I wanted to visit this country even before my dad moved there, but there won't be much skimpy clothing."

"No," Jackson replied as their mouths inched closer. "But I see many *more* vacations in our future." He then pressed his lips to hers and everything around them blurred.

Author's Note
____

I hope you enjoyed Book Two in the Timing is Everything Series that will continue with *The Time We Met*. Each book can stand alone, but it's recommended they're read in series order for maximum enjoyment.

And if you have a moment, please feel free to leave a rating and brief review at wherever you purchased the book. Authors always appreciate and need honest reader reviews.

About the Author

Christine Miles is a full-time writer living in Albuquerque, New Mexico.

An avid reader and writer since elementary school, her passion for literature inspired her to pursue a BA in English and an MA in Creative Writing. She writes YA and Adult Contemporary Romances with sassy, independent heroines and swoony heroes who love them for their strength.

When not writing romances, she loves traveling, binge-watching shows on streaming apps, reading mysteries and thrillers, listening to music, and spending quality time with her family, friends, and dog.

You can find her on Facebook and Instagram. Sign up for her newsletter to get ARC's and updates at www.christinemilesauthor.com.

facebook.com/ChristineMilesAuthor

instagram.com/christinemilesauthor

amazon.com/author/christinemilesya

bookbub.com/authors/christine-miles

goodreads.com/christinemilesauthor

9 781962 092050